This item is du
m
u

POWER SHIFT

POWER SHIFT

Judith Cutler

ISIS
LARGE PRINT
Oxford

First published in Great Britain 2003
by Hodder & Stoughton Ltd,
a division of Hodder Headline

Published in Large Print 2004 by ISIS Publishing Ltd,
7 Centremead, Osney Mead, Oxford OX2 0ES
by arrangement with
Hodder & Stoughton Ltd,
a division of Hodder Headline

British Library Cataloguing in Publication Data
Cutler, Judith
  Power shift. – Large print ed.
  1. Power, Kate (Fictitious character) – Fiction
  2. Policewomen – England – Birmingham – Fiction
  3. Detective and mystery stories
  4. Large type books
  I. Title
  823.9'14 [F]

ISBN 0–7531–7037–X (hb)
ISBN 0–7531–7038–8 (pb)

Printed and bound by Antony Rowe, Chippenham

This one's for Jon, with my love

Acknowledgements

I am grateful to the West Midlands Police for their help, and in particular to Inspector Mark Bramwell, in charge of the real Scala House team. His patience and enthusiasm were exemplary. Thanks too, to John Rose of Birmingham Environmental and Consumer Services.

CHAPTER
ONE

At six thirty on any normal Monday morning in December, Kate would have expected an easy run into the city. But this time she was heading not to the centre, but towards the covered wholesale market, where laden lorries and utility trucks were causing chaos as they pushed their way back into the pre-rush-hour traffic. Kate was almost pleased: it showed that there were still some independent retailers left in the world of supermarkets. Not when she was cut up like that, though. She swore fluently, wondering whether to pull the driver over and give him an official earful. She didn't like being pushed off the road in the dark, and especially not at a time when most sensible people would be hoping their partner would do the decent thing and organise a cup of tea in bed. Kate had been up before six, driving through the suburbs; she'd been tempted once or twice to pick up a forlorn knot of damp commuters waiting for an early brightly lit bus. From time to time a kitchen or bathroom light snapped on, as if prompted like a security device by the movement of her car past the window.

Shrugging — if she stopped the guy she'd only get soaking wet and achieve not a lot — she picked her way through yet another one-way diversion: Birmingham was rising phoenix-like from the concrete chaos that had once been the Bull Ring, but was taking its time about it. Soon there'd be a city to be proud of, not just because at last top retailers had decided to join international musicians, actors and restaurateurs, but also because of the stylish architecture and imaginative use of space. Meanwhile, as each flattened site was developed, you had to deal with the constantly changing traffic layout and the fact that your bus stop had disappeared from where you left it last night.

Damn. Kate had got into the wrong lane, to be blasted by a container lorry as she edged into the correct one. There. At last she pulled on to the space reserved for police vehicles near the indoor market. A security guard stopped her. Good. She preferred people to do what they were supposed to do. It would have been nice to have to flash her new ID, but the sight of her uniform silenced him. Another day she'd change at work, like everyone else. Today — yes, she wanted to establish herself somehow. This was a big day: there ought to be some sort of initiation, even if it was simply shaking the man's hand and introducing herself.

"Kate Power," she said, with a friendly grin, proffering her hand.

Perhaps six thirty was too early for security men to crack their faces. In any case, he needed one hand to hold the ballpoint he used to run down his list, the other to hold the clipboard. "Registration number? And are you just visiting or here for a bit?"

2

"Here for the foreseeable future." At least the next six months.

"OK. And next time, it's better to reverse in."

She nodded, popping on her hat. At least it would keep the cold, thin rain off, although she'd never felt the lack when she was in plain clothes. She'd never looked good in one when she was a rookie constable. No reason for her to do so now.

She strode up Hurst Street towards Smallbrook Ringway. What a weird mixture, greasy-spoon cafés cheek by jowl with a very exclusive-looking Chinese casino. Rod's favourite Indian restaurant, brilliant for an after-the-opera meal, was being refurbished. She hesitated: should she stop for a take-out coffee? No, better to see what system operated at Scala House. So she turned left on Smallbrook Ringway, and headed for Holloway Head, a traffic island proclaiming it was the gateway to the Chinese Quarter by means of a pagoda-like structure slap in the middle. But it was also home to a vulnerable-looking sculpture of a nymph. A few mixed messages. It was the boundary too of Brum's gay village: what would its denizens have wanted if they'd been asked to choose a boundary marker? A big pink ribbon? Perhaps not. In any case, up the road in Centenary Square, Birmingham already had a statue in a curious shade of pink, the sort she associated with old ladies' corsets.

And so into Scala House, with its uninspired entrance staircase. For this wasn't an ordinary police station, with all the foyer bustle that that implied. No cells, either. It was a small outpost of admin offices in

3

an ordinary commercial block, the ground floor of which was occupied by a gay bar. OK, then — onwards and upwards.

She managed to walk past the nameplate screwed to the door without a backward glance. At least, she conceded, not a visible backward glance. It would have been nice if the nameplate had been screwed on straight, but what mattered most was that it was there.

INSPECTOR
KATE POWER

Yes! It took maximum effort not to punch the air in triumph.

There was also a desktop version, smart in gold-blocked wood, but she stowed that away for the time being. No point in over-egging the pudding. The pips on her shoulders made the point about her rank, anyway. Not to mention what she hoped would grow into an air of authority: at the moment she was a new girl and everyone knew it — herself especially.

She shook off the hat and raincoat and looked for somewhere to hang them. Hmm, John Twiss, her predecessor, had been well over six foot. She'd have to bring a drill in and put the hook within reach. And stick a mirror on the wall — she didn't like peeping into a compact mirror like a dowager prinking her lipstick. DCI Sue Rowley, her old CID boss at Steelhouse Lane nick, had never appeared even in the women's locker rooms looking anything less than immaculate, hair apart, that is, whether in plain clothes or in uniform.

Part of the job, she'd always said, to show the underlings you were in control, no matter how egalitarian you might prefer to be.

From the desk at the far end — yes, if you looked up you could see who was coming through the door or, better still, who was going past it — Kate looked round her new office. Apart from the lofty hook, her predecessor had left little evidence of his occupation: on the wall by her left arm was a chart summarising official performance indicators and another beside it showing how the unit was matching up. On the wall facing her, above an empty waist-high bookcase, was a large-scale road map of the immediate area, her manor's boundaries outlined in thick green felt pen. On the right-hand wall, opposite the window, were a white board and a noticeboard with coloured pins herded together neatly in the bottom right corner. Despite herself, she got up to peer behind the vertical blinds: a fingertip drawn across the window came up grey. Well, she could do something about that. She could do less about the view the blinds concealed: cupping her hands round her eyes, she found an unattractive vista of fire escapes and dingy walls, with a flat roof immediately in front of her. The puddles were a soup of litter peppered with fag ends. She had a nasty feeling it would all look rather worse by daylight.

Hell, she should have been over the moon at achieving another step on what she hoped would be a steady ladder of promotion. She was. Of course she was. She was just a bit lacklustre after the last case, which hadn't gone entirely to plan. And, to be honest, she'd never been a morning woman — especially when Rod had done no more than hunch a naked shoulder and move over to the middle of the bed when she kissed him goodbye.

She turned from the window. No, it wouldn't be so bad. Not when she'd personalised the place a bit. She had a tiny furniture budget, which would extend to a coffee table and a couple of easy chairs. The computer would provide a reassuring presence on the acres of empty desk. Most of her colleagues filled the rest with personal photos: a silent reminder of why you were doing the job. But it would be tactless at this stage to introduce a photo of Rod. Love of her life he might be, but in the minds of unpromoted officers he no doubt figured as Superintendent Sugar Daddy, giving her a leg up in exchange for a leg over. Very well: all the more reason to prove herself a good officer.

Her neck was itching already. She ran an irritated finger round her collar. Much as she'd like to shed the clip-on tie and undo the top button, she knew she ought to follow the Sue Rowley tradition, noblesse obliging her to be a stickler over her own appearance before she could raise so much as an eyebrow at anyone else's lapses. However smart the crisp poplin blouses and serge skirts or trousers, after years of dressing as she pleased — within, it had to be said, self-prescribed parameters very like Sue's — she was bound to find them irksome, wasn't she? Heavens above, this was what most policewomen wore day in, day out. So what if her bra showed quite clearly though the shirt? So what if the trousers made her neat size-ten bum look like a saggy sixteen? Grow up, woman. She straightened. That was better. And she'd better try to regard carrying all the equipment a uniformed officer was issued with as the equivalent of permanent weight training. It was only for a few months anyway: until she earned enough Brownie points to get back into CID. Everyone agreed that that was where her career lay. It was simply policy to have a break from plain-clothes work, taking on responsibility in uniform for a period.

Kate looked at her watch. Six fifty. Time for the early shift to be taking over from the night shift. That was something else she wasn't looking forward to. OK, as a detective sergeant she'd never worked anything like a nine-till-five day, but at least there'd been a semblance of routine, except — as often — when there was a crisis. Now she and Rod would have to keep elaborate diaries — wall-charts on both kitchen walls would be helpful. But at least they could be together some hours out of the twenty-four. And it was good for everyone concerned that she wouldn't be working in one of his murder-investigation teams. She needed to be able to grow and function apart from him.

"Ma'am." The doorway was filled with the solid presence of one of her sergeants. He'd be about forty, already showing signs of a gut he'd end up having to support on his uniform belt.

She was fairly sure she hadn't heard his polite tap on her doorframe because there hadn't been one. And there was no lift at the end of the sentence to show any hesitation. But perhaps that was how John Twiss had preferred things — informal to the point of casual.

However much she'd have liked to follow suit, she had a nasty feeling that what was seen as affable when the boss was a six-foot-five rugby-playing alpha male might be construed as weakness when you were a five-foot-five untested young woman.

"Morning, Sergeant Drew. Neil, isn't it?" She stuck out a hand, coming from behind her desk and smiling a welcome. "I'd offer you a seat only there don't seem to be any." There was certainly a question in her voice: now she came to think about it, easy chairs were standard issue.

"There's a furniture budget."

"Which is tight. And I'd rather it wasn't spent on visitors' chairs when I'm sure some of the office chairs could do with upgrading. So it'd be nice if the ones from in here wandered back from wherever they've wandered off to. Come on, Neil, there's evidence: you can see the marks on the carpet there. Eight neat little indentations." She pointed. "Plus four bigger ones — are we talking coffee-table here? Hmm? No questions asked if they're back here by the end of tonight's shift."

"Ma'am." He looked as sullen as a schoolboy.

"Are you ready to brief the early shift?"

"Just going to."

"I'll slip in while you're doing it."

"Thought you'd be busy."

"I am. But it gives you a chance to introduce me when it's most convenient, least disruptive. I'll be doing the same for each relief."

"Long day."

She shrugged. "When was it ever a nine-till-five job?"

8

The briefing didn't make good listening. Neil Drew's team was down to four out of its full complement of seven.

"But not to worry. We don't have to argue about who gets the car today."

"*The* car?" she repeated, before remembering she should have been coolly observing and waiting for her grand moment. "You've — *we*'ve only got the one?"

"Two. One's double-crewed for fast response. The other is shared between the rest of the relief for routine calls."

She ignored the swift turn of heads. "And car number two is?"

"In dock. Gearbox. Supposed to be under bloody warranty, but the suppliers and manufacturers are arguing the toss."

"Haven't they ever heard of courtesy cars? I'll get on to it. Can't manage without wheels. So who's on sickie today?"

The consequent snigger took her straight back to the school-room. Ah.

"The usual suspects, ma'am."

"Gaffer," she corrected crisply. "Who are?"

"WPC Kerr. She's got a lot of problems, m — gaffer: women's troubles, like." Neil Drew's sneer was a challenge.

"WPC Kerr's pregnant, we think," said a stout African-Caribbean WPC, probably in her forties.

"Well, that's certainly a woman thing." Kate grinned. "And the other officers? Men's or women's troubles?"

"PC Parker's got a bad back. Has had on and off for a year or more."

Kate made a note: Occupational Health. "And . . ."

"Master Bates," Neil Drew said.

"Does he now? And what else is the matter with PC Bates?"

"Bad stomach."

"Bad regularly?"

"Judging by how often he farts, bad all the bleeding time. But he's here more often than he's away."

"Just about," added the WPC, *sotto voce*.

Another one for Occupational Health, then. "OK. You've prioritised today's duties then, Neil? Anything you can't cover?"

"A meeting with the Chinese elders."

"Time?"

"Three, I think."

"Let me know for certain, and I'll try to clear a slot in the diary. And if you've got any other stuff someone new could tackle, let me have it."

So far, so good. There'd been a distinct frisson of what sounded like approval and she had a sense that she'd started off on the right foot — at least with those who were there. What if the staffing problems were repeated on the other shifts? She might be able to cover the odd meeting and do bits of follow-up, but essentially she wasn't here as a roving WPC. And although she was going to stay on till after the night shift had reported, she couldn't work till ten every night. She'd seen other bosses try to do everything and end up as one of their own sick-leave statistics. At training courses, the importance of proper breaks for everyone, including herself, had been dinned into her. R and R; regular meals. No dashing off to the pub at the end of each shift. Think healthy to stay healthy. So one inviolable item on today's agenda would be lunch. She'd already promised herself that. And now that the Home Office thought it was a Good Idea for police officers to eat in local cafés, she would attach herself to one of her officers and kill two birds with one stone: get to know the officer, exercise a little, eat and see the officer ate too. Four birds. And a fifth — getting her face known in the community.

She was just heading for the outer office — the team's name for it, though the office wasn't even on the outside of the building — when she heard voices.

"I heard she got a collar on her last job. A big one." Who was that? Not Neil Drew. Parker? No, he was the bad back. Timms. Steve Timms.

"Yes. Undercover. Down in Devon. But she lost one of her team." That was Drew all right.

Losing a colleague was never good news. Suddenly she was on the back foot — or would be, if she wasn't careful. Risk time. She stepped forward, saying easily, "Don't let the detective superintendent in charge hear you call it my team. Craig and I were just foot soldiers."

"But he died," Drew said. It was a statement, not a question.

"You take risks undercover."

"Wasn't there rumour of an official complaint against you before he died?"

11

She raised her eyebrows: Drew was going much too far. Everyone knew it. Timms, Drew, Kate, and the African-Caribbean WPC — Hale, she thought — who'd padded up behind her.

"You have been doing your homework well, Sergeant. But I'm sure you've got other things to do than check up on what a sick man did before he took a crazy risk that lost him his life. Post-traumatic stress disorder," she added parenthetically.

"I thought it was post-traumatic stress syndrome," Drew observed.

"When you have it long and badly enough it becomes a disorder, as I'm sure your research will tell you. We'll talk later, Sergeant. In the meantime, where do you people take lunch? And if you tell me lunch is only for wimps, let me tell you that current research doesn't support that theory."

CHAPTER
TWO

"Before you ask," Euphronia Hale said, as Kate carried two baguettes bulging healthily with salad across to the table the WPC had grabbed in the café window, "Neil Drew wasn't after your job. Nor was he backing any of his mates to get it."

"So why's he so angry? And resentful?" Kate waved aside Euphronia's purse. "On me. I'll be treating everyone the same. Even Neil. Especially Neil."

"And will you be asking him the same questions?"

"I should have asked him before I asked you," Kate observed, trying not to flush. It was her first major failure as manager.

Although Euphronia nodded, she didn't seem to be scoring any points. "You should." She shrugged wide shoulders. "But he might not have told you. In fact, he'd have denied everything and blustered and got more and more hostile. *That's* why I'm telling you, not because you asked. Another thing, you'll hear people talking about 'Ronnie': that's me. I don't like the name, but it's better than my given one."

"So you're happy for me to call you that?"

Euphronia-Ronnie shrugged. "Till we all come up with something better. I'm working on it, gaffer. Not 'ma'am', I notice." She picked at a shred of lettuce.

"Kate when we're off duty. And only 'ma'am' if I'm bollocking people. I've had some good gaffers here in Brum. Both genders. I'd like to become one myself."

Ronnie chuckled quietly. "You know, some of the lads — and lasses — reckon you've only got the job because you're sleeping with Top Brass. I don't think they're right."

With a woman like this perhaps you could afford to be honest. You couldn't afford to be anything less. "I'm in a long-term relationship with a superintendent. But I came into the service on the accelerated-promotion scheme, so I don't think sleeping with Rod has much to do with it."

"Might even have slowed you down a bit?" Ronnie looked at her over the top of her baguette. "You know, people thinking if you've got personal commitments you won't be able to cut the mustard?"

Kate shook her head. "I honestly don't know." And then her phone went.

"Sergeant Drew here." His voice was tinnily formal. "I've just had a call from the Chinese elders wondering where you are."

She was on her feet. "It's never three already?"

"It's thirteen hundred. Ma'am."

"Where's the meeting?" She scribbled on the napkin Ronnie shoved her way. "Let them know I'm on my way. And we'll talk about why you told me three, not one, when I get back."

14

Ronnie was on her feet too, wrapping both Kate's and her own baguette in a spare napkin. "You'll never be able to park there. I'll drop you off."

They were both puffed by the time they reached the car park, Ronnie especially having no breath to talk. Kate, too, would have to up her fitness levels. Ronnie extricated her car, a handsome number distinctly smarter and newer than Kate's, with apparent ease. "This bloody traffic gets worse every day. Look at it!"

Kate looked. She wasn't sure whether it would have been possible to make much more progress in a response vehicle, flashing blue light notwithstanding. "You're sure I wouldn't be faster on foot?"

"Probably. But you'd arrive hot and bothered, and that'd show disrespect. Big on respect, the Chinese."

Kate nodded, dabbing powder. And a smear of natural lipstick. At least her eye makeup hadn't gone to that mysterious place where it always seems to go. And the bloody hat would cover a multitude of sinfully dishevelled hair.

"The problem with Neil," Ronnie said slowly, but quite deliberately, "is that he doesn't like people to know in case they feel sorry for him and try to take over work he should be doing."

"Know what?"

"Wandering wife. Leaving him with the kids."

"How wandering? Permanently?"

"Worse. From time to time. Poor bugger just gets things sorted and back she comes. Creates a few weeks' mayhem. Spoils the kids rotten. Gets everyone thinking everything'll be OK, then she ups and offs again. And when she's off, he's mum and dad and psychotherapist and everything else to those girls. But he'll never let on."

"How does he survive?"

"You've just seen."

"How do you know all this if he won't talk?"

"I know one of the teachers at their school. Quite well. An absolute nutter, his wife, she says. Completely destabilises the kids when she comes and when she goes. And Neil, come to think of it. Now, do you know anything about this afternoon's do?"

"I was going to mug up as soon as I got back from lunch. Who am I taking over from?"

"Dave Bush. Sergeant Bush. Looks like an overgrown student. He's on annual leave — nothing dodgy about his health. Good old-fashioned cop, despite his fancy title, field intelligence officer. He's really doing his homework — he knows the people who own and run the casinos, the gambling clubs, the restaurants. You name it. Rumour has it he's even learning Cantonese so he can talk to people better — or at least impress them that he's trying."

"Like learning a little Greek when you pop off to Crete."

"Exactly. Only, knowing Dave, he might make it quite a lot of Cantonese. There you are — over there. That new building with all those small windows. Cherish House."

"Seriously?"

16

"Seriously. Because that's what they do. They may need an old folks' home for their oldies, but they treat them right, cherish them."

It was a good job, Kate reflected, that she'd had no more than a bite of her baguette. The community leaders awaiting her politely at Cherish House had provided nibbles more delectable than any she'd ever come across, and she regretted that manners and a burning desire not to make any more gaffes prevented her grabbing fistfuls. Or did she dimly remember that eating a lot was a sign of good manners in some cultures? Why hadn't she taken the time to brief herself properly? You simply couldn't cruise through meetings like this with a smile and shiny buttons. The best she could do was continually apologise for Sergeant Bush's absence. It seemed he was more alert than she: he'd already written to apologise, and had e-mailed his good wishes for the reception this lunchtime. Kate had an idea she and Bush would be able to do business.

Meanwhile Mr Choi, a sleek fifty-year-old with an English accent as pure as her own, was apparently to be her escort. She hated the clichéd thought that he was impenetrable, but forced herself to admit that he was. While quietly dressed and almost self-effacing, he couldn't have been taken by the most naïve person as a nobody. No, Mr Choi was Someone, just as the chief constable or a prominent industrialist was Someone. She must ask Dave Bush about him. Now he was presenting her to a question-mark-shaped woman with ravine-deep wrinkles. At a hundred and two Mrs Peng

17

was the most senior of the cherished seniors. All Kate could do was smile and bow over the claw of a hand. She was hard put to it not to curtsy. She told Mr Choi that her great-aunt was eighty-five, but Mrs Peng, receiving the information with a sharp nod, didn't seem overly impressed. She was the only resident who made an impression on Kate: the rest passed in a blur of handshakes and platitudes. Goodness, was this how the Queen felt?

But the Queen knew what was expected of her and, if she forgot, could rely on a quiet prompt. Kate blundered on, waiting for — something? A speech? An adjournment to a meeting room to get on with some unspecified nitty-gritty? Or should she make her excuses and beat it? Perhaps they'd stop circulating food and wine as a signal. At last, feeling unbearably gauche, she drew Mr Choi slightly to one side.

He responded to her enquiry with what seemed like unfeigned laughter. "My dear Inspector, this is what that admirable novelist E. M. Forster would have called a bridge party. The representatives — in this case in the singular, alas — of law and order meeting the natives."

Kate had never liked *Passage to India*, but clearly it would have been a terrible lapse of etiquette to embark on a discussion of the book's literary merits.

"To be fair, this is perhaps more of a celebration than that implies. A celebration of our successful co-operation. Cherish House itself. The youth project your colleagues and mine initiated. The continued work for New Year and other festivals."

18

Kate nodded and smiled as if none of these projects was news. Of course, she'd heard of the street procession for the Chinese New Year, but had never yet been able to see it for herself. But she'd no idea how well the police and the Chinese community were working together. To her shame, all the Chinese connections her brain would make were with tongs and triads, table tennis and takeaways.

So if this was no more than a social event, how long ought she stay? Mr Choi had given her no hint, but he was so suavely polite that she suspected he wouldn't have turned an immaculate hair if she'd been supposed to do no more than appear, eat a spring roll and flit. To her enormous relief her phone rang.

Ronnie: "Better get yourself back here, gaffer. Can you walk or shall I send a car?" For all the world as if they had a limo at their disposal!

"Better send the rapid-response vehicle," Kate snapped, for Mr Choi's benefit, not Ronnie's. But she doubted that he was taken in.

"So what was all that about?" Kate demanded, as Ronnie brought a mug of tea into her office. One of these days she'd have to tell them how she liked her brew, which wasn't strong and milky.

"I looked in the diary. It said thirteen hundred to thirteen forty-five. So I thought you might need rescuing. Dave knows the drill, you see. The guy before him used to spend whole afternoons with the godfathers."

" 'Godfathers'? You mean I've been hobnobbing with —"

"Oh, yes. Dave'll fill you in when he comes back. I won't spoil it for you. But there was a phone call from Tim Wilde — he's our tame geek — and he said he could come in this evening to show you the ropes if that'd help. About eight, he said."

"Wonderful. I take it it's his own time?"

"Actually he's on the night shift, so he shouldn't be here till ten. But he said most folk couldn't deal with IT when the sun had gone beyond the yardarm."

"Nor can I," Kate lied. After the last IT course she'd been on, she'd just have to pretend to be an apt pupil: not for anything would she put off a willing worker. "How do we contact him?"

"E-mail. I'll tell him yes, shall I?"

"Please. And is Sergeant Drew anywhere around?"

She wasn't looking forward to this. To bollock or to offer a sympathetic ear? He'd almost certainly respect her more if she tore him off several strips. So would most officers of his age. What would Sue Rowley do? But Sue had both age and experience on her side, and could turn on that quasi-motherly exasperation she used to speak to her teenage kids whenever she wanted to put miscreants in their place. Kate couldn't do motherly, not without sounding like a cross between Mary Poppins and a football manager.

It seemed that Neil Drew wasn't anywhere around. He'd gone out of radio contact. This wouldn't be school-run time, would it? Someone would have to collect the kids, and if the wife had gone walkabout again presumably it had to be Neil. And he could have gone with her blessing so long as she'd known in advance. Sod the bloody stupid man. She'd kill him!

Except that — she slapped her forehead — she was back in the world of shifts, wasn't she? Neil had been here well before seven and could go off at two, quite legitimately. It wasn't like CID, where you worked flexible days but were expected to come in and leave at whatever times the boss chose. Another little gradient on the already steep learning curve.

So what the hell had Ronnie Hale been doing hanging back after hours briefing her and making her tea? Being a good colleague, that was what.

The damned lunchtime drinkies had made her miss the start of the two till ten shift. Hell. Looking like a PC Party-goer was the last thing she wanted. OK, there was no reason why she couldn't simply walk round and introduce herself informally. Jesus! More faces after the kaleidoscope of new ones this morning and at lunchtime. Then there'd be the night shift. The way she was feeling, Tim the Geek would find her a far from apt pupil.

Time for a prowl, then, and another cup of tea. Ronnie's brew had been so strong she felt as jumpy as if she'd had three black coffees. DCI Graham Harvey had always drunk much healthier herbal brews to preserve his blood pressure. She'd never liked them much, but they were better than twitchiness. Maybe she could find other caffeine-free alternatives.

The tiny kitchen wasn't as clean as she'd have liked. A few weeks as a professional cleaner had given her a taste for taps without any slime even at the back and for regularly wiped work-surfaces. She might have to have a word with the contract cleaner. While she was at it, she'd check the loos, both women's and men's. That meant a chaperon. The only uniformed officer she could see was a slightly built Asian of about her age, chewing his ballpoint over a mound of files. Heart swelling with fellow-feeling, she tapped lightly on the frame of his open door and grinned, gesturing him back into his chair when he leapt with alarmed precision to attention, gabbling name and number. "It's OK. You're not in a POW camp. You must be Zayn Ara? Kate Power." She leant across the desk to shake his hand.

Mistake. He didn't know whether to stand or stay sitting, and compromised with an awkward bend, which couldn't have done his back any good.

"I'm actually looking for someone to escort me to the gents'," she said, laughing with what was rapidly becoming an embarrassment to match his. "If I'm going to run a tight ship I'd like to make sure it's shipshape." Hell, why had she embarked on that particular image? "Seriously," she continued, "as a new officer in charge I want to make sure everything's as it should be."

"I hear you've already sorted the second car," he said, getting to his feet properly this time.

"Yes. It should be here first thing tomorrow. They wanted to give us one with 'Courtesy Car' splashed all over it," she added.

"Haven't Them Upstairs already mooted that idea? Sponsored cars, like sponsored traffic islands."

22

"Lovely idea! Let's think. Sponsored speed cameras. Cells courtesy of Dolphin Showers. Desks by MFI."

"Inspectors might have one from IKEA," he mused.

She had a feeling this lad should go far.

The loos were no better than average.

"What about the locker rooms?"

"My mum would say it was like my bedroom. Lots of fluff underneath the lockers. Only it's my wardrobe, of course." He blushed, as if recalling their difference in rank again.

"You sort your bedroom, I'll sort this. You're not married, then?" They stopped by the kitchen. She filled the kettle.

He grimaced. "I'm what you might call on the shelf, aren't I?"

"Can blokes be on shelves?"

"My mum reckons I threw up my best chances while I was at uni. All the girls that are left are too plain or too dim, she says."

She'd have liked to ask what he thought, but probably inspectors shouldn't be gossiping with their constables about their marital status. In any case, their roles reversed, enquiries like that might be construed as racist or sexist.

"Tea? Coffee?"

He shook his head politely. "It's Ramadan, gaffer."

"And you're working full shifts without — heavens, Zayn, I take my hat off to you." She remembered another Muslim colleague's needs. "What about prayers?"

"I take Fridays off as annual leave if the shift roster doesn't give me time off, which it mostly does. And, of course, working nights helps. And it'll be Eid, soon." A phone rang. "Mine! Excuse me, gaffer!"

The only other person around was their clerical support, deep in transcribing some policy-meeting notes, which, she told Kate with a straight face, she'd find she needed the following day. Mrs Kathleen Speed. In this relatively egalitarian set-up, she seemed more a Mrs Speed than a Kathleen. Nothing to do with her age, which was probably not much more than fifty, more the effect of a tight bun and pursed mouth.

In the meantime, there was plenty of stuff in Kate's in-tray, which had materialised on her desk while she was out. Someone had stuck an adhesive label over her predecessor's name — Mrs Speed, perhaps. Cases she knew nothing about; meetings to schedule; most of all a huge file crammed with government papers outlining the latest Home Office initiatives. She flicked through them, attacking the margins with a magic marker, which had arrived as part of the stationery complement at the same time as the in-tray. Mrs Speed was clearly worth cultivating.

"Here's the list of e-mail addresses you'll use most often," Tim Wilde, tall, blond and scrawny, said, passing her a sheet. "This is such a small unit it's rare to be able to talk face to face with people you need, so we do it this way."

"Hang on. As it's a small unit surely I should be able to talk to everyone directly."

He laughed. "Small but chaotically formed. Take yourself. You're on shifts — yes? So you want to talk to, say, me? About some IT problem? But I'm on a different shift. You could leave a note and I could leave a note in return, or you could e-mail me, so we've both got copies. It's the system Inspector Twiss set up when he discovered he was Mr Meetings."

"Am I about to discover I'm Ms Meetings?"

"I wouldn't bet your pension you're not. Anyway, assuming you know all about e-mail?"

"Enough."

"Good. Well, this is how you organise the shift roster — just a matter of putting the info in and pressing a few buttons."

Kate pressed experimentally. "What about making changes — if someone needs a dental appointment, say, and doesn't want to sacrifice annual leave?"

"Most people here seem to have a good set of teeth." He grinned, showing his own. "But it can be done."

"Who does it? Can people change it themselves?"

"Only sergeants. I believe they're supposed to consult with you first. Do you want me to change it?"

"So it's a free-for-all? No, thanks. In fact, until I know everyone, I'd rather they all had to come to me first. Even sergeants. Not because I don't trust people, Tim, so that I can get to know them and any problems they may have regarding time off and so on."

"Like N — I mean, yes, good idea." Tim blushed.

God, he was so like the man she'd worked for when she was undercover! For a weird moment she was back, putting pressure on what she'd hoped was an innocent man. No. The past was past. The law had done its bit — now it was time for justice to see what it could do. All through that case, all she'd really wanted was to go home. And that was what she wanted now, completely and overwhelmingly. She swallowed a yawn, refused to stretch. She must concentrate on the next bit of information Tim was bringing to the screen. There was a great deal she hadn't learnt on that course.

"You're not doing this again," Rod said flatly. "Out of the house at six, back home at eleven." But he tempered his words, or augmented them, by digging his thumbs deep into the muscles knotted round her shoulders and neck. "There's not even a panic on to justify it. If you work silly hours when you don't have to you've got no reserves when there's a crisis."

She tried to nod, but his thumbs had found another tangle of tissue.

"And," he continued, "if you don't promise to be good in future, I shan't get you a drink."

"I'd die for a drink. Or you may need it to resuscitate me if you go on like this! Ouch!"

He brought her her drink as she soaked in the bath. They'd fallen into such easy, relaxed ways with each other she couldn't think why she'd hesitated when he'd asked her to move in with him. Well, she could. There was the matter of Aunt Cassie and her house. But she spent so little time there now that next time he suggested it she'd agree. Yes. She might even raise it herself. Later tonight.

She was asleep before he set the alarm. Almost. But not quite.

"OK. Six thirty," she mumbled.

CHAPTER
THREE

The next morning Rod and she got up together — and by common consent immediately returned to bed for a few energetic minutes. Rod appeared pleased with his efforts. "It's nice to see a glow on your cheeks, sweetheart. You've been looking less yourself than usual." He stroked her cheek.

"I'm fine. Honestly."

"You weren't in the night. How many hours' sleep did you get?" He pushed back her hair and tenderly scrutinised her eyes.

"I didn't keep you awake, did I, Rod? I'm so sorry."

"I was asking about *you*. You still haven't got over that last case, have you? And now you've been plunged willy-nilly into the Brave New World that's police middle management."

She shot him a hard look. Could he be patronising her? After all, he was much higher up the food chain than middle management. And it wasn't as if he was likely to stick at superintendent: he was as hardworking as he was ambitious and talented.

If he registered it, he ignored it. "When you're in the ranks," he expanded, "you can always blame other people, especially your bosses. When you're a boss, you can blame the incompetent idiots in the ranks. Inspectors and CIs get blamed by everyone. I've still got the scars on my back, somewhere."

She grinned. It was impossible to get on your high horse with a naked man holding a hopeful hand under the shower jet.

She hadn't been entirely accurate when she'd told Ronnie Hale that she and Rod were in a long-term relationship. The truth was that she hoped, no, believed that they were, and that this was just the start of it. Certainly she'd got to the point where she couldn't imagine life without him. They'd once had, yes, an affair. Almost immediately they'd had a major falling-out over her working methods, but had then slowly but surely become friends. Almost as soon as they'd both found that they were more than ready to become lovers again, Kate's work had taken her undercover. She'd been afraid that their time apart would re-erect barriers, but had dismissed her fears, even when she'd found it impossible to settle in her own house, still felt a visitor in his. But Rod had been his usual urbane self, rather more domesticated, in fact, as if caring for an invalid: she smiled again. Surely only a man in love would spend so much time after a day's work at least as tough as her own processing vegetables to make her soup and preparing delicate sandwiches. And only a woman in love would welcome his dripping embrace as he vacated the shower, which he left running for her. As she dried her hair, she heard him calling upstairs that he was making porridge to ensure she had at least one decent meal today.

He raised an eyebrow when she entered the kitchen in mufti.

"I feel more me if I go in like this. And change there," she added. Hell, she sounded like a defiant schoolgirl, not his lover.

"I did like those black stockings, though," he said mock-wistfully.

"I'll wear some specially for you. And some big fierce hand-cuffs?"

"Only if they're pink and fluffy. You'd think they could make non-stick porridge to go with non-stick pans, wouldn't you?"

"You could always microwave it in dishes," she suggested, leaning her head against his shoulder as she peered into the saucepan.

He kissed her hair. "No. It never tastes the same. How on earth can stuff this colour and texture be so good for you? Now, I've put you some teabags in that caddy — a selection. If you drink the stuff they make there you'll end up with insides like leather."

She peered inside. "Rod, your mother gave you these."

"And you liked them, or claimed to, and I loathed them. And I know you won't grass me up. Will you?" He put his head on one side like a guilty choirboy.

Her reply was an extravagant hug. This lovely man didn't deserve anyone to snub him. "Not if I can liberate something else — those china mugs at the back of that cupboard . . ."

"The relentlessly pretty ones with jolly country flowers on? Auntie Winnie's last Christmas present."

He clasped his hand to his forehead. "Just think, I thought I was going to have to pay someone to take them away." He added, more seriously, "You can't really want those, not for work?"

"They're better than anything we've got. And they'll do until I can buy something less, er, cheerful."

"I shall be for ever in your debt," he declared, burrowing for them. "Especially if you take them straight to a charity shop when you've finished with them."

"And how will you settle your debt?"

Still on his knees, he said, "By doing whatever you ask, your slave for ever."

She kissed his forehead. "I think I may enjoy having you in my debt."

"Sick? Neil Drew? Jesus, why didn't you phone me, Ronnie? I'd have come in early again." Not that she was late. It was only seven forty now. What the hell was the usual procedure? Should a sergeant be brought in from another nick? Should one of the constables be made acting sergeant? She must get on to Personnel immediately.

Ronnie Hale looked up at her from behind her desk, for all the world like an inspector rebuking a rookie WPC. "I assumed you'd be in at the same time as you were yesterday. You didn't tell me you were coming in late."

"Unless there's an emergency, this week I'm simply on the day shift, not the early. You have all my phone numbers: I expect you to use each one till you find me. All right, who did the shift briefing?"

"I did."

So the obvious person to make up was Ronnie herself.

"It was nothing out of the ordinary. We're an experienced team, ma'am, and we know what we have to do." Ronnie returned her gaze to her papers.

Completely wrong-footed, Kate wanted to stamp and yell, "Don't call me 'ma'am', call me 'gaffer'!" The issue wasn't any longer the absence of a surly sergeant, but the chilling behaviour of a subordinate. But she'd already treated the subordinate as an equal. It was her own fault that she was now being — what? Put in her place? No problem — except it was the wrong place.

She gathered together the shreds of her dignity. "I'm sure you do. All of you. But in future one of the things you must do is notify me. Is that understood?"

"Ma'am." Ronnie looked her briefly in the eye, before returning to her task.

"Thank you." She must keep cool no matter how much she wanted to yell. "Did Sergeant Drew give any indication how long he was likely to be off?"

"None."

"Or of what was the matter?"

"Tummy bug." It couldn't have mattered less to her, could it? Or was she silently seething because Kate hadn't mentioned a temporary upgrading?

Kate had got as far as the door. She turned. "And we're sure it's him, not one of his kids?"

32

"Now you're asking," Ronnie said. At last she looked up. "Trouble is, what does a single dad do if one of his kids isn't up to school?"

"I should imagine he's run out of annual leave?"

"Pretty nearly. Except what he's saving for Christmas, which isn't much. And he can't manage without it then, that's for sure."

"I wouldn't want him to." She'd no idea how to tackle this one, but she wasn't about to admit it to Ronnie. "Apart from Neil, do we have a full complement?" Dreadful she should only just have remembered to ask.

"Phil Bates says he should be in tomorrow."

"Maybe he passed his bug on to Neil . . ." Kate murmured hopefully, but Ronnie merely continued, "Parker's sent in a sick note for his back — self-certification. And Kerr's here, but looks as if she shouldn't be."

"Is her pregnancy still a rumour or has she confirmed it yet? Because I don't want her belting round the streets if —"

"Hang on, gaffer. Pregnancy isn't an illness, you know. I worked up to thirty-six weeks with both of mine."

"Normal or light duties?"

"Normal, until the bosses got embarrassed by my size. Then they pulled me indoors. Wasn't my choice, believe me."

Kate did. "Point taken. It's a matter for Helen, her doctor and Personnel. And then me."

Ronnie's expression declared that single, childless women ought to say nothing about things they knew nothing about. But she didn't speak.

"Where is Helen?"

"What are you going to say to her?"

"You know that that's between her and me, Ronnie. In any case, what sort of gaffer would you think I was if I didn't meet everyone in my team as soon as I could? Now, who's staffing the rapid-response vehicle?"

"Me, in a couple of minutes. And it should have been Helen, but I'm not stopping at every set of traffic lights while she spews, so it'll be Mick Roskell. He was at the briefing yesterday."

"Didn't register him."

"You wouldn't. He lurks behind the door and doesn't say anything, but put him in a tight spot and he's the best cop I know."

"So that leaves just Steve Timms and me to hold the fort. OK." She smiled. "Thanks for all you did this morning, Ronnie, but remember, I have to be informed next time."

"OK, gaffer." Ronnie sketched a salute and smiled for the first time that morning.

The person she needed to speak to in Personnel wasn't in yet, so Kate left a message. Then she slapped her head: the simplest thing would be for her to transfer to the early shift herself and simply stay on as long as it took. Simplest — but what would Rod say? Meanwhile, she'd better have a quick word with Helen Kerr. There was no sign of her in the offices: Kate assumed that she was out. Until, checking the loos again for cleanliness, she found her in one of the cubicles on her hands and knees. She was a big, tough-looking woman, built as if she wouldn't disgrace a male rugby team. Kate felt for her, being caught at such a disadvantage by someone half her size. Giving her a moment or two to tidy up, Kate fetched a chair and a glass of water.

When she returned, Helen was on her feet in front of the mirror, shoving furious fingers through unyielding hair. "I'm OK. Quite OK. Fine." Even those few words betrayed a thick Black Country accent.

"And will be all the finer for a quiet sit-down." Kate waited: yes, the woman was going to obey what they both knew was an implicit order. "Here, even if you do no more than wash your mouth out. That's better. Is it something you've eaten? Or this bug that seems to be going round? Phil and Neil's?"

"Some fucking bug! Phil Bates has got a sodding ulcer and that thing that makes you fart all the time."

"Irritable bowel syndrome?"

"Great fun sharing an office with him. Or a car. And Drew'll be on the skive again."

Not a woman for being loyal to her colleagues, then. "But it's you I'm concerned about at the moment," Kate said repressively. "Are you well enough to be in work?"

"I'm all right if folk don't fuss."

"You're mistaken. I'm not fussing and I don't think you're well enough to be here. Do you?"

"I told you, I'm all right. I'm just up the fucking duff. It's fucking morning sickness, isn't it?"

"Is it? Are congratulations in order?"

"Not specially. I still haven't decided whether to keep it."

Kate tried not to flinch. She would have died to protect a woman's right to choose, but this brutality shocked her. Helen might have been discussing nothing more important than a new pair of curtains. "You've had counselling?"

"Waste of sodding time that'd be."

"Sometimes it helps clarify things. I'm sure Personnel could refer —"

"And have it down on my sodding records that I need a fucking shrink? No bloody thanks."

"I believe that nothing's written down, and certainly the counselling's confidential." But Kate wouldn't admit to this woman that she'd had therapy herself. You had to be very careful before you put that sort of ammunition into anyone's hands. In police terms, it was still better to have a broken bone than a damaged mind, even if the damage was just as real and caused by something as powerful as, if less visible than, a bullet. "Now, are you up to another sip of water?"

"For fuck's sake, don't nanny me!"

"'For fuck's sake, don't nanny me, *gaffer*,'" Kate corrected her quietly. "Remember, I'm responsible for the health and safety of all my officers. As soon as you're up to it, come and talk to me in my office. OK? . . . I said, 'OK?'"

"Gaffer."

★ ★ ★

Before Kate could even begin to plan what she should say to Helen Kerr, Kathleen Speed knocked on her door, tight-lipped in apparent disapproval at finding it ajar. She certainly closed it emphatically behind her as she stepped in, dropping equally firmly a pile of glossy folders on Kate's desk. "Goodness knows how much they spend on these. They could print them out on plain paper — just as easy to read, and very much cheaper." She looked accusingly at Kate.

"Absolutely. And leave several forests of trees standing."

"Of course, they do grow some trees specially for paper," Mrs Speed demurred. "And some of this might even be recycled." She started to check through but Kate held up a restraining hand.

"When do I have to have read these?"

Mrs Speed consulted a black-bound desk diary. "Local problems of law and disorder — there's a meeting about that tomorrow morning at ten. You could delegate, I suppose, but Inspector Twiss always insisted on going to that sort of meeting himself."

"Why did he think it was valuable?"

"Because he met members of the community. Shopkeepers, restauranteurs, not just the Chinese leaders. Which reminds me, you've got one of them wanting to see you. A Mr Choi."

"We're keeping him waiting while we talk about Home Office initiatives! Here, there's room in the top drawer of that cabinet if you squash things up a bit. Shove everything in there. Good. Now, show him in and get the kettle on. We'll use the new mugs in that carrier-bag there."

Mrs Speed repressed a disdainful sniff, but placed two on the corner of Kate's desk.

"Thanks. And a variety of teas. What are we waiting for, Mrs Speed? We mustn't keep Joe Public waiting if we don't have to."

"I'd have thought it made a point —"

"What point? Joe Public pays our wages, Mrs Speed. The least we can do is be courteous to our employer."

At least she had a chair on which to seat her visitor. The coffee table had returned too. As pieces of furniture neither would have moved Rod to rapture, but they didn't disgrace the police service either. Mrs Speed showed in Mr Choi, returning almost instantly, and certainly before Kate asked her, with a tray bearing a kettle, which she plugged into a handy power-point, the tea caddy and a plate of biscuits. If Mr Choi was amused by the lack of sophistication, he was too polite to show it.

Mr Choi's preliminaries took for ever, but Kate sensed that there was no rushing him. He would say whatever he had to say in his own time.

At last he coughed politely in the middle of a discussion of English metaphors. He'd touched on *toeing the line, beating a retreat* and *keeping mum*. Kate had floundered, but managed to offer *the witching hour, the dead of night* and *dead tired*. She was hoping that Mr Choi hadn't realised how much of her present state she'd revealed, when he said, "And there is a strange word to describe the capacity in which I present myself to you this morning. Snout. I'm here as your snout, Inspector Power."

Enough of idiom. "You have information for us, Mr Choi?"

"Information? A complaint? A very strong rumour?"

"Complaint?"

"Not against the police, my dear Inspector Power. Possibly but not definitely against some of my confrères."

God, the bugger knew French, too.

"Against any in particular?"

"If I knew exactly whom, I could take action. Believe me, Inspector, I could take action." Neither his face nor his voice had changed. But he exuded menace.

"I'd much rather you left any action to us, sir." She hoped her protest wasn't as feeble as it sounded to her own ears.

"Of course. And since in any case I don't know the source of our problems, I have no option. Illegal immigrants, Inspector Power. That is the nature of my complaint. I own legitimate restaurants and retail outlets. I do not employ what they call 'indentured labour'. A euphemism, I believe you call it."

"Not so much indentured as slave? Working for virtually nothing to pay off exorbitant fees to traffickers for smuggling them into the country?"

Choi nodded. "Exactly so. You have clearly done a great deal of homework in the last thirty hours, Inspector. Allow me to congratulate you."

Kate blushed but didn't argue. She'd no idea where her brain had been yesterday, but at least some of the things she'd learnt on all those courses returned to it today. Or was it simply something she'd read in the newspapers? Whatever. "Do you have any idea who's responsible? Enough for us to work on, if not for you?" She smiled, ironically. "Which organisations are benefiting?"

He shook his head. "I'm sure my intelligence will produce something for you soon. As for access, they come in via the wholesale market, I presume."

She thought of the traffic in the area. "In a container lorry. One of the hundreds, if not thousands, coming in every night."

"Quite so. A pleasant little conundrum for you to solve, Inspector." He sipped his tea for the first time. "This is a very unusual flavour, Miss Power."

"If it's like mine, it's not so much unusual as rather nasty." She laughed. "But at least it's healthily nasty. The station brew is —"

"I know. Absolutely disgusting. Stewed and then diluted with milk." He flicked his wrist.

Was it a genuine Rolex? Kate didn't doubt it for a second. "Aren't you taking a risk, wearing that round here?"

"On the contrary, I'm safer wearing it round here than anywhere else." She was sure his smile was deliberately enigmatic. He got to his feet, the herbal tea unfinished. "Rest assured, I will supply you with any information that reaches me. I know from experience, alas, that you are unable to reciprocate."

She walked with him to the top of the stairs, wishing the surroundings were more appropriate. They shook hands, both bowing slightly.

"I look forward to working with you, Inspector."

"And I with you."

But as she watched him descend, assured, polished, dangerous, she wasn't at all sure that she was.

CHAPTER
FOUR

Helen Kerr, arms akimbo, was waiting for Kate when she got back to her office. Kate suppressed a sigh: instead of getting her head round an allegation about major international crime, she was in for a truculent discussion about pregnancy.

"Come on in," she said, more mildly than she wanted. She held the door, closing it gently on the two of them. "Are you feeling better? Come on, sit down."

Helen remained on her feet. "The thing is, I was out of order then. Way out of order."

Kate gestured at one of the chairs, with what she hoped was authority, but said noncommittally, "Hormones do funny things, don't they?"

"Fucking right. I thought PMT was bad enough but this! Any road, I was out of order. Gaffer."

Kate nodded a friendly acknowledgement. "Look, sit down. I'd offer you tea but this is a herbal brew and disgusting stuff."

"I'm off tea. Makes me throw up. Maybe that stuff'd suit me better."

"Try it." Perhaps this was the way forward. Kate reboiled the kettle and poured water on to a pinkish bag.

Helen sniffed at the resulting pale raspberry-coloured liquid with interest, swirling the bag around for a couple of minutes before fishing it out and slinging it accurately into a bin. She even volunteered a smile as she took the first sip. "Ah, it's not half bad."

Which Kate took as approval. It was a risk, but she'd take it: "Which part of the Black Country are you from?"

A beam lifted the heavy face. "Ah, I come from down Lower Gornal — d'you know it?"

"No, but my best mate comes from Tividale. He would."

"Ah, he would. But don't take no notice of anything he says. They think we're thick down Lower Gornal. Thick as pig shit."

"I might think you're thick as pig shit if you come in when you're poorly," Kate ventured.

"If I really was bad, you'm right. But, honestly, it's just this business of throwing up me guts for a bit. Then I'm fit as a flea. So long as you don't offer me tea."

"Tell me, how long does it take each morning before you're well? An hour? A couple of hours? And then you really are OK?"

"Suppose. Yeah, by ten I'd say I was in the clear."

"So why don't we swap shifts, this week at least?" She was almost thinking aloud. "I'm supposed to be on days, but if Neil Drew's off I ought to come in early anyway. And you could come in when you felt up to it, and complete your shift eight hours later."

"Hey, that's a bosting idea. Why didn't I think of that?"

Because you're too busy being angry about being pregnant. Should she push any further? Just a very little. "Now, we ought to meet to see how this arrangement's working, but I can't see us fitting it in for a couple of days."

"I bet you don't know if you're on your arse or your elbow, do you? I mean, our bloody paperwork's outside of enough, but yours must be . . ." She shook her head.

"Quite. But if it is working, we could see if we can fix a swap for you with someone next week too. And then someone else, until your morning sickness is over."

"It'd be over fast enough if I got rid of the bab."

Kate said nothing. She looked steadily at Helen, whose heavy jaw and strong brows were knotted with baffled anger.

"It's not that I don't want it, like," she said at last, tugging at her hair. Her hands were remarkably elegant, with beautifully shaped nails. Not cared-for, of course. Cuticles like fringes. But she hadn't bitten the nails down. "Not as such. But it's turning my life upside down — you know what I mean? I mean, I don't even smell like me any more. As for my tits . . ."

Kate got up and reached for her diary, scribbling on a scrap of paper a number from the back. "You could always try these people. This is their direct line. So Personnel don't ever have to know."

Local Problems of Law and Disorder: well, perhaps they were more local than the Home Office had anticipated. But she'd do no more than put the policy document in her bag to read at home. She couldn't

44

leave Steve Timms to carry the day's load. It wasn't fair on him and would only add to the contents of steepling in-trays that dominated everyone's desks.

She found Timms, hands in pockets, glowering down at Mrs Speed, who was reciprocating with a hard, sideways glance in the direction of Kate's room. The kettle! Hoping she hadn't been noticed, she slipped back and returned to produce it with a magician's flourish. "Da-dah! Any chance of a proper cuppa? But not *too* strong. I'll just go and wash those mugs."

Timms was looking anxious when she returned, hands still wet since the roller towel had expired. She was going to have a significant conversation with the cleaner.

He cleared his throat. "I was wondering, gaffer, if you'd like to try some of my tea. Green tea. Very refreshing and very good at mopping up free radicals."

"I didn't know they'd let any out." Kate grinned.

No one else did.

The green tea was better than anything Kate had yet drunk at Scala House, and she popped into the office to tell Steve so.

"Steve, what do you do for lunch?" When he hesitated she continued, "I want to spend a little time with everyone here, and lunchtime is as good an opportunity as any. Do you have any plans for today?"

"I — I usually bring my own." He reached into a torn Safeway carrier for a couple of round plastic food boxes, an apple, a banana and a bottle of mineral water.

"How about I nip and get a sarnie and we eat here together?"

His Adam's apple, which hitherto she'd hardly noticed, wobbled convulsively. "I could nip out and get it for you?"

She ought to argue that a bit of fresh air would do her good, but he seemed so eager that it might be churlish to refuse. "Cheese salad, please." She wouldn't want to offend someone who might well be a veggie by asking for anything meaty. She fished in her purse. "About one? Meanwhile is there anything in your in-tray that has to be done today and I could do for you?"

He pointed. One more note, a single sheet would cause a veritable Niagara of paper. "All urgent. Or they were last week. Maybe the week before that." He patted a pile of files. "And that's all paperwork that's got to be completed before the DPP will even look at the cases."

"What one thing would make life easier for you?"

He laughed drily.

"No. Seriously."

"Get rid of the Home Secretary. We've got so many bloody initiatives we don't know where we are. And X is top of the list one week, Y the next."

"I hold him, you shoot him. What about more local help?"

This time he almost wriggled with embarrassment.

"Between ourselves, Steve."

"A full team all the time'd be nice. So I don't have to worry about other people's jobs as well as mine."

46

"You don't have to worry about them anyway. That's up to me. Meanwhile, hand over a couple of cases; get on with your own priorities, and we'll chew the fat over lunch."

At least she had a full shift, sergeant and seven constables, to greet at the start of the two till ten shift. The sergeant, Jill Todd, looked vacuously pretty: she wouldn't be much above thirty, and had doll-like blue eyes, a milkmaid, not a metermaid, complexion, and blonde hair wisping out of a knot. Kate told herself to suspend judgement. She herself might not be pretty, except perhaps in Rod's eyes, but she was young, too, and had been on the receiving end of enough bias to cure her of it towards others. Furthermore, she hadn't been told of any other fast-track graduates in the nick, so she must assume that Jill had got where she was simply through being a good cop.

"I know you're all under pressure," she began, to a predictable groan, "but a rumour's come my way that's worth taking notice of. Illegal immigrants. Coming in via the wholesale market, of course, and being distributed around local retail and food outlets."

"Mr Choi paid you a visit, has he, gaffer?" Jill asked. "Is he a regular?"

"He seems to get a kick out of visiting us here. Twiss had to fend him off for us."

" 'Fend off'? Sounds as if he was an unwelcome visitor."

There was a gentle rumble of assent.

"He's all buddy-buddy, that's the trouble. He sees it as if he's some sort of ambassador — building bridges."

"He used the same term to me when we first met, at Cherish House."

Jill raised her eyebrows. "I thought Dave Bush always went to those dos."

"Annual leave. He's your expert, is he? We could do with him here now."

"He'll be back this weekend," someone volunteered.

"I'm not sure that this will wait till the weekend. Unless you really all doubt Mr Choi as a reliable source of info, I'd like you to keep your eyes extra wide. Especially whoever's patrolling the wholesale market."

Jill looked around the group, none of whom seemed entirely comfortable. "Why don't I finish the briefing, and then talk to you?"

"Good idea. Thanks. Now, I've got a meeting tomorrow about local problems of law and disorder, in lines with the latest directive. If anyone has any ideas you want putting forward, or if any of you want to come with me, my door's always open. Thanks, ladies and gentlemen."

Kate was regarding a gift-wrapped parcel sitting on her desk when Jill tapped and came in. "That didn't take long. It'll be Mr Choi's first present," she explained.

"Are you sure?" Kate glanced up, startled.

"I'd put a fiver on it. You'll find it's tasteful, just what you needed, not cheap, but certainly not expensive enough to call it a bribe. And it's certainly too small to return to him without causing offence."

Kate laughed. "You've had experience of this."

"No. But Twiss used to talk to me when he got them."

"We're not talking set of golf clubs."

"Much less pricy. But more expensive than tees. Oh, do you play golf? Because —"

"'Fraid not. Tennis when I get a chance. OK, so what did Mark get?"

"A teddy bear when his first baby was born. Nothing wrong with that. Several local traders gave him things. He was a good community cop, as well as a good boss. He'll be a hard act to follow."

Kate nodded. She wasn't sure how to read the observation she'd rather have made herself. "Anything else from Choi?" she prompted.

"One day our electric kettle blew while he was here. A new one arrived within minutes of his leaving. And that microwave out there."

"But that's a big present. Almost a bribe."

"Not when it's for the whole lot of us. And when he fixes for the community newspaper to take his picture presenting it."

"Any road up, as Helen Kerr would say, shall I open the box?"

"How's Helen's morning sickness?" Jill asked, as Kate tackled the adhesive tape, without notable success.

It was general knowledge, was it? "Hell, that's the trouble with having short fingernails!"

"Is she going to keep it?"

"That's her business, not for us to —"

"Silly cow, it'll soon be too late to get rid of it."

Perhaps that was what she wanted — a pregnancy by default, as it were. Kate ignored the comment. "Well, that's the first layer. Do you think Choi's got shares in Sellotape?" She worked away, removing the gift-wrapping at last to reveal a gift box. "Wow, this will have cost him a fiver in itself."

Jill jumped up and down with possibly feigned excitement. "Come on! What's inside?"

"Look." She held up a bone china mug, one of half a dozen nestling in tissue.

"No teapot?"

"No. But look what he's packed into the mugs — teabags. All sorts of different ones."

Jill was upending the mugs. "No trademarks — they look good, but they're not Royal Worcester or anything."

"So I can't send them back as being too expensive a gift."

"Precisely. And, if you don't mind my saying so, they're a bit nicer than yours."

"I don't at all. These are due for a charity shop: I promised Rod they'd never darken his kitchen again."

"Rod? Oh, Rod Neville. You're the one he's with, are you?"

Kate stepped back a pace. " 'The one'?"

"Everyone knows he's with some high-flyer. So it's you. Well, I hope you'll be very happy."

Should she take the good wishes at face value or judge their sincerity by the tone of voice in which they had been delivered? "Thanks," she said positively.

"How did you cope being undercover? Being apart from each other?"

"How does anyone cope? Anyway, we're back together now, that's all that matters." Kate hoped Jill wouldn't notice that her palms were sweating. How stupid to be getting so worked up over a girlie talk about boys. Why not try patting the ball back into the other woman's court? "Are you involved with anyone?"

"I was. But it seems to be over now. Quite over."

"Someone in the service? Or a civilian?"

"What's it matter if it's over? Yes, a policeman. Someone quite senior."

Kate hoped her smile looked more sincere than it felt. "Anyone I know?"

"Sorry, gaffer, I'd rather not talk about it. Footloose and fancy-free — that's me. I might even make a play for Mr Choi." Her grin seemed forced.

"Make sure he gives you mugs with a manufacturer's name stamped underneath if you do. Royal Worcester or Doulton," Kate said lightly. "Is his information genuine, do you think?" She retired behind her desk: yes, she meant business.

"Let's just say it suits him to tell you." Jill sat too. "I'm sure if it was in his interests to keep mum he'd have done so."

Despite herself, Kate grinned. "Funny, that was one of the expressions Mr Choi and I were discussing. He seemed very interested in the English language."

Jill laughed. "Oh, that's because he's heard you're a graduate. He thinks all graduates are intellectuals."

Did that imply Jill Todd wasn't? Another reason for shoulder chips? "He's missed his mark as far as I'm concerned. Anyway, how seriously do we take his information? Just maintain the routine, only more so — or go all out to find what's going on?"

"You could annoy some very influential people if you do — even more influential than Choi. Who is, we reckon, quite high in a triad."

Kate's eyebrows shot up.

"Oh, don't worry. He's unlikely to bother us. We never have difficulties with the heads of triads. To all intents and purposes they're simply respectable and influential businessmen. They're — unofficially — in charge of districts. Here's Choi's." She got up to outline a section on the street map with her index finger. "Dave Bush knows more about them than I do. All their nicknames, everything. Basically they control the area by fear, latent violence. Nothing actual."

"So far as we know. So Choi's allegation could be simply to put pressure on another gang. Or, of course, it could be genuine. Which is what I want us to find out."

"Some of the other duty teams are very short-handed." Jill's tone said hers was put upon quite enough as it was. When and why had management decided on the trendy term *duty team*, not *shift* or *relief*?

"We find evidence of what Choi's alleging and we'll get help. Probably more help that we'd like. Whose beat takes them round the market? In your team, at least."

52

"There's not much happening at this time of day, of course, but at night, when it's really busy, it's Pam or Tony. Sometimes both."

"So the duty team currently on nights are really the ones to talk to?" She'd have to hang on here till ten.

"Yes, but you don't have to do it in person. Hasn't Tim shown you the e-mail system? Twiss used to brief by e-mail. After all, we're only human beings. If you get in at seven you're entitled to your evenings free. And if you're in a new relationship —"

"Free to do my homework for the next day's meetings!" Kate interrupted. "Now, was there anything you wanted to raise particularly?"

"E-mailing seems a very good option to me," Rod said, as they sat over the risotto and salad he'd prepared.

"All the same," Kate muttered, failing to stab a piece of chicken.

"Who suggested it? An old hand? Because if they did, I'd take it as a sign they trusted you."

"No. A young hand. A very attractive woman called Jill Todd." Was his silence suspicious? Or was he simply too busily engaged in tearing bread to mop the last of the salad dressing? "Have you met her?"

"Heavens, Kate, it's an enormous force! Why should I?"

"Well, you said you'd been to Scala House."

"Did I?" He produced a puzzled frown.

"You said their tea was awful, so I presume you've tasted it. And Jill's not the sort of person you'd forget if you'd ever met her."

His frown deepened. "I met a female mountain. And the most waspish civilian clerk it's ever been my misfortune to encounter."

"That's Kathleen Speed. She didn't approve of those mugs, by the way. No, Jill's a sort of slender and intelligent Marilyn Monroe."

"Didn't my A-level teacher tell me that that was an oxymoron? A contradiction in terms?"

"A sergeant. My age. No? But you might have met her at one of your superintendents' balls — if you have such things."

"If she's a sergeant —"

"But she's been seeing a senior officer. On-off. Now off, apparently. I just wondered —"

He shook his head emphatically. "Not all my colleagues are as indiscreet about their love lives as I am, Kate. Whereas I flaunt you for all to see, others hide their partners in holes and corners. Now, if you really insist on going back in to brief the night duty team, may I suggest an admirable way of getting you poised and relaxed before you leave?"

"I know just the thing," she said, only half amused. "The paperwork for the local problems of law and disorder meeting at ten tomorrow."

CHAPTER
FIVE

The night shift, which, like the late relief, had a mercifully full complement, seemed quite pleased that she'd made the effort to come in, especially when she said she'd probably see them again as they left at seven. They took Mr Choi's hint seriously, and agreed to step up their regular patrols of the wholesale market.

"Go and get yourself back home, gaffer," Alan White, the sergeant, told her. He was a kindly looking man with a sagging chin and stomach who might have stepped from the set of *Heartbeat*. "It's going to be a cold 'un tonight."

It was. She huddled closely under her jacket as she scuttled back to the car park, and wasted valuable time scraping frost from the windows. Perhaps she should have a classier car to reflect her new status: Rod's had all sorts of enviable gizmos, and both windscreen and rear screen could melt their own ice. It even told you the outside temperature. That was one thing she could manage without tonight: it must be −3 or 4 degrees Celsius. But the kids milling round the clubs and restaurants were in shirtsleeves, the girls showing as much bare flesh as they would on a beach in Ibiza. And, she observed to herself in a close approximation of Aunt Cassie's shocked tones, at this time of night on a weekday, too. What sort of state would they be in at work the next morning?

And they were still pouring into Smallbrook Ringway, parking wherever they could. Look at them! She managed at last to squeeze past bumpers and pedestrians straying on to the road and inch on to the Holloway Head island, heading for Rod's Harborne home as fast as she safely could on newly gritted and salted roads. They wouldn't have done the little cul-de-sac he lived in, so she took the corner at dictation speed.

There was no sign of Rod's car.

Heart sinking, she let herself in, tapping in the alarm code. It was no surprise to find a note on the dining table.

Sweetheart,
Yes, there's a problem. With luck it shouldn't take me long to sort it. If not, don't forget your porridge tomorrow morning.
R XXXXXX

If only she'd gone back to Kings Heath: her own home always felt less empty than his.

But Rod was there to cook her porridge, not even bleary after his return at about midnight. The delight on his face at finding her curled up under his duvet was enough to silence any joking complaints she might have made about being woken by nasty bright lights (he'd used one bedside lamp), cold questing hands and icy feet. But she couldn't settle to sleep, despite his best efforts. This time her mind was circling round Great Aunt Cassie. Dismissing Kate's parents as generally unsatisfactory, Cassie had made a point of providing a home for her during the school holidays. They were closer than Kate had ever been to a couple about whom she secretly tended to agree with the old lady. When, a couple of years ago, Kate, burdened by negative equity on her London house, had transferred to the West Midlands CID, Cassie had opted for a retirement home, handing over her home to Kate, with enough money to turn it from a drably decayed terrace house into a bijou among other bijoux. She would be dreadfully hurt if Kate moved out. Or would she? She'd be profoundly irritated, more like. She had maintained for thirty-odd years a relationship with a wealthy jeweller, but she'd never given up her independence. Kate, however, was sure that the state of the Worksop Road house — even basic maintenance had been neglected — was an indication of how little time Cassie had actually spent in it. She'd let the lover clothe her and give her jewels that Kate was convinced she later sold, hoarding every penny, not forgetting a small cache of diamonds under a floorboard, so she could enjoy an old age as comfortable as modern medicine and a luxurious room could make it. But the house had been there when she needed it, and there to pass on to Kate.

Rod was happy to stay the night in Kings Heath occasionally, but there was no doubting which was the more pleasant home. If it was hard to find space to park all the residents' cars, it was almost impossible to edge in visitors', and Rod was only classed as a visitor. Then there was noise from her neighbours either side: the Victorian artisans for whom the houses had been built might have been superior enough to have three bedrooms and an upstairs bathroom, but they hadn't demanded soundproofing, and Kate's nights had been disturbed by far less agreeable things than Rod's chilly embrace. Neighbours' nightmares, neighbours' rows — and even neighbours' lovemaking. Since Rod favoured an uninhibited approach to the last, his detached house, all other factors notwithstanding, was a better choice.

And it was a lovely house, well considered. Whereas Kate had stuck with furniture and ornaments that fitted the period of her house, Rod had gone for an eclectic mix, risking modern pottery and sculpture on Georgian bookshelves. There were *objets trouvés* — even a heap of stones in one corner — and fine silver. But the house worked in a simple, uncluttered way that defied Kate's analysis. Perhaps it had something to do with the cool colour scheme. Whatever it was, she always returned home with a feeling that she had tried hard and missed. But it was home, and she wouldn't want to give it up if that meant giving Aunt Cassie pain.

On the other hand, Rod and she almost never spent nights apart, except when he was called out on a case, and enjoyed any spare time in each other's company. People had started to invite them to meals as a couple; they indulged Rod's taste for music by going to concerts at Symphony Hall, and were beginning to sort out his garden. Except that all that was about to change, wasn't it? How would he react to the change in her hours to shifts, and irregular shifts at that? It was quite likely they'd not see each other for a week at a time. How would they deal with that? Should she simply drop back into her Kings Heath life for a week? It would make sense. But she couldn't bear not seeing him for so very long.

Oh, she was behaving and thinking — or not thinking — like a teenager with nothing to worry about except love. She had a new job to consider — and it irritated her that, despite a couple of hours' pouring over glossy documents and making both marginal jottings and notes, she was still going to have to tap and acro her way through the morning's meeting. *Tap and acro* — now *that* was a phrase that might interest Mr Choi. Something to do with the circus, perhaps, tap-dancing and acrobatics . . .

Perhaps Rod sensed she was still awake. Still asleep himself, she thought, he rolled over and gathered her to him, her back against his chest and stomach. Lulled by his deep, steady breathing, she slowly drifted off.

The meeting about local problems of law and disorder hadn't gone badly. She had taken care not to push herself forward, but the few suggestions she'd made had been welcomed with surprising enthusiasm. All she had to do was persuade the powers-that-be that they should invest time and resources in them. And her own human resources were better that morning. She'd turned up at five to seven to find Neil Drew drinking weak tea and pecking at dry toast. He was very pale: perhaps it had really been he, not his kids, who'd had the stomach bug. He'd responded without special enthusiasm to her suggestion that she should shout him lunch at the end of his shift, merely pointing out that he had to be off by two forty-five or he wouldn't be able to pick up his kids.

"A quick lunch it is, then," she'd said. "At two. And, Neil, get the time right, will you? You really dropped me in it at Cherish House."

"Sorry, gaffer." He looked genuinely apologetic.

In the same café as the one she'd begun her meal with Ronnie Hale, she bought another salad baguette for herself and a bowl of soup for Neil. "Time for ten minutes' peace and quiet," she said, sighing as she sat opposite him. "And the bonus for you is that you can mark it down as unpaid overtime so you can take it off later as time off in lieu."

He looked at her with swift suspicion. She kept her face bland. After all, it was a perfectly good way for officers to accrue time to go to the dentist, for family responsibilities, and so on. She'd earned an enormous amount of time while she'd been undercover: one of these days she'd have to think about using it. But there was an unspoken code that it should be used in small bursts, not put together to enable you to take a week on the piste. And how much time could she spend having her teeth whitened, even if the thought had remotely appealed to her? She suspected her TOIL would lapse.

He toyed with the soup as if it were poison.

"You're still not well, are you? Why did you come in?"

He snorted. "I should have thought that was obvious. You were down to three yesterday, and no doubt Ronnie Hale was strutting round as if she was officially acting sergeant."

"Someone had to take charge of things," Kate said mildly, "and I'm certainly not up to speed yet. Not Kathleen's speed, anyway."

Ignoring the pallid quip, he picked at the roll that came with the soup, pushing the butter pat to one side. "I don't eat butter at the best of times," he said. "Have to watch the cholesterol, my age. I'm not a health freak," he added quickly, as if that would be a matter of shame, "don't get me wrong. Not like young Steve Timms. Raw beansprouts and all those supplements. Tablets for this, pills for that. Shake him and he'd bloody rattle."

"He doesn't just know his onions, he knows what's in them?"

"Right. Now, I know there's no such thing as a free lunch. What was it you wanted? Mind, I've only got twenty minutes before I hit the road."

"No ulterior motive, Neil. I just want to get to know everyone. Have some idea of what makes them tick, and find out for myself, not just from hearsay."

"There's plenty of that in this nick."

She looked at him with cool amusement. "We're none of us above a bit of gossip, though, are we, Neil?"

He dropped his eyes. "Well, you know how it is. Your last case — that bloke you asked about the drug-dealer, Earle Grey. He's a mate of mine."

"I hope you can put him right about what happened. Craig — the man I was supposed to live with, not just work with — wasn't your ideal partner, Neil. Dead prickly and as cocky as a farmyard full of roosters." Another for Mr Choi's collection. "Like I said, I'm convinced he had post-traumatic stress disorder. I never found out what caused it."

He swallowed more soup. "Must be a bit of a culture shock for you, being your own woman undercover, and now back in uniform."

"I was in uniform then." She laughed. "A cleaner's uniform. Which reminds me, I must do something about the loos. I take it the men's are as uninspired as the women's? I asked young Zayn to chaperon me, but he was too embarrassed for me to have a real poke round."

"You women and your clean bogs!"

"Hygiene, Neil. Helps prevent the transmission of tummy bugs. And there are few things more satisfying than really clean bogs, in my book at least."

"As one who's seen enough of them in the last thirty hours, I can't disagree." He managed a dry laugh.

"What about your kids? Have they steered clear so far?"

He half stood. "Is that what this is all about? My kids and their single dad? God, those bastards — got to bloody grass up a mate, haven't they?"

"Get off your high horse, Neil. I told you, I'm trying to get a bit of time with everyone. Ronnie and Steve, so far. You're third. I thought there might be things you could tell me that'd make me more efficient — a better gaffer."

"You mean, grassing like they did? I bet they told you all about Helen." He scowled furiously and shut up as Kate laughed.

"We all do it, don't we? Come on, Neil. You're an experienced sergeant, which is more than I ever was, come to think of it. That's the trouble with the accelerated-promotion scheme — you're only in the job five minutes before you're doing something else."

"Ah. Police Constable CV. Or Detective Constable CV in your case, I suppose."

She smiled obligingly. It was a standard joke, after all — people resented high-flyers like herself apparently cherry-picking jobs and flitting off to the next. "I could do with guff, not gossip — though there's a fine line, I admit. Mr Choi, is he the Godfather that Sergeant Todd paints him as?"

He looked uneasy. "I should think you'd want to watch her." In response to her raised eyebrows he added, "Well, you know . . ."

"I don't know. Care to tell me?" She tried to keep her voice light but was sure she'd failed.

"Well, you've both got a taste for —" he stopped short, swallowing bread "— for promotion. That's it." He looked with huge relief at his watch. "Thanks for lunch, gaffer, but I'm off on the school run."

She rose too. "We'll continue this conversation first thing tomorrow, Neil."

"I thought you were on days."

"I've done a short-term swap with Helen so she doesn't have to come in till she's over her sickness. I'll be in before seven." She narrowed her eyes. "Then you can tell me what you really meant to say."

Though she was technically free, there was no way she could leave the office for the delights of Christmas shopping. Apart from battling through more policy documents, there was a little matter of clearing up crime in the city, and there were several items from Steve Timms's in-tray that she should be able to wrap up by the time Rod was finishing work. They'd agreed, more or less at his insistence, to have a drink and a meal out. He claimed to have exhausted his repertory of recipes, and they both knew she was no cook. She was running out of clothes and ought to check her mail: a quick foray to Kings Heath was in order, too. But, as Neil had pointed out, it was school-run time, and there was no point in trying to get into Worksop Road, let alone to park there, until well after three thirty. She'd wait till four-ish to push open a window of opportunity. There was plenty to tackle in the meantime.

She made sure that none of the taps dripped and drained the outside loo, checking that some fuchsias and geraniums she was trying to over-winter in there were well wrapped up in fleece. Suddenly depressed by the house's reproachful reminder that she'd put a great deal of time, money and energy into it, she stuffed the mail into a carrier. She'd take it with her. She was checking that she'd double-locked the front door — shades of Aunt Cassie — when her neighbour hailed her.

Zenia nodded at the carrier. "Wouldn't it be easier to have it redirected? I mean, you're not with us much these days, more's the pity. Love, is it? That nice, sexy Rod?"

Kate blushed.

"Good for you. Better than that other creep, making you look furtive in your own home."

Kate turned the conversation to Zenia's own family.

"And Royston's got himself a job! Not much of one, but it's a start and it gets him up in the morning."

"He'll be all right, Zenia."

"He's got more brains than he uses, that's the trouble."

"Haven't most kids? He'll end up going to college one of these days, you mark my words . . . Now, just in case the place burns down, would you mind having my address and phone number? You can even e-mail me at work." She wrote down her details.

"But you're not going altogether? Not yet?"

"It's OK — no new neighbours to run in, Zenia. Not yet," she added, under her breath.

At last she headed back to work. At least it was much easier driving back into the city, against the flow of rush-hour traffic. She found some music on the radio: perhaps that'd cheer her up.

Mrs Speed raised an eyebrow as she came back in. "I thought you'd gone home for the day."

"I wish. No, I shall be here till seven if anyone wants me. I've switched to the early shift for a while: they're still short of bodies."

So what did Mrs Speed mean by that nod?

Dropping the carrier full of letters on to her desk, she stopped dead. There was a slight smell of perfume in the room. Or was it aftershave? Who had paid her room a visit in her absence? Well, there was no reason why someone shouldn't have popped their head round the door — she hadn't left it locked. But heads weren't where you put perfume. And whoever it was must have spent long enough in here to leave such a trace. But even as she sniffed again to try to imprint it in her memory, it had gone. Well, if she didn't like her territory being invaded, she must do the obvious thing — make sure she locked it in future. Which meant getting a key.

Mrs Speed was just putting her coat on, barely pausing to listen to Kate's request, but she admitted grudgingly that keeping the keys might be one of her responsibilities. "They're locked away. Would tomorrow do?"

"Of course. Mind how you go — it's freezing already."

Back in her office she tipped the post on to her desk, then shoved the carrier into a bottom drawer in case it ever came in handy. Apart from the bills — not too many, she noticed, offering a prayer of thanks for direct debits — it was mostly junk, which she filed swiftly in the bin for recycling. But there were a couple of handwritten envelopes. She didn't recognise one script at all, but the other was familiar. She held it, staring at it till the characters flowed and merged. Why should Graham Harvey, her old DCI, be writing to her? Surely everything that had ever been between them was best forgotten. She didn't want to open it. There was a knock at the door and, with a waft of perfume, Jill Todd entered. Kate laid the envelope quickly back on the desk.

Jill smiled. "I thought you'd like to know I've shoved Helen off for some counselling — stood over her while she made the call."

Kate rubbed her ear doubtfully. She didn't want Helen talked into an abortion just because a colleague thought she ought to have one.

"Well, you can't hang around with these things," Jill said briskly.

Perhaps she was right. "So long as we all support her whatever the outcome," Kate said. "I don't want any locker-room sniggering. Is she in a stable relationship?"

"Her! God, it must be like shagging a carthorse!"

Whatever Kate did would be wrong, wouldn't it? If she didn't laugh it'd show she lacked that essential for being a police officer, a sense of humour. If she did, it would betray what was clearly a vulnerable woman. She allowed herself a half-smile, quickly removed. "She doesn't wear a ring, but that doesn't mean anything, of course. But she didn't mention a partner, and I'd have thought he might want some say in the proceedings." Rod certainly would, if she fell pregnant. The thought was so intense she clapped a hand to her mouth to keep it in.

"Do you want me to find out?"

Kate shook her head. "It's not our business. We're just here to support her and —"

"Hang on, it's more than that. It's a major problem. We'll have an officer on extended light duties, we'll need maternity cover and, God knows, most women who take maternity leave don't come back but chicken out and stay at home. Fraud, really."

"Let Personnel worry about that. She's a colleague, Jill, let's treat her as that, not as a problem." Kate stood and reached for her briefcase: the discussion was definitely over.

Jill shrugged. "If you say so. Off now, are you?"

"Yes. Twelve hours is more than enough if there isn't an emergency on. I've got a date with a washing-machine."

"Not with Rod?"

Funny, she no longer thought of time spent with him as a date. "Maybe I should invite his shirts to join mine in the spin cycle," she said lightly. "Anything else I should know about before I go home?" She started them both towards the door.

"Nothing that won't keep till tomorrow."

"Fine. Don't work any later than necessary. Or let your team. We've all got homes to go to. Good night."

She closed the door behind her.

CHAPTER
SIX

"You were asking about Jill Todd," Rod said. He waited, but more, it seemed, out of courtesy than embarrassment: the waiter had arrived to take away the remains of their main course. He topped up her glass. "Last night — remember? I wasn't entirely honest about her. And the trouble I went to sort out last night wasn't police trouble, it was personal."

Kate's wine slopped. Rod mopped it, but took her hand. He still seemed entirely calm: he neither fawned nor blustered. "I did see her, after we split up." This time he grimaced: the break-up had been his conventional reaction to a maverick move on her part. A highly successful maverick move, as it happened. "And I could see you were preoccupied with Graham Harvey."

Kate nodded, feeling the blood come up her neck. She wasn't especially proud of her affair with her DCI. It wasn't that she'd been sleeping with her boss that worried her — after all, Rod was senior to Graham, and she had no qualms about that. She wasn't even sure it was because Graham was married. It was more to do with what Zenia had rightly called the furtiveness, not to mention the constant waiting for the phone and the regular disappointment — all the problems of being just the mistress or, less glamorously, Graham's bit on the side. She'd never felt herself an equal partner, not as she did with Rod. Almost always, at least.

Rod dropped his eyes — whether to spare her or because he was less in control of his own emotions than he liked she didn't know. "Jill did something you've never done. She made demands."

"What sort of demands? I'm sorry, I —"

"You're entitled to know. She wanted to trade sexual favours for — well, she knew I couldn't promote her, not as such, but she'd have liked . . . Anyway, as soon as she started that little game, I finished the relationship — it was so brief I don't know if it can be called that. You and I, we became friends all over again, didn't we?" His smile washed over her, warm with the delight of some of their shared moments, times they'd shared purely and simply as companions. "Jill wouldn't give up — she tried to start things up again from time to time. But I wasn't interested. In any case, by then I realised that however much you and I were 'friends' I wanted more. And since September and that weird trip to Hythe I've known I wanted no one else."

Her face and mouth wouldn't form the words she wanted. Even if she'd known what they were. Anger, disappointment, relief? Any or all. At last, she took his hand. As he raised hers to his lips, the waiter brought the dessert menu. Rod took it with an irritated frown, but laid it unopened on the table.

"Such timing! But Jill's tenacious. She phoned again last night. So I went round. To tell her everything was

70

absolutely over and that was that. I don't know whether I'm ashamed to say this or not. I took a tape-recorder. In case you — you . . . I don't know. Needed proof?"

She shook her head. Absolutely not.

"You — recently you've been quite . . . distant, almost," he continued, "and I was afraid. After all, you didn't exactly leap at the chance of our being together properly."

"Not distant. Anxious. That undercover work seemed to knock me off balance more than I knew. I just wanted to bed down and pull the duvet over me."

"I'm all for that. So long as I'm under it with you. But that's all?"

"Quite all. And if you're worried about me and Graham . . ." Her throat was dry. "The funny thing is there was a letter I suspect was from him waiting for me when I went back home."

"I shall be glad when you call my house home," he said. "I'm sorry. I interrupted."

She smiled both her own apology and forgiveness. "I gathered a load of clean clothes and all my post and took it into Scala House. Bills, junk mostly. But a couple of proper letters. I think one was from Graham. But someone — Jill, actually — came in and said some things I disapproved of about one of our WPCs and I just wanted to come . . . home so I left them there. You'll have to wait till this time tomorrow for a full report," she ended, trying to make her voice light.

He shook his head, dashing the menu to the floor as his hands cut any suggestion. "I don't need a report."

"Any more than I need a tape of you telling Jill where to go. All the same." She smiled. "Tell you what, let's forget dessert. I'd have thought coffee and a liqueur at *home*," she emphasised the word slightly, "would be nicer."

"Under that duvet," he agreed, and called for the bill.

"If you think it's so important, I'll go myself," Neil Drew grumbled. As well he might. It was bitterly cold and no one in their senses would want to go out in the pre-dawn gloom. A light drizzle had turned the freezing roads and pavements into ice-rinks.

"I'll come with you," Kate said. "I want to know what we're talking about."

"You! But you're the gaffer."

"Exactly. And if I'm going to be as good as my predecessor was, I need to know my patch as well as he did. Let me just get my gloves and scarf and we'll be off."

They walked a good deal more briskly than the regular beat pace, not having enough breath left for much conversation, which in any case was blown away by the vicious wind. From time to time Kate felt Neil glancing at her — perhaps he was trying to make her out, trying to decide if she'd make a good gaffer despite his prejudices.

At last he said, "Are you sure this touchy-feely stuff you're going in for's the right thing? A lot of folk like their bosses to be bosses."

72

"I can be authoritative if you want me to. But don't you find women who try that end up as vixens?"

"Bloody right. I've known some absolute harpies in my time."

"But that doesn't mean that if you think I'm too soft, you shouldn't tell me so. I'd welcome your advice, Neil. Even if I don't always take it."

He grunted in acknowledgement. Then he grabbed her, pulling her backwards. A container lorry had put wheels on the pavement in an attempt to get round a tight bend.

"Thanks. The bastard! Did you get his number?"

"Tried, but —"

"No problem. I wouldn't have liked to be squashed before the end of my first week. Thanks again, Neil."

She thought for a moment he was going to be solicitous enough to take her elbow to guide her across the next road. But they arrived at the entrance to the market with no further incident, and by then they were firmly in patrol mode, stolid, impregnable, as they presented themselves to the security check-in. This was staffed by a burly man, old enough to be ex-police or ex-services. He wore a uniform with something approaching pride, but cupped a no doubt illicit cigarette in his right hand, which was richly tattooed.

" 'Morning, sarge," he greeted Neil. "Fancy a cuppa?"

"Later, Mick, if we've got time. This is our new gaffer. Inspector Power."

"Don't tell me, Power by name, power by nature." After their dutiful laugh, he continued, "What happened to the last geezer, Neil?"

"Upwards and onwards, mate. Involved in training, so they say."

"Hmm. Pity a bloke like him's got to be behind a desk. I suppose that's where you'll be most of the time, miss."

"I dare say. But on a lovely morning like this who could resist coming for a bit of a walk?"

"Ah, and there's supposed to be bloody global warming and all. We could do with a bit more, that's all I can say."

"But —" Neil took a breath and swallowed whatever it was he'd been about to say.

"We'll hold you to that offer of a cuppa." Kate grinned. "See you in — when d'you reckon, Neil?"

"Give us, say, half an hour, Mick?"

"OK. Half an hour, or thereabouts."

"I'd say he's got something to pass on, gaffer," Neil muttered, as they headed into the Aladdin's cave of fresh produce, half saluting various stallholders and drivers as they walked along the vegetable-spattered pavement. It wasn't just banana skins they had to dodge, but outer leaves of cauliflowers and cabbages, and various unidentifiable fruits already crushed to slime.

After the diesel-fume-laden streets, Kate's nostrils took time to sort out the components, which came in waves according to where they were walking. She liked the earthiness of sacks of potatoes, didn't relish cabbage: it was like waiting for school dinners all over again. Half of her would have liked to hug the huge bunches of flowers they came across, but lovely as they were they didn't smell.

"No. They're hothouse flowers from Africa, see," Neil said. He tutted. "Seems such a waste to me — people spending pounds and pounds on stuff that doesn't smell and which is ruining the environment. And when folk start joking about global warming! It really gets to me, I tell you."

Kate stopped short and stared.

"Oh, yes. My lad was doing this project about it. It's not the big laugh Mick thinks it is. The British Isles could end up colder, for one thing. And you know air travel's one of the worst offenders, in terms of pollution — well, imagine jetting flowers from Kenya or wherever! And it isn't as if it does the environment out there any good. They build these polythene cities they have to irrigate, which takes water from the water-table and ruins ordinary food crops and — Sorry, I didn't mean to rabbit on."

"You weren't rabbiting. I never knew, honestly. I mean, I thought I was being green saving all my paper and taking bottles to the bottle bank and —"

"Well, all that's a start. So long as you take them on foot." He made a visible effort to change gear. "Now, over here's this all-night café, and I tell you, gaffer, you won't find better hot chocolate anywhere. Or bacon sandwiches."

She could believe it. The smell had her salivating. "Is your stomach up to a sandwich?"

"Still a bit queasy, to be frank. But don't let me stop you."

"No, I'll save myself for Mick's tea. So did your son get a good mark for his project?"

"An A plus," he said, with simple pride. "He'll go far, my Simon. Jenny's not so bright, but she'll do OK. Really painstaking and meticulous. She'll make up in effort for what she doesn't have upstairs. Seen all you want?"

"Where's the lorry bay? Don't worry, I'm not going to be a one-woman sniffer dog, hunting for traces of human occupation. I just want to get clear in my mind where things are."

"Down here. See? Where the big guys are pulling out? The time you really want to see it is one or two in the morning. Then the trading starts — what, three-ish, four-ish. You can see it's more a matter of packing up now, getting rid of rubbish."

"Where does that go?"

"There's a big crusher — do you want to see it? Because it pongs a bit, mind."

"I think we can give that a miss. How many of these people do you know? Hey, mind your back!"

A utility truck, almost certainly overladen, was heading for the exit more quickly than it ought.

"Some two-bit corner shop buying cheap, picking up odds and ends no one else would touch," Neil said. "I think I should warn you about Mick's tea, gaffer. If you don't like our brew, you won't like his. I reckon it rots the enamel of your teeth quicker than acid. Not to mention what it does to your stomach."

"Would you rather give it a miss?"

"Nah. Don't want to give offence. And, like I say, you never know what he's going to come up with."

"You know me, silent as the grave," Mick said, putting four spoonfuls of sugar into each mug.

Kate wrapped her hands round hers and sipped, tentatively. If you drank it purely as a hot sweet liquid, it was OK. It was only when you tried to classify it as tea that things went wrong.

"OK?" Mick asked anxiously.

"Fine."

"Good. There are some that don't like the whisky I always put in," he said seriously.

There was a little pause.

"Any tips for us?" Neil asked. Not subtle, then.

"Only the Baggies against the Blues this weekend."

"Or? Come on, Mick, I told my gaffer you had your ear to the ground. Why else should she come out on a day like this? Look, it's still not light, is it?"

"They say there's a big smash-up on Spaghetti Junction," Mick said, as if agreeing. "All these folks driving too fast for the road conditions. It'll mean a lot of people being late in for work today."

They all nodded solemnly. Kate sipped a little more tea — she noticed Neil had given up on his, and was gathering his gloves and helmet.

"We don't need a traffic report, Mick. Come on, who's doing what to whom?"

"What have you heard, then?"

"We only get the rumours third hand. Come on, you old bastard, you can't let me down in front of a lady."

Kate raised an eyebrow, amused or ironic or however these two chose to take it.

Mick touched his nose with a thick forefinger. "You want to check out the car-boot sale this Sunday."

"Fuck it, Mick, we want to check it out every Sunday. They bloody queue up here on a Saturday night, gaffer, cars and vans bulging with stolen property. If we could ever mount a proper sweep . . ."

She nodded. "Who knows? Anything else, Mick? Neil said you were great on the latest, but I don't know that this lot was worth getting out of bed for."

He shrugged. "There's nothing else, miss, not that I know. But I'll keep my eyes and ears open. You can depend on me. And no one can say fairer than that."

"Indeed they can't," she agreed, false hearty. "OK, Neil, we'd best be harassing a few hapless motorists."

They walked in silence till they were well clear of the building.

Neil turned to her, shaking his head. "You know what I think, gaffer? I think —"

"He's been nobbled, Neil. That's what I think. Either that or he's an old soak well over his limit."

Neil had continued with his normal patrol route, but had pointed out that since it was usually covered by a single officer, there wasn't a lot of point in Kate getting chilled to the bone when she'd probably got a lot on her plate anyway. After a token argument, Kate had agreed, heading with great relief and a full bladder —

78

was that tea of Mick's pure diuretic? — back to Scala House. She was greeted by a commotion just outside Mrs Speed's office. Ronnie Hale was huddled on a chair, with Mrs Speed, Steve Timms and a PC Kate didn't recognise kneeling beside her.

Timms noticed Kate first. "She had a bad turn in the loo, ma'am. We think it's that stomach bug. She said she'd been bad in the night, but she insisted she was all right. Then, well, you can see —"

"Ambulance?"

"I wouldn't have thought —" he began.

"I'll be with you in a second," Kate said, bolting to the loo. She wasn't going to pee herself in public, but everyone would assume she'd got the bug too. Let them.

By the time she was back, Ronnie was conscious, and refusing absolutely to have anything to do with an ambulance or hospital.

"Fine," said Kate, "but we've got to get you home."

She struggled to her feet, swaying as she tried to straighten. "But, gaffer —"

"But nothing." She pressed her gently back on to the chair. "I'm not having my officers at work when they're ill. If you've got this bug, you go to bed. Simple as that. OK?"

It patently wasn't, but Steve Timms, with a stroke of something like genius, chimed in, "We don't want Helen getting this. Not in her condition. I'll run her home, ma'am."

"It ought to be a woman," Mrs Speed observed. "In case she's unwell."

A euphemism for *sicking up her guts*, no doubt.

"Remind me, who's her usual partner?"

"I am. Phil Bates, ma'am. But with my stomach I wouldn't — I daren't —"

Kate didn't know whether to wring his neck for cowardice or applaud his common sense. "I'll take you, Ronnie," she said. "Where are your keys?"

So that was half the morning gone, and since Ronnie had obviously felt too ill to talk Kate had achieved nothing except exposing herself to a bug she'd certainly rather not have. Phil Bates picked her up in the courtesy car and brought her back from the neat, detached house in Handsworth Wood that Ronnie shared with her teacher husband. Perhaps this was the moment to talk to him, especially as he was chomping on something that smelt remarkably like the stomach tablets Aunt Cassie relied on if she'd had too much wine — oh, yes, the retirement home was remarkably liberal about such things.

"This isn't the tummy bug, but your usual indigestion, is it?"

"Indigestion? It's a gastric ulcer. And these," he fished a sheet of bubble-packed capsules from his pocket, "are for my IBS."

She might as well lead with her chin. "What do the doctors think caused them?"

"Doctors? I don't need them to tell me. Stress, of course."

"What is it that's causing you stress?" Even to her ears it sounded a stupid question.

"How about colleagues who don't bother showing up for their shift, consequent excessive overtime, mostly unpaid, missed meals, no canteen, inadequate transport, too much work for too few officers?"

"And that's just for starters. So, how could things be improved?"

"Sack half the relief for a start. Or put a rocket under their arses to get them pulling their weight."

"That's them. How about you?"

"Oh, 'no man is an island', ma'am. Get them sorted and you'll find I'm a new man."

And you'll find I'm the Queen of Sheba! "Point taken. But what'd improve your life? Regular meals? So we'd have to get you off shift work, for the time being at least."

He pointed vigorously skyward. She craned to see. "Flying pigs, ma'am. I should believe a nine-till-five when I got it. And, if I may make a humble observation, pigs aren't very likely birds." Wincing, he reached for another bubble-pack — yes, Aunt Cassie's favourite brand. "Probably a good job when you consider their droppings."

She didn't join in his laughter. "You might choose to specialise in a particular area — get sent on a training course then put in a post enabling you to use your new expertise. Computing?"

"Oh, ah, and end up like young Tim? He's supposed to be our nick's resident geek, but I haven't noticed them taking him off shifts."

That was something worth checking out. She'd no idea how expert Tim was, and if he had any specialist ambitions. Maybe he was as miserable and depressed as Phil.

She tried again. "That's Tim's problem — if he sees it as a problem. But I'm concerned that you're in constant pain."

"It isn't just that. I never know when I'm going to have to have a shit."

"What does your gastroenterologist say?" She preened herself — that was the right term, wasn't it?

"My how much? My own doctor's not interested. Just tells me to eat regular little meals and take my medicine."

"I'd have thought it was worth going back to him and making a fuss. The NHS can do very clever things."

"Once you get on the waiting list. You know there's a waiting list to get on the waiting list, these days? And how do I get to see a doctor? When do I get time to do that?"

"You've had a couple of days off this week — couldn't you have —"

"Couldn't stir from the bathroom. Agony, I was in. And the GP only sees emergencies the day you phone — otherwise you have to wait a couple of weeks and you're better by then."

"If you were that bad, I'd have thought that constituted an emergency."

"I told you, I couldn't stir from the bog."

The way he was making her feel, soon he wouldn't be able to stir far from A and E. She spoke very quietly and clearly: "Listen, Phil. You are ill. You are entitled to take time off for a GP's appointment, whichever week you get it. You say you've worked overtime so you can take time off in lieu. When we get back, the first thing I want you to do is get a doctor's appointment — this week, next week, whenever. Understood? Now, I'd mind that cyclist, if I were you. I think the car people would prefer this back the way they lent it us."

It was only when she'd got back, gasping for a cup of Mr Choi's excellent tea, that she found she was going to be late for a meeting to which she was unexpectedly bidden at Lloyd House, back in the city centre. It wasn't a meeting Rod would be at either, though he was based there, since he headed the murder-investigation teams throughout the region and this was about public satisfaction with grassroots policing. Laugh-a-minute time. And Rod had a meeting of his own to worry about when she phoned to suggest a late lunch.

So that was her afternoon wrapped up too — finding on computer the action plan Twiss had begun and left for her to finish. And finishing it. Which she did by seven thirty.

Phoning Rod to say she was on her way and that she'd pick up a takeaway, she started to stow her things in her bag.

Her things. Including the post she'd left there last night. So where was it? Not on the desk, or anywhere in it. Not in the waste-bin. And certainly not in her bag. So what the hell had happened to it?

And what had happened to her memory? She'd still got no key to lock up behind her. Muttering things about stable doors, she scrawled a note to remind her to talk to Mrs Speed the following morning. And then, in somewhat neater writing, she wrote a note to Mrs Speed, which she dropped on that lady's desk, anchoring it with a pen in each corner. There. That was better.

But it didn't help find the missing letters.

CHAPTER
SEVEN

Friday was a court day for Rod, so he was looking even more spruce than usual as he picked up his briefcase. "Now, you're not to worry about contacting Graham Harvey — not on my account, anyway," Rod said, continuing the previous night's conversation. "But —"

"He's entitled to know that someone's stolen mail he almost certainly regarded as private."

"I'd still rather not —"

"If you're protecting my sensibilities, please don't. If it's your own, that's a different matter." Despite his efforts, she detected anxiety in his voice.

"I'll phone him this morning," she said, picking up her car keys.

"To be honest, Phil Bates is a total pain in the arse," Neil agreed, steadying a pile of files on the corner of his desk. "And what really gets me is this business of blaming other people."

"That's between ourselves, mind," Kate reminded him sharply. "But you'd have no objections to my referring him to Occupational Health?"

"You can refer him to Dudley Zoo and welcome. 'Specially if they keep him there. He'll be starting nights come Sunday, and I leave it to you to guess how many shifts he'll actually work. Big round zero. Maybe one, if he thinks you're trying to make things better for him."

"How good a cop is he?"

"Barely up to speed. He's one of these late-entry people — can't make a go of any other job so he thinks he'll be brilliant in the police."

"Are you thinking what I'm thinking?"

"He'll complain the stress is so bad he deserves massive compensation and swan off and enjoy himself. A lot of folk do."

Kate nodded but wouldn't commit herself. "Family?"

"I'll try to find out. Tell you what, Kate, half the time we're bleeding social workers for young offenders, the other half we're nannying our colleagues."

Kate. Well, something had upped her in his estimation. So it was with a lighter heart than she expected that she dialled DCI Graham Harvey's number. But, none the less, with an irritatingly shaking hand. And when she got his answerphone she was enraged to find that her voice cracked. She cleared her throat and tried again.

"Graham, I had some mail stolen the other day, and I think one item may have come from you." Or did she mean *might*? Rod would know. "Could you call me, please?"

There was a time when she'd have spent the rest of the day staring at the phone, willing it to ring, but even if she'd wanted to, she didn't have that luxury today. There was no Ronnie Hale, still no Tony Parker, and

Helen Kerr looked as if she might as well not be in at all. Perhaps Mrs Speed hadn't liked the tone of the memo that had greeted her on her arrival: she always found something vital to bury herself in whenever Kate hove into view. Thwarted, Kate passed five invigorating minutes in a forthright conversation with the cleaner about the lavatories.

She had just finished her action plan in response to the meeting about public satisfaction with grassroots policing when Neil appeared. "Thought you'd like to know we've got Helen Kerr locked in a lavatory." He grinned. "But at least it'll be a clean lavatory, won't it, gaffer?"

She looked at him sideways.

"No, I'm not taking the piss, honest. You're right — there is something about grotty bogs that makes you feel all no-how. I don't know how you did it but you made that dippy Irish cow —"

"In the interests of equal opportunities and non-racist language let's just call her Thelma." But Kate grinned to take the sting out of the rebuke.

"Thelma, then. Never knew that. She's broken the habit of a lifetime and put in her full hours and you could eat your dinner in the gents'."

"Hope you won't have to. I noticed you didn't touch Mick's tea — you're sure your tum's behaving itself?"

"No point in taking risks. You're up for the Police Medal, sinking the lot. Anyway, what shall I do about Helen?"

"What you mean is, what am *I* going to do about Helen? OK, I'm on my way."

★ ★ ★

"You phone a vulnerable woman at home and tell her she should have a termination! How dare you?" This was the first time Kate had ever withdrawn to the far side of her desk so that she could lean forward and plant her fists on it. "The last thing I said to you was that she was a colleague who needed support, not a junior officer who needed kicking into a decision to suit us."

Jill Todd stood her ground. "I gave her the best advice as I saw it. Great lump — how could she manage a baby on her own?"

"We don't know she is on her own and I know a lot of great lumps who make better mothers than honours graduates. But it isn't our business to judge. It was great that you persuaded her to go for counselling — though I'd have preferred you to be more subtle in your approach. But counselling is where you're enabled to make up your own mind." Having extracted a promise from Helen that she'd at least talk to her partner about it — the young woman's bovine eyes lit up when she mentioned her Vince — Kate felt she'd done all she could to right the balance.

"Oh, of course, Inspector Power." Jill crossed her arms and leaned back, shifting her weight on to one leg. "Power: Irish background. Roman Catholic, of course. I might have known you'd be a pro-lifer."

It was like being back in the playground. "I'm an English Baptist, and I'm pro-choice. Her choice. Not your choice or my choice. And it's my belief she wants that baby more than she'll admit. Now, sergeant, if I hear that you've spoken to WPC Kerr on this or any other personal matter I shall have you up for a disciplinary before you can blink. Do I make myself clear?"

The phone rang. She let it. Mrs Speed could intercept.

"Well? Do I make myself clear?

Jill stood to something like attention. "Yes, ma'am."

At least something had penetrated her arrogant skull.

"OK. Now, we're supposed to be fighting crime, not each other, so I suggest — Damn!"

The phone rang again. This time it didn't stop. Kate offered a chilly nod of dismissal, and picked up the handset.

Jill didn't move, except to shift her weight to the other hip. Kate covered the mouthpiece and raised an eyebrow.

"Don't you want to hear what I've picked up about the market?"

Much as she'd have loved to box the woman's ears, Kate spoke briskly into the mouthpiece: "Kate Power here. I'm in the middle of a meeting. Could you give me your number and I'll phone you back? Thanks."

At least Graham had taken the hint. Just as if he were a stranger he dictated his number. Kate, who knew it better than her own, decided — not quite on impulse, in view of the missing letter — to write it down religiously. But she transposed digits as she went. Anyone trying to dial the number would reach goodness knew whom. And she trusted Graham to have enough sense to have blocked the automatic return call facility before he dialled. "Thanks. I'll get back to you as soon as I can."

She sat down, indicating that Jill might too. "Well?"

"There's a security guard there called Mick. Very reliable source of information. He says he thinks something's going on. He'd like to see a big operation some time soon."

"Preferably at a time he isn't there, no doubt." Kate grinned sardonically, standing to show the meeting was well and truly over. "Nice one, Jill."

"What do you mean?"

"When I spoke to him this morning, he didn't say anything except that the car-boot sale would involve dodgy stuff. How clever of you to have wormed this out of him where Sergeant Drew and I failed."

The phone again. This time she didn't recognise the voice, but she did recognise the rank. You'd didn't put assistant chief constables (crime) on hold. Not even when they'd lent you to their Devon colleagues at a time when you'd much rather have been with your lover in Birmingham. She nodded Jill from the room.

"Got a job for you, Power. Urgent."

She might have thought that the admin priority was public satisfaction with grassroots policing: indeed, from what he said, the ACC thought so too. "Thing is, Power, the PM himself is now laser-beam focused on street crime. So we now have to prioritise. And, God bless us, the chief needs figures now. Especially if they show that we're winning. Bloody hell, who'd be a police officer these days?"

90

Kate laughed, but decided to take a risk. "Tell me, sir, how keen are the government to sort out illegal immigration? Because I've had a tip-off from one of the Chinese community about things going on in the wholesale food market."

"How seriously do you take it?"

Kate explained its provenance. Then the opinions of two of her sergeants.

"Hmm. Anything else?" Was it resources or experience that made him sound reluctant?

"Only that Sergeant Drew suspected one of the security men knew something was up but was saying nothing."

"Your nose telling you anything?"

"It is, actually. It's saying, 'Watch and wait.' But call up extra resources as and when."

"How long have you been in post, Kate?"

"Feels like for ever. But — what day is it today? Thursday?"

"Friday!"

"In that case, about four and a half days, sir."

"Good for you, Kate."

Why? What was good about that?

His laugh indulged her, like a doting uncle's. "Got over that Devon business yet?"

"I didn't like losing my colleague, sir."

"And, of course, the jungle drums have told everyone that it was your fault. Buggers, aren't they? But you're over it?"

"Getting back to normal, sir. Except for one thing . . ." She hoped her pause was dramatic enough.

"Well?" He sounded genuinely concerned.

"I seem to be obsessed with clean lavatories."

He roared with laughter. "Good girl. Now, you'll let me have those statistics by — what — three this afternoon?"

"Of course, sir."

So that was her lunchtime gone. Sometimes people reported crimes but wanted to have no action taken. They might be talked out of action by an officer who could see that successful apprehension and prosecution were extremely doubtful — or, of course, by an officer who simply didn't want to take any action. Other victims resisted such a line, demanding that action be taken, whatever the odds of success. Still others who claimed to be victims were simply lying, usually so they could make inflated insurance claims. If you made sure you used the recorded crime figures only, massaging out the crimes simply reported, with no action to be taken, they looked marginally better than the previous quarter's. It'd be nice to be able to eradicate the spurious crimes, but these couldn't be expunged even if the alleged victim was actually charged with wasting police time. Sighing, she tapped away on her calculator.

It was three before she realised she had neither eaten nor phoned Graham. On the grounds that all dodgy jobs were better done on a full stomach she slipped on her jacket and headed out into drizzly rain for a baguette. And realised, just as she was going back into Scala House, that she didn't want to eat and might never want to eat again. She did what many of her colleagues had done that week: bolted for the loo. There was, as Neil Drew had agreed, much to be said for a clean loo when you were clearly going to be intimately acquainted with it.

Staggering back to her desk, she remembered she had to get the figures and the rest of her report through to the ACC. Thank goodness for e-mail. Then she bolted again.

There was no alternative. She must go home. As soon as she could, scattering messages for her teams like so much cyber-confetti, she set out. She knew she had to be extra careful with her driving: her attention was very much elsewhere. So while she was shuffling out of her parking space — it was tight enough to make her bless her manoeuvrable Fiesta — she double and triple-checked each corner. She knew exactly where her rear and front bumpers were.

So how did this woman come to be sprawled across her bonnet?

Even at two miles an hour, she braked hard enough to shake most things off. The woman didn't fall off. But now Kate couldn't get out of the driver's door — not at this angle. Passenger side — yes. An awkward scramble, but there she was.

The woman clung on. Woman? She couldn't have been more than fifteen, if that. Thin, pale, and wearing nothing — in the most literal sense — but a cropped T-shirt, exposing a midriff covered in nothing but goose pimples, tiny skirt and high boots. At last she peeled herself from her resting-place and threw herself at

Kate, falling on the ground and clasping her knees with icy hands and arms.

"Police. Lady, police. Asylum. Lady, asylum. Slave. Sex slave."

Tearing off her jacket — it couldn't be much above freezing and goodness knew what the wind-chill factor must be — and reaching for her radio, Kate wondered if hers was the sort of bug you could work through. It better had be.

OK, prostitutes were supposed to be dealt with by local stations. But this wasn't your average tom, was it? So the first call was to the paedophilia and pornography unit, conveniently based just down the road at Digbeth nick. But what about Immigration Control at the airport? The child plainly wasn't British and, stomach bug notwithstanding, Kate would have eaten her uniform hat if she had a legitimate passport and visa. She huddled the poor kid into her car. But she was retching again already — just made it to the gutter. Hell. She'd better head straight for Digbeth. Let them deal.

Let them, indeed. As Kate introduced her new acquaintance — she'd managed to extract the name Natasha — you could almost see the word "paperwork" appearing in her colleagues' eyes. They were inclined to think that, since it was Kate's collar, she should take responsibility. No point in pleading your stomach in these circumstances, clearly. But she could at least do what she'd never done before: she pulled rank. She ticked off on her fingers: interpreter; social worker; rape suite; police surgeon. And then, to her embarrassment and probably theirs, she fainted slowly but inexorably at their feet.

CHAPTER
EIGHT

"Not bloody likely! I don't need a damned ambulance!" Kate protested. But she couldn't claim to be well. So in the end she had to consent to be shipped to the first-aid room, to sip water, to lie down, even, swathed in a red blanket comfortingly like those that had covered period-pain sufferers at school. She might even have closed her eyes. But she left the clearest instructions that she was to be roused after ten minutes, no matter how deeply asleep she might appear to be.

She didn't sleep at all, of course. She was on her mobile phone briefing her Scala House colleagues, and insisting on their prioritising the wholesale market on their patrols. She also phoned Rod to say she might be late.

"Late? How late?"

"Not sure."

"What's up?"

My guts might have been an honest answer, but it wasn't one she chose to give Rod. She gave a very brief explanation involving the girl. But the lavatory became the most urgent priority, and she cut him off.

Who the hell was she trying to kid? She ought to be at home in bed, with Rod producing water with replacement salts for her to sip: he'd do it with as much panache as if he were serving champagne.

But there had to be one of her Scala House team ready to join in the interviews. Who would it be now? Jill Todd. There was no doubt about it — this was definitely the sort of bug you could work through.

"Romanian! Well, I could see the poor kid wasn't Chinese," Kate added, stupidly. "How did she get here?"

"That's what we'd like to find out," the paedophilia and pornography unit inspector, Ray Baird, said grimly. He came from the far side of his desk to look at her more closely. "Are you sure you're all right?"

"Fairly sure I'm not, actually," she said. "There's a bug going round Scala House and it's chosen me as its latest host."

He backed away visibly. "Shouldn't you be at home?" He retreated behind his desk again. Perhaps he thought his heaps of files would act as a barricade.

"There's a job to do here. I found the kid in the middle of my patch and I want to know what's going on."

"Just as well we can't get hold of an interpreter till tomorrow, then," he said, smiling thinly. "He'll be here at ten."

"So will I."

★   ★   ★

And she was. Largely thanks to Rod's ministrations and entirely against his advice, Kate forced herself into her uniform — it seemed to have been that that had inspired the kid yesterday.

"Just remember that this is officially your free time," he said.

"Since when did that stop you working at weekends?" she only half joked.

"When murders have the decency to occur during the week, it does."

"Oh, yeah," she jeered affectionately.

As she drove carefully round to Digbeth, the city centre already packed with Christmas shoppers, she knew he'd been right. She was so wobbly that if she'd had any sense she'd have turned round and gone home to bed. Home. She'd meant to Rod's. There. She'd done it again. Meanwhile, since she was nearly at work, she might as well stay.

But not in the room she'd been allocated. Every old nick like Digbeth was constantly in a state of refurbishment to bring its interior up to modern standards. Interview rooms were part of this process; while some, if not the height of luxury, were inoffensive, others were so tatty you expected to see Bill Sykes's or Magwitch's name on the board outside. So why had they put Natasha in one of these? She surely didn't need to be intimidated any more than she was at the moment, her eyes so wide you could see the whites. She was chaperoned by a woman of about forty, wearing the most nondescript clothes imaginable, and schooling her basically gentle features into an extremely stern expression.

"Kate Power. I'm the inspector from Scala House, on whose patch this young lady was found. Or, rather, found us." Kate smiled encouragingly at the child, now clothed in a jogging suit and trainers and pulling bits of pink varnish off badly manicured nails. She was dropping the detritus on to the floor.

"DS Meg Walker," the chaperon said. "One of Ray Baird's team."

Kate flapped a hand in acknowledgement. "Look, this room's dreadful. All these brown tiles and heavy furniture are going to scare Natasha to death. I'll go and find somewhere more user-friendly."

It didn't take long. During the small hours, the station would be seething with minor criminals whom it was her colleagues' job to adjudge mentally ill or simply pissed out of their minds, and deal with accordingly. There were also the victims of their crimes to talk to. Now the processes of law would be dealing with all three groups, and Kate more or less had her choice of room.

"But why ever did you put her there in the first place?" she asked the hapless duty sergeant.

"She's an illegal, isn't she?"

"She may be an illegal immigrant, she may be an asylum seeker, not even bogus. I'd say she was some sort of victim — she called herself a sex slave, and that sounds like a victim to me. So next time use your loaf, for God's sake."

"Ma'am."

Kate hadn't the energy to sustain her anger. "OK. See if you can run to earth something hot to drink. And eat. Poor kid looks half-starved."

She opened the door, saying gaily, "We're on the move! Come!"

Natasha flung herself across the room. Meg Walker made a grab. She missed. Kate braced herself for an assault. But, as before, Natasha simply fell at Kate's feet, embracing her knees. "Lady, lady. Please." She pointed at the corner out of Kate's range.

"Come on. Up you get. No one's going to hurt you." Kate tried to ease her to her feet. She looked at Meg. "What's going on?"

"It's just —"

Kate tried to take a step forward, but the weight of the child prevented her. Damn this stupid weakness. Any moment her knees would buckle. "Don't tell me it's a bloody spider."

"Allow me to introduce myself, ma'am," a young man said, stepping forward, hand outstretched. "I'm Mihail Antonescu. I'm the accredited interpreter." He had more teeth than any human being was entitled to, arranged with such precision Kate was sure he must have paid fistfuls to an American orthodontist. Come to think of it, his accent was vaguely American. He would have been handsome but for his pockmarked skin: his cheekbones were film-star quality, his eyes a lovely limpid blue.

Since the child was now clutching at her hands, Kate had to ignore his gesture. She smiled coolly. "I see we

100

have a problem here. Would you be kind enough to wait a few moments? And would you come with me?" she asked Meg. She took the child's hands and pulled her to her feet, not quite dragging her out of the interview room with her. In any case, once she got the idea, the girl came willingly, cowering against Kate's shoulder as soon as Kate came to a standstill.

"What the hell's all this about?"

"She was fine till the interpreter turned up."

"So why doesn't she like him?"

Meg looked at her sideways. "It'd take another interpreter to discover that."

"So what happens to her now? Until we find one."

"Back to the detention centre."

"No. To a safe-house. Innocent till proved guilty." Kate turned to Natasha. "Have you eaten?" She spoke slowly and mimed.

Negative. That was clear. By now the duty sergeant was hovering. "I've found another room for you, ma'am — this way. And I've organised a bit of breakfast. I found some croissants and got them to heat them up for you."

"You're my hero," Kate declared. She smiled warmly. He was certainly using his head now.

Meg Walker was busy with a pencil and paper. Natasha fell on the croissants as if she hadn't seen food for three weeks. As she ate, the sleeve of the tracksuit was pulled back. Bruises, in so many colours that the damage must have been done over a period of days, if not weeks. Kate touched one, very gently.

The girl nodded vigorously, pulled back the other cuff, then unzipped her top.

"Jesus," Kate gasped.

Meg looked up. She'd drawn the outline of a woman, and now shaded the wrists and neck. She passed paper and ballpoint to Natasha, who twigged rapidly, shading in other areas. She then drew a powder compact and mimed patting powder over her face and neck. Kate clapped and smiled. They'd eventually need an interpreter, if not the exquisite Mihail, to get fine detail, but in the meantime, they could make a lot of progress, the three of them.

A map of Europe: at least eight out of ten for accuracy — how many English GCSE students could have done as well? Then Natasha mimed, pointing at her pencil then at her lips: both women stared first at her, then at each other.

"Lipstick?" Meg dug in her bag.

Natasha shook her head vigorously. And mimed writing again.

"A red pen? Is that what she wants?" Meg wondered.

"See what the duty sarge can produce. Be nice to him. I was ratty earlier and he didn't altogether deserve it."

Meg returned in two minutes, clutching a cornucopia of coloured pens. "Seems he's used to having to find something to entertain kids," she said. "And he's got more paper if we need it." She laid some scrap in front of Natasha.

The girl picked up pen after pen. Kate was suddenly back in Aunt Cassie's kitchen, with the crayon set she'd always craved, thirty-six, maybe forty-eight, pristine paint, pristine points. Her mother would have said, "But you can only have them if you promise not to chew them." That had been her besetting sin at the time. Aunt Cassie simply offered them as they were. And Kate's promise to herself was far stronger than any her mother could have coerced from her. Not a toothmark would sully the paint. Ever. Nor did it. When Kate had transferred her attention to her nails, biting them down to the quick, Aunt Cassie had produced a dream kit, a palette of eye, lip and nail colours.

How could she possibly sell Aunt Cassie's house?

What would Natasha make of such a kit? Yesterday, so far as she could remember anything, the girl had been masked with makeup. Today she wore absolutely none, her skin sallow and muddy, as if she hadn't slept enough or eaten decent food. Well, not enough food. Ever.

At last Natasha selected a pen to her taste, the one Kate wouldn't have expected her to touch. Brown. She traced a line from what Kate thought was Romania down to the Balkans and then across to the coast facing Italy.

"Where's that?" Meg asked.

Kate shook her head doubtfully: had this bloody bug rendered her completely useless? "Hang on — it's where an especially nasty sort of Communism hung on longer than anywhere else. Orphanages." She clicked her fingers in irritation.

"Albania," Meg supplied. "Doesn't say much for our knowledge of geography, does it?"

"Don't tell Miss Firth." Kate giggled. "She'd come back from teacher heaven to haunt me."

"A martinet?"

"Absolutely. All the same, she taught me how to read maps like words. But you forget other important things like place names, don't you?"

"We did, anyhow. But I know that's Italy. Naples? And that's Rome. Good girl. Well done."

Natasha nodded, helped herself to another croissant and changed pens. This one was black. She drew a line up to what was clearly Belgium. Then she hesitated. Another colour? At last, she decided to continue with black, but with little lines crossing the main one.

Meg made a *ch-ch-ch* sound. "Train?"

Yes, Brussels to London.

Then she changed colour, with a big smile at Kate. A nice cheerful pink brought her to Birmingham.

"So you reckon she's telling the truth?" Rod asked, presenting her with a glass of water. "To your complete recovery, sweetheart."

"Thank you. And to your escaping the nasty little bug." She toasted him.

He sat at the other end of the sofa and gathered her feet on to his lap. Bliss.

"I don't know what she's got to gain by lying," she said. "We have certain facts. One, she's between thirteen and fifteen: she says fourteen. Two, she's had various sexually transmitted diseases, she says, and the

104

police surgeon thinks she's currently got chlamydia. She's prescribed her two sorts of antibiotics, just in case."

"Which corroborates the sex-slave theory."

"Indeed. And maybe her dislike of Mihail the interpreter does, too." She explained.

"A rather extreme reaction."

"Very. But perhaps she's just off young men in a big way after her experiences."

"I take it she illustrated those too?"

"With modest little pin men and women. She's better on geography than on portraiture. But she did a very good container lorry. We're still not sure how the driver was involved. Meg thinks he's a goodie who gave a terrified girl a lift. I'm less sure. But until we get a female interpreter, who can tell? Meanwhile, I've asked everyone to step up their patrols of the wholesale market tomorrow night and to call in the instant they see anything suspicious. Not that they won't tonight, but it'll be all those car-booters unloading their ill-gotten gains. I'm going to have to do something about that, you know," she added, struggling to sit up.

"Not tonight, you're not. Tonight, Kate, is your first proper night off since you started the job, and you're going to stay here and have your feet stroked."

Maybe she should have argued. She didn't.

CHAPTER
NINE

Kate replaced the bedside phone. She'd been about to slam it down, but Rod had caught her eye with an ironic gleam in his own. "Surely you should draw the line at violence on the Sabbath."

She stuck out her tongue. "No Romanian interpreter available till Monday, damn it."

"In that case you can do the sensible thing and come back to bed and enjoy the Sundays." He rustled the *Observer* invitingly and patted the space beside him.

"But, Rod —"

"But nothing, sweetheart." He ran a hand down her back, fingering her ribs. "You're fading before my eyes — when was the last solid meal you had? It's your legitimate day off. By some miracle no one's contrived to get him or herself murdered so I'm off duty too. Three good reasons for us to have some quality time together. Agreed?"

"Agreed." She was less reluctant than she pretended. Altogether less reluctant. Especially the way his hand was moving now. She snuggled back under the duvet. "I do believe my appetite's coming back."

★ ★ ★

For all Rod had suggested they read the quality broadsheets and enjoy other minor dissipations, they both knew that Sunday was a day for catching up on paperwork they hadn't had time for during the week. Rod had his study, of course. And Kate had hers. The only problem was that it was back in Kings Heath and, if she were entirely honest, she couldn't face the prospect of driving through sleet to a cold house — OK, she'd left the central heating on, but it would feel cold anyway — to work on her own. Was it the drive or the empty house? In any case, she reasoned, she'd come back to Rod's for the evening: he'd rented a video and promised to cook more invalid food. But she had to be there to brief the night relief. "It's changeover day: early shift back to night, late to early and —"

He laid a finger to her lips. "I *have* worked shifts, my love. Before I took to my Zimmer frame. Though as I recall we worked shifts that started later and later, not earlier and earlier."

"It's part of some Home Office research — to see which disrupts sleep patterns less," she explained.

"Which means that soon the nation's police will be working the most disruptive pattern possible."

She nodded. "But the point is, I need to be there to set things up."

"No. Absolutely not. And I'm speaking as one who made — makes! — mistakes through being over-eager myself, Kate. You've got an experienced sergeant to whom you've sent long, long e-mails so he knows exactly what you want doing. He's got a team he's used to working with, at least some of whom, you say, are good, reliable officers. What does it say about your trust in them if you turn up, pinched and ill, to tell them how to do a job they've been doing for years? Well?"

She pulled a face. She knew just how much both Neil Drew and Ronnie Hale liked being treated like beginners.

"It was fine playing silly buggers dashing in and out last week, when you were trying to get to know people. Though I have to say that if you'd worked reasonable hours you might not have succumbed to this bug of yours. You'd do the West Midlands Police far more good if you had a nice early night and turned up at a sensible hour tomorrow." He grinned. "Say, '*Ja*, Uncle Hans.'"

"Why? Oh, Christ, because you were talking like a Dutch uncle. Goodness, does that mean we're committing incest?"

He looked around his study. "Not at the moment, I'd have thought." He got to his feet, taking her hand. "But that doesn't mean it can't be immediately arranged."

Kate insisted — and Rod didn't argue overmuch — that she should be there to debrief the night team as they came back to base on Monday morning. She had the kettle boiling and had even boosted the office heating to welcome them in from the bitter Birmingham pre-dawn.

Neil Drew, however, had steam clouds of anger puffing from his ears, as he wrapped his hands gratefully round a mug of hot chocolate. "Fucking Bates. What the hell does he think he's doing? I radio for assistance — oh, some kid pulls a knife on me — and he's the nearest, since he's in the wholesale market, and he never comes."

"Are you all right?" She pointed to some blood on his cuff.

"Don't worry, gaffer. I'd played that game before. He hadn't. The little shit's gracing the cells at Digbeth. And because he's now their collar, I don't even have to worry about the paperwork."

"That's a bonus, anyway. What does Bates have to say?"

"Fuck all. I've tried to make contact God knows how many times and not a bloody peep from him. Not a sodding sausage."

Ronnie Hale looked at him with disdain. "He's got the gastroenteritis bug, hasn't he? And with a stomach like his is supposed to be, he's probably got it bad."

"Too bad to radio in?" Kate asked.

"Well, we *are* talking Phil Bates here, gaffer."

Neil grimaced. "So we are. OK, gaffer. Not quite all present and correct, as you can see."

"Have you had time to call Bates on his mobile?"

She was glad she'd phrased it that way. She was spared anything more than an ironic lift of Neil's eyebrow. "Switched off. And his home answerphone's on."

"I'll keep trying," Kate said. "His numbers will be on computer?"

"His numbers are in my head — no, engraved on my heart, more like. Here, I'll write them down."

"And his address, too, please. Just in case."

Neil wrote, but said quietly, head hardly raised so she had to strain to hear him: "Don't put yourself out over this, Kate. He's a bleeding rotten little skiver, always has been, and a pain in the arse to boot."

"Point taken," she murmured back. "But even so."

Kate was making her sixth attempt to phone Bates when Jill Todd breezed in wearing a new perfume. "Feeling better, gaffer? I hear you had quite a moment of drama at Digbeth."

Well, a civilised question deserved a polite answer — even if she found it hard to notch up to friendly. "Much, thanks. It was only this stomach bug. You're all right? Your team?"

"All here and raring to go." Jill added an ironic smile.

"I can guess. Has the sleet turned to snow yet?"

"Yes — and we've had the first couple of shunts on the Holloway Head island."

"Already? I'd have thought that would have been a priority for gritting and salting. So we're in for an exciting day. Now, you remember that Mr Choi warned us about people-trafficking via the wholesale market? Well, we may not have people in the plural, but we do have a person in the singular." She explained about Natasha.

"Not the sort of thing Mr Choi was on about, surely," Jill objected coolly.

"Possibly not. But just in case it is, I want to prioritise the wholesale market again for today's beats. I know, I know, but the girl arrived at the market in a

110

container lorry, and people may have seen something useful."

"There are quite a lot of container lorries at the market." Jill might have been talking to a kindergarten child.

Best to ignore it. "And it looks as if Phil Bates succumbed to the bug last night. He never finished his stint there."

"He bothered to turn up at all? Well, that's a first, in weather like this. Has to look after his sinuses or some such."

"Well, I'd like to find out why he didn't bother phoning in sick. And why he hasn't answered his phone."

"Well, he couldn't, not if he's throwing up and shitting." The words came slightly oddly from such a delicate-looking woman.

A delicate-looking woman who may have taken two letters from your desk, Kate. Another job for today: talking to Graham. And chasing Mrs Speed for a key. And speculating whose number Todd here might have been dialling if she took the bait of the phone number.

"Well, I shall keep trying until I have to go down to Digbeth, to talk to the Romanian kid."

"I could do that," Jill objected.

"Of course you could. But you've got a full in-tray and the silly girl seems to think the sun shines out of my ears."

She might have heard the other woman mutter, "Or somewhere lower." Might.

"So I'll be off at about nine forty-five. It seems interpreters don't get up at the same time as the rest of us. Meanwhile . . ." She picked up the phone and pressed the redial button: she held the handset so Jill could hear the endless ringing. "Who's the least busy in your team? Because I'd like these numbers dialled alternately every ten minutes till we get a reply. In fact," she patted her own in-tray, "whoever you choose could take over from me right now. I've got to get my head round these figures about half an hour ago."

She couldn't fairly have used the verb "snatch" to describe Jill's action, but she came close to using the verb "flounce" as the sergeant left the room. On impulse — and, on reflection, she should have done it much earlier — she posted a missing-letters note for everyone on the e-mail system. She wanted to make sure she'd not misjudged her sergeant. She seemed to have misjudged one of her staff. As soon as she neared her desk, Mrs Speed held up triumphantly a pair of shiny new keys.

"Two?"

"One to wash and one to wear, my mother used to say. Or one to use and one to lose."

"Good idea. So I keep one and you lock the other away."

"You're sure you wouldn't rather have both of them?"

Kate smiled, handing over the spare. "I'm sure you've got a system. So long as I know what the system is."

Mrs Speed gave the side of her nose a conspiratorial tap. "In here." She produced an old-fashioned cashbox. "Hitherto only I have ever had a key. But I think you should have a duplicate, don't you?"

Perhaps Kate was winning. She hoped so. Because it was clear she'd have to have further words with Thelma — she was beginning to agree with Neil's description of the cleaner — about the state of the washbasins, so mucky she couldn't even understand how they'd ever got that way.

The interpreter who presented herself at Digbeth wore a huge, shapeless fur coat and a battered turban, skewered in place by a dramatic hatpin. She looked so like a teddy bear that Kate almost laughed out loud. But she was reassuringly female, which was all that mattered to Natasha, she hoped. And when she removed the coat, she looked a normal enough elderly lady, face pinched with cold despite the deplorable hat.

But before they could get under way, there was a very long exchange between the two Romanians. Natasha didn't seem to find the new interpreter at all to her taste, but Kate was determined to stick with her, all other things being equal.

"What's the problem?" she asked Madame Constantinou.

"She wanted to know all about my family and the region I came from." Madame Constantinou shook her head and jowls sadly. "It seems to me that our young friend may have been betrayed by people she thought she could rely on."

"But she's happy to trust you?"

"She seems to think me acceptable," she replied. Her voice was heavy with irony, which intensified as she added, "For the time being. Why does she have that paper and all those felt-tip pens?"

Kate explained about Saturday's communication exercise. "And I think Natasha likes drawing anyway. It's nice she's got something to keep her happy in the safe-house. Poor kid."

Madame Constantinou nodded. "She has been treated more like a woman than a child."

At last Meg Walker bustled up, absolutely transformed by a new haircut and highlights. Kate ventured an unobtrusive thumbs-up, but Natasha bounded across the room, laughing and touching the blonde streaks with delight. Kate felt a frisson of relief: if Natasha took a shine to Meg, then the questioning could be left in her hands while Kate turned to other Scala House cases.

Natasha shot a couple of questions; Madame Constantinou sniffed with disapproval.

"Well?"

"She wants to know when she can have her hair done like Sergeant Walker's. And when she can have her breakfast."

Now they had Natasha talking, it was impossible to stop her. But whereas Kate wanted, at this stage, a brief explanation of the events Natasha had depicted on Saturday, the girl wanted to dwell on the details. It took almost an hour to get through the first part of her story.

It was bad enough, and Kate felt guilty for wanting to urge her on when Natasha seemed to need the sheer therapy of sharing her experiences.

She'd been the only daughter of a minor civil servant. He had never been a calm man. Her mother had been truly a saint, enduring his bad temper and occasional violence, except when it was directed at Natasha. From time to time she'd had to send her away to her cousins in Oradea, but she'd always come back, of course. At last she'd realised her mother was ill, and she described her protracted suffering and eventual death from breast cancer.

Natasha broke down and cried. She couldn't be patted better by all three women, so Kate slipped out to organise more food and ring back to Scala House: no, still no news of Phil Bates. From Jill Todd's offhand response, she couldn't be sure how much effort had been made to run him to earth, but that wasn't her problem now.

The next hour was occupied with Natasha's father's response to his wife's death. Drink, almost predictably, and violence. And, of course, there was no mother to protect her. Natasha and Madame Constantinou drew a combined veil over what Kate strongly suspected was an episode of at least attempted sexual abuse. So she went of her own accord to stay with her northern cousins, only to have her father turn up, yelling and breaking things. While he cooled his heels in the town gaol, her cousins sent her to safety, to some dear friends in Yugoslavia.

Was the irony in the word "dear" Madame Constantinou's own, or had it come from Natasha?

Before such essentials as school could be organised, or work, for that matter, Natasha — "I was quite pretty then" — attracted the attention of what she called "nasty people". She glossed over how this came about. Perhaps she was lured by the promise of money; perhaps her contact betrayed her. However it happened — Natasha's fatalistic shrug was grotesquely echoed by Madame Constantinou's — she had to become a dancing girl in a nightclub. It had to be spelt out, no matter how much they'd have preferred the euphemism for Natasha's sake. Dancing meant stripping and having sex with the clients.

Time for another break.

"We're going to need all sorts of support here," Kate murmured to Meg Walker as they left the room. "I don't mean just obvious things like rustling up some winter-weight clothes. She's going to need counselling and —"

"I've already spoken to some of the women in the Steelhouse Lane rape team. And I'm on to Social Services. And the DSS. And I've raided my girls' wardrobe."

"You've actually brought in some clothes? Meg, you're a star."

Meg shrugged. "It's last year's fashion to them. I hoped it might be up to the minute for her. But the poor girl's as worldly as they come."

"But she is still a kid — look at the way she loves those felt-tips."

116

"I nicked some makeup for her too. When shall I hand it over?"

"How about at lunchtime? We'll need a break from all this emotion and I've got to shoot back to Scala House to —"

Meg folded her arms. "Does that mean you're skipping lunch? Well, let me tell you, Gaffer, you don't do that after the bug you've had. A nice light lunch, maybe, but how can you expect to get better if you don't look after yourself?"

"There's no sign of him?" Rod echoed over a glass of wine that evening.

"None. He's just vanished. And I'm worried. Really worried."

"Talk me through this slowly. You've got a constable who's a total waste of space who buggers off for the day and you go dashing off to Erdington to look for him?"

"Before you ask, I am not off my head. I know the obvious person to do it is someone from the same team. But they're working nights, and it'd look very good, wouldn't it, if they started banging on Bates' front door and hollering their heads off in a nice residential road —"

"Are there any in Erdington? Are we talking about the same place?"

"— in the middle of the night? He's spoken to me about his health problems; I was about to contact Occupational Health about him. Seems to me it's my job. Plus," she added, tongue in cheek, "to lose an officer may be regarded as a misfortune; to lose one at a possible scene of crime looks like carelessness."

Obligingly Rod threw back his head and laughed. "Nothing from the neighbours?"

"Nothing. Neither next-door neighbour has a key, either. Salad?"

"Please. We'll talk about this properly while we drive over to see Aunt Cassie."

"You're coming too?" She was both pleased on her own account and touched on Cassie's.

"I saw quite a lot of her while you were working in Devon, remember. And I fancy it's easier with two people."

She put her head on one side, grinning. "You wouldn't have an ulterior motive? Such as if you drive me you can make sure I don't stop off at Scala House and spend half the night there?"

"Hmm. Now, no more shop while we eat. Not for the next half-hour. Remember our pact: meals to be crime-free zones. It may be honoured more in the breach than the observance — I think Shakespeare caps Wilde, by the way — but we have to stay sane."

She nodded, lifting her wineglass. "To sanity!"

CHAPTER
TEN

"There's no ice." Aunt Cassie's fingers worked in her lap. "I kept reminding whatshername . . ."

"Your care worker? Izzie?" Rod prompted her. He squatted beside her.

"That's her. Izzie. Bright enough girl for all she's got those rings and things in her nose and goodness knows where else. But she wasn't herself today," Aunt Cassie grumbled. "She even left Mrs Nelmes on her commode for half an hour this morning."

"A commode! Ugh! Why didn't Mrs Nelmes use the lavatory, like everyone else? It's *en suite*, after all. She can't expect care assistants to —" Kate stopped. Her stomach wasn't as clever as she'd thought it was.

"You tell me. Mrs Nelmes *claims* she was poorly, but she was up in the dining-room at six o'clock. And a jolly good meal she had, too — an extra sweet. Anyway, there's no ice, as I was telling you. And I did fancy a nip of gin," she added, as wistfully as if she didn't have one every night. "Especially with these nice fresh lemons. And a lime!" Which had come courtesy of an open-all-hours Asian corner shop.

Clearly, one of them had to go for ice. Since Aunt Cassie was currently holding Rod's hand, it had better be Kate. She took the ice bucket — one of Rod's innovations while she'd been away — and headed for the kitchen.

She'd almost reached the service stairs when she heard an urgent whisper: "Kate!"

She couldn't have said she'd been dreading the moment but she'd certainly hoped that this wouldn't be a night on which Graham Harvey chose to visit his mother-in-law, the Mrs Nelmes whose toilet habits had so offended Kate.

Where on earth had he been lurking, anyway?

"Graham." She turned with a social smile in place. At least by calling her he'd given her enough time to prepare it.

As if he were her boss, catching her sneaking off early, he charged towards her, head thrust forward. "Why the hell didn't you phone me back?"

"Why the hell did you write to me?" she countered. No, she wouldn't play any of his guilt games, not now she was with Rod.

"To lose a letter like that!" He jabbed towards her chest with a rigid index finger.

"To have it stolen."

"But what possessed you take it into work?"

"Because I didn't have time to read it or any of my other mail at home. It's my first week at Scala House, remember." Now was not the time to tell him about her domestic arrangements.

"So you didn't even have time to phone me back," he sneered.

How could she ever have loved this man?

120

"I'd have thought everyone in the West Midlands Police would know by now that I passed out cold at Digbeth nick. The gastric bug that's doing the rounds." She gave him half a second to ask how she was now. He didn't. "I suppose I could have phoned you at home this weekend. From my sick bed." She allowed a little sarcasm into her voice.

"Today?"

No, she wouldn't tell him about her missing constable. Hierarchies were all-important in the police, and if she told him before she told Personnel and the chief superintendent at Steelhouse Lane, the commander of her operational control unit, she could be in the shit good and proper.

"How many spare hours did you have to spend on the phone in private conversations? Well, then."

He seemed to crumple. "Meet me for lunch one day this week." There was no missing the yearning in his voice.

She said as gently as she could: "You know I'm with Rod now."

"Rumour had reached me," he said bitterly. She'd never realised how easily his face fell into bitter lines. She'd always thought of him as a rather tired schoolmaster in posture as well as expression. Then hope transformed his face. "Tomorrow?"

"Maybe. If I don't phone you, no."

"But . . ." He put a detaining hand on her arm. He more than held her back: he gripped, tightly.

In the past, she'd been happy to carry his bruises on her arms: a sign of his passion for her. In the past.

"For God's sake, Graham, when you had a panic on, did you ever put me first?"

She was probably still flushed when she returned with the ice. Rod certainly registered something, but confined himself to laughing when Aunt Cassie observed, the first swig safely down, "We thought you'd gone to the Arctic to get it, didn't we?"

"I'll walk with you," Rod insisted. "It's one thing a woman officer striding round here. But at the moment you're simply a woman, my woman, to be more precise, and I hate the thought of you being vulnerable to attack."

"I could tell you all sorts of statistics about street crime in the area — and the age, social and sexual profiles of victims," she said, smiling across the car roof as he locked up.

"You're asking for a quotation about lies and damned lies," he said, taking her hand and tucking it into his pocket, wrapped in his own.

If one of the Scala House teams saw them like this it would be round the West Midlands Police even faster than the stomach virus. Which was presumably what he intended: he'd rather be blatant than risk rumours. She wasn't sure. She still wanted to prove herself on her own merits, not as the boss's woman. He had nothing to prove except that he could pull a younger woman.

Once in her office, however, he sat quietly on one of the visitors' chairs while she went off to speak to Neil Drew.

"If Phil Bates doesn't turn up tonight, Neil — and maybe we should allow him ten minutes' grace — I want to start pulling out the official stops."

"Go round to his place, like?"

"I've already done that. The house was locked. No sightings by neighbours, no key-holders."

His face said she was mad.

"I have a feeling, Neil. A copper's feeling." She knew he wouldn't argue with that.

"So we'd better find out who his relatives are."

"I'll sign the authorisation to get hold of the next-of-kin form before I go."

"And you want me to start the formal questioning of other officers, gaffer?"

"Absolutely. We know he's a whinger, Neil, but that could be stress. I want self-harm ruled out. I want every fact on my desk tomorrow when I have to tell Chief Superintendent Oxnard. *I*s dotted, *t*s crossed."

"This isn't how you wanted to start your first command, is it?" He gave a rueful smile.

"Quite. And I've already got a reputation for losing colleagues," she reflected, more to herself than as criticism of his gossiping: she'd almost forgotten how hostile he was only a week ago.

"You haven't lost this one. He's done a runner. And from what I've heard, that mate of yours was less of a mate than a liability." He pulled himself upright. "So I'd like to offer a formal —"

She clapped him on the shoulder. "Forget it, Neil. Let's just get on with our jobs. I'll be in as early as I can tomorrow. Unless you need me now?"

"Look, Kate, anyone can see you're not a hundred per cent yet. When Oxnard accepts he's a missing person —"

"Which he won't surely, not for a couple of days."

"We'll see. But when he does, it'll be all hands to the plough time. And you'll need to be fit then."

She nodded. "You're right, of course. You're properly over it? And the family — did they escape?"

"Both had a spot of tummy-ache — but you know what kids are. They bounce back."

She crossed her fingers. "I'll be here before the end of the night shift. But tell you what, Neil, I'd appreciate a call if Phil does turn up."

When she undressed, Rod couldn't possibly miss the marks on her arm. Any conversation about them would be better before bedtime. So she said, as they locked up for the night, "Graham was at the home tonight."

"I thought you looked rattled. Problems?"

"Only these." She pulled back her jumper and touched the bruises. "He seems a very troubled man, Rod. He's not happy that I lost his letter."

"It still hasn't shown up?"

"No. Nor the other one that went at the same time." She'd kept quiet about her suspicions of Jill Todd's involvement. Probably she hadn't needed to say anything. "He wants to meet me this week. Lunch."

It was impossible to read his expression.

"I'm very busy, Rod. And I don't know that a conversation between us would be helpful at this stage."

To her surprise he started to laugh. "You're beginning to sound like me — or were you taking the piss?" He added, more seriously, "Unless you feel that talking with you would enable him to gain closure."

"And you're beginning to sound like a cod-psychology self-help book."

They agreed, at last, that should Kate want to see him — assuming, and it was a big assumption, that she had time — then she would go with Rod's blessing.

She really would have to have another word with Thelma about standards of hygiene in the loos. This time it was the sanitary-disposal receptacle that wasn't closed properly. Hell. Someone had jammed something in it, that was why. She might be pernickety, but Kate found she didn't want to investigate without the benefit of gloves. At least there were always some latex ones around in a nick: they were used for handling evidence. But it was, as she found when, suitably protected, she went foraging, only a balled-up piece of paper. Well, a bit more. Paper in an envelope.

Laying it on the surface beside the washbasin, she flattened it out. Guess what: one of her letters. But not the one from Graham. Should she get an evidence bag, so it could be tested for fingerprints, or would that be making too much of a fuss? Absolutely. She wanted her teams' respect, not their mockery.

The letter — the envelope had been opened but the flap was pushed back against the adhesive strip — was on familiar headed paper: from Aunt Cassie's solicitor, the one who'd made over the house to Kate and who'd overseen an interest-free loan from her aunt so that necessary repairs could be undertaken. As soon as she'd sold her Croydon house, Kate had repaid the loan, of course, but there was no doubt that she couldn't be living as well as she was without the gift of the house.

The letter was marked STRICTLY CONFIDENTIAL, and the opening sentence begged her not to tell Aunt Cassie of its existence. Kate could see why. It seemed that Cassie's reserves, largely in shares, had suffered so badly in the recent stock-market fall that it was extremely doubtful if they'd support her at the home as long as she'd hoped. So it might be wise for Kate to seek other — cheaper — accommodation for her aunt now.

Like hell!

Cassie was, Mrs Nelmes apart, extremely happy where she was. Come to think of it, Mrs Nelmes added a piquancy that Cassie enjoyed enormously. She hated it when one of them wasn't well enough to spar with the other. The answer was obvious: Kate would have to sell the house — or officially buy it — to support her. Goodness knows, it had shot up in value since the repairs and since the general surge in property values. She'd fax the solicitor a note to that effect, with a note of apology for the delay: that would be quicker than a letter, and safer than relying on an opportunity to use the phone.

What if Graham's letter was also in the bin? She'd no idea what happened to the soiled items within, but rather thought that she didn't want to contact the company concerned to see if a letter could be retrieved. Perhaps it was an appropriate destination — if only she could be sure that that was where it had gone.

Meanwhile there were other, more urgent matters: it was time to hear from Neil Drew what he'd discovered about Phil Bates.

"His nearest and dearest are in Manchester and Telford," Neil said, "so we've got the local police to go round." His smile was ironic.

"Just so that I don't go buzzing off myself," she said, not quite suppressing a yawn. All this early rising didn't suit her, did it?

"Quite. Like I said, gaffer, you've got to keep a bit in hand. I didn't know you'd spent your weekend working — how you managed when you'd got the bug, goodness knows."

"Natasha —"

"That's the foreign tom?"

"She's fourteen, Neil. Just a kid. More a victim than a tom. Which is why I stuck with her as long as I could. Some time today I'll have to make time to pop down to Digbeth and see how she's getting on. Now, did you get anything out of anyone at the market?"

"Zilch. Like so many wise monkeys. But we're working on it. There's one bloke down there I've been tempted to get on our books as Sarbut — that's an official informer, gaffer."

"Quite." Kate nodded curtly — no need to point out that she was quite familiar with the lingo. "If you think he'll be any use, sort out the paperwork and move.

127

Tonight, I mean. Not now. That security man — Mick?"

"About as useful as a chocolate lavatory. I reckon he's doubled the amount of whisky he puts in his tea."

"Scared or just cold?"

"Who can tell?"

"Might be worth a conversation. I'll pop in on my way to Digbeth."

He started to say something but stopped.

"Go on."

"I was just going to say, don't go on your own. I made sure there were two of us last night."

She looked him full in the eye. "You're thinking what I'm thinking." It was a statement, not a question.

"If he isn't anywhere else, where can he be?"

She felt the blood draining from her face. "The crusher —"

"Or with his feet up in Telford. Mustn't go jumping to conclusions." He stifled a yawn.

"Come on, Neil, what's sauce for the gander is sauce for the goose. Off you go, now. Have a good zizz."

"Some zizz. Got to take the kids to school first. But I will push off, if it's all the same to you. Nice quiet night otherwise, by the way. Nothing like a good hard frost to make people law-abiding."

Chief Superintendent Robert Oxnard looked down at her report, tapping it with an index finger stained with nicotine. He was one of the old school, military in bearing with salt-and-pepper hair and moustache. He must be due for retirement — the sooner the better, if

128

this morning's performance was anything to go by. He sat, keeping her standing — rather as Graham used to do, come to think of it. At last he put down her report, opening instead a card folder — Phil Bates's personnel record, from what she could see. "Look at this. This man Bates has missed a couple of courses he was down for, sloped off a day early at another. A list of excuses and reasons as long as your arm. The bugger's a known skiver and you've got everyone at action stations already!"

"Hardly that, sir."

"He's not even officially missing yet."

"No. But the report details the action I've taken so far and that I would propose should be taken if our investigations prove fruitless." She was careful about the phrasing: she knew they'd almost certainly lose the investigation if and when Bates became a missing person.

Oxnard tapped the report again. "New broom, aren't you, Power?"

"Sir."

"Doing this to suck up, are you? Or just to impress the troops, eh?"

"Most of them are of your opinion, sir. Except the sergeant in charge of his team."

"Who's anxious to please his new gaffer."

"Who disagreed violently at first. But there are some interesting coincidences, which I've outlined here, sir." Her turn to touch her report.

In an ideal world, he'd have invited her to sit and talk him through them. As it was, he picked up the papers as if they were so much cold ash and tipped them into his in-tray.

So much for that hour's work, then.

It was nice to be greeted by Natasha as a long-lost cousin. In Meg Walker's daughters' cast-offs she looked much less like a waif. She hadn't yet cajoled anyone into letting her have her hair done, but had at least clipped it up in fashionable tufts. As for the makeup, she'd applied it with gusto rather than finesse, but presumably that was what her former boss had wanted. For that was the latest development. She'd had a boss. A pimp, more like. As first he'd seemed a saviour, rescuing her from the strip joint. Vladi.

Madame Constantinou was by now so involved with the tale that she wrung her hands just as Natasha was wringing hers. Vladi had been a client at the club. Oh, so tall and handsome and with such lovely eyes. He'd been generous, too: he hadn't tried to hurt her when he'd — Madame Constantinou flailed in vain for a polite synonym. The word "fuck" was clearly beneath her, though Kate thought it was the nearest to the brutal words she was sure Natasha was using.

"He didn't hurt her when they — made love," Madame Constantinou concluded lamely.

As if making love involved hurting your partner.

"And he gave her presents. Not enough to annoy the club owner but enough to make Natasha feel special. So when one night he announced she didn't have to strip at the club ever again, nor have sex with the

130

fatbellies again . . ." Madame Constantinou paused to check the term: Natasha nodded ". . . she was happy."

Fatbellies. Gross men humping their flab up and down on and in Natasha's slender body. Kate fought to suppress a shudder. She must. She was supposed to be a professional.

"Vladi is boyfriend!" Natasha declared, triumphantly.

All the women nodded approvingly at the change in her fortunes.

"He took her home in his big car, and gave her good food and wine. At last she could be happy!" Madame Constantinou was really getting into the spirit of things. "But the following day, Vladi left her alone in his flat. Suddenly some men burst in, who tied her up and put her in a boat — not a proper boat, you understand, but one you blow up?" Madame Constantinou looked puzzled.

"An inflatable. Go on."

"There were terrible storms, and Natasha was very . . . unwell."

It was clear from Natasha's graphic mime that she had been very sick. What would she have made of her interpreter's euphemisms?

They'd taken her to Italy, and she was driven in a car boot to Naples. This time there was no stripping. Just sex, with many, many fatbellies. One evening, just as she was going out for the hundredth time that day — Madame Constantinou seemed embarrassed by something: the precision? The imprecision? — a big car had pulled up and out stepped Vladi. Her hero. She embraced his knees: he would rescue her again.

So why was Natasha here now?

CHAPTER
ELEVEN

A constable Kate didn't recognise was stooping over the photocopier, anxiously comparing what it ejected with the textbook pages he was copying. Although his hair was cut as brutally short as many of his colleagues', his trendy wire-framed spectacles made him look curiously innocent, in a studious sort of way. Going for the cliché, she thought he might be the missing Chinese scholar.

"Good morning," she said cheerily.

"Ma'am." He studied his feet, blushing, hands a-flap.

"You wouldn't be Sergeant Dave Bush?"

"Yes, ma'am." He gave another awkward shuffle. Yet he wasn't as young as she'd thought — he'd be older than she was, perhaps in his late thirties.

"So you're the officer whose worth is beyond rubies! You're Mr Choi's favourite officer!" she declared triumphantly. "As soon as you've finished, make yourself a cup of tea and bring it into my office."

When he came, he inched in, and stood guiltily in front of her desk.

She stood to greet him. "No tea?"

"Well, in the circumstances . . ."

She was puzzled. "What circumstances, Dave?"

"The photocopying, ma'am. It wasn't — police business."

"Why not sit down and tell me about it?"

He looked for a chair but, having put his hand on the back of it, remained half sitting, half standing.

"Look, Dave, I've been wanting to speak to you for the last week. Why not tell me what's wrong, then go and make your tea and bring it in here? I think we're in for a long session."

"I was photocopying something for my course, ma'am." It was just like her, years ago, confessing to Miss Firth that she'd forgotten her geography homework.

"This is your Cantonese course?"

"You know about it?" He smiled, straightening, a different man. "Yes. I was only messing about at first, you know, thinking it might be useful. But now I'm doing an evening a week at the Brasshouse Centre — the languages centre in Ryland Street — when I can make it, that is."

"It seems to me that we should ensure you can make it every week. A skill like that's invaluable round here."

Like a teenager, he flushed with pleasure.

"You've obviously got the personal respect of the Chinese community," she continued, "and I was so impressed the way you'd contacted Cherish House to wish them well for their reception. You were sadly missed, all the same."

He blushed. "It sounds as if I've passed over. To the other side."

"As in 'gone before'?" She pulled a face.

"Yes, ma'am. As in shuffling and mortal coils."

No wonder he got on well with Mr Choi. "In that case you deserve a cuppa. I'll ask Mrs Speed to get us both one. China tea for you, I presume?"

"Actually, ma'am, I hate it. I only drink it to be sociable. I'm really a coffee man, ma'am."

"And I'm really a gaffer woman, Dave. Kate when we're not on duty, gaffer when we are. OK? Otherwise I feel I should be in a gilded coach, waving."

"But isn't that pronounced, 'mam', ma'am, to rhyme with 'jam'?"

"As opposed to rhyming with 'harm'? Or," she added, when all she heard from the phone was noises she couldn't place, "rhyming with 'alarm'?"

She'd better check what was up. Nothing was up, but Mrs Speed was down, face down, to be precise on the desk, surrounded by a knot of officers. Tim Wilde was the only one she recognised. Replacing the handset someone had left on the desk, Kate joined her colleagues.

"The tummy bug?" she asked. "Better call an ambulance."

These might have been the words to rally both her and Ronnie Hale, but they didn't stir Mrs Speed. Nor did the efforts of Sergeant White, who presented himself as their duty first-aider. So the ambulance it was — with a very sober group of officers watching while Mrs Speed was carried away, accompanied by Sergeant White. Someone fiddled with the phone in the hope that it would put all calls direct to the extension required — when that failed, Kate asked Tim to get on to the central police switchboard.

After this it was almost a relief to return to her conversation with Dave Bush, who'd quietly made an excellent cup of coffee for them both.

"Mr Choi seemed to be warning me that there was something illicit going on in the wholesale market. Not everyone thought his warning was . . . shall we say, disinterested? Now, two things have happened. The first, as you're probably aware, is that Phil Bates has disappeared."

"You don't want to worry about him, gaffer. He's as reliable as an eleven pence piece. He'll be off with his mates, fishing."

"In this weather? For seals? Through a hole in the ice? Look, Dave, the last time anyone saw Phil he was setting off on his regular beat incorporating the market. Since then, nothing. So I'm worried. Now we've had this Romanian child turn up: she came in some container lorry, she says. In the cab, not in some airless compartment, at least. So that's two things possibly involving the market. Would either of them be what Mr Choi was talking about?"

"Wouldn't have thought so. Not one tom, anyway. If it was coachloads of illegal immigrants coming to work in the warehouses and restaurants round here, that'd be more his line."

That had been more or less Jill Todd's opinion. Perhaps she should have believed her. "You wouldn't fancy an act of personal sacrifice, would you, Dave?"

His eyes widened.

"Go and drink China tea with Mr Choi and dig as deeply as you can. And when you've finished with him, get out there and talk to as many other people as you have time to. But, Dave," she called him back, "for goodness' sake take care. We're enough people short round here already without losing you." She grinned ironically.

He managed to grin back, flapping a bony hand in acknowledgement.

She was suddenly hungry. Hell, she'd forgotten to have any lunch. Stupid, stupid, stupid, especially as she'd passed so many places where she could have picked up a sandwich; she could even have joined her colleagues in the canteen at Digbeth nick. But it was three already: she'd be eating with Rod at seven or thereabouts. Was it worth bothering now?

An extra-loud rumble told her it was. Selfish as it might seem, she'd take the long way round.

It was her patch, after all, and any time spent where locals could see her and, better still, talk to her was more than justifiable — a positive investment in good policing. The fact that it was a dazzling afternoon, with the sort of cloudless sky that presages a hard frost, was a bonus.

As she pushed open the outer door on her return, she could hear the phone. She ran back up the stairs, clutching her BLT. The caller wanted Sergeant Bush. Feeling a complete idiot, she ran to his office and yelled. OK: the call to the switchboard hadn't worked. Should she sit and take any calls while she ate?

She mustn't. She wasn't the office junior. She was the gaffer. And gaffers didn't sit trying to answer the phone while chewing an unmanageable baguette. Gaffers sat in the privacy of their own rooms, drumming the desk and wondering furiously how long they were going to be without clerical back-up, and phoned Personnel to demand instant action. Only lowly cops worried about how long the poor woman was going to be ill.

So this was what management did to you.

Management also made you cunning. Her colleagues with the National Crime Intelligence Service must have information on Romanian prostitutes and their Albanian pimps. How could she access it? Of course, it was none of her business. Not really. As and when Phil Bates was finally declared a missing person, investigating his absence would be more than likely taken away from her and her colleagues and made the responsibility of a murder-investigation team. One of Rod's MITs. And although there was no competition between her and Rod, and he would almost certainly have nothing to do with the day-to-day running of the case, she still wanted to have done as much as possible before handing over "her" case. She owed it to the Scala House people. Uniformed officers always felt their CID opposite numbers had a bob on themselves. Worse, when a CID officer messed up, part of the disciplinary action against him usually involved a return to the uniformed ranks. OK, there was more supervision there — but also the distinct impression that the ranks were second rate, not premier league. No, mention to Neil

Drew or Dave Bush the possibility of outside "help" and they'd work round the clock to avoid it.

If God helped those who helped themselves, she had an idea of whom she might be able to call on for help. And it would kill several birds with one stone. Graham Harvey had a friend quite high up at NCIS. Having someone she could talk to unofficially was almost worth the lunch Graham was bound to press her to accept. She might have avoided it today, but he wouldn't let go, would he?

"Geoff French?" His voice sounded tinny over the phone. "Yes, I'm sure he'd help. Mention my name."

Oh, I will — never fear. "Thanks, Graham. Now, your letter. The other one's turned up — stuffed into a bin in the ladies' loo. But there's no sign of yours yet. I'm hoping that's in the bin too." *Irretrievably.* Talking to him on the phone was much less hard than face to face. Perhaps she had an extra nano-second in which to react; perhaps she was simply less aware of a body with which she'd been so intimate.

"Had the other one been read?"

"Possibly. The envelope had been resealed."

"I wonder if mine's been tampered with. You haven't checked the bin yet?"

"It's a sealed sanitary disposal bin: there's no way I can get in."

"I still can't think why you had to take it into work."

"I explained, Graham. I've hardly seen my house recently and I wanted to check that I hadn't forgotten to pay any bills and was going to have something essential cut off."

"You should pay by direct debit — much safer."

Stop being so bloody didactic! "And I'm not so sure it was a good idea to write at all, Graham, knowing that I'm with someone else. He might have been the jealous type." She waited: no response. "So, what did you say in the letter?"

"I can't go into that now. I'm up to my eyes in something for one of the ACCs." With a bit of luck that might mean he was too busy for lunch this week.

"OK. Why don't you phone me when —"

"Oh, Kate." He groaned.

Is he really in pain or is he just giving me a hard time? "Graham, I —" *I couldn't go on destroying both our lives, knowing that you'd never get a divorce in a million years, and that if we'd ever got together I simply wouldn't have been good enough for you. Ever. Come in, someone, anyone — please!*

"You'll meet me for lunch one day? Really?" It came out in a rush.

He might have heard her sigh. Well, it would get the damned business over. "As a friend, yes." *And poor lonely Graham could do with a friend, couldn't he? That's probably what drew him to me — loneliness. Much the same as what drew me to him, come to think of it.*

"Friday?"

"Provided nothing comes up — for either of us. Any idea where?"

"I'll — I'll have to think about it. I'll call you."

The poor man hasn't worked through the implications, has he? Somewhere big and impersonal or small and noisy — above all, somewhere where neither of us is known.

To her horror — she must be back in management mode again — she was coolly dialling DI Geoff French's number within five seconds of Graham's putting down the phone.

French seemed happy to help, but rather more interested in what she had to offer. "How did you say you'd come across this child?"

She explained briefly. "Geoff, this is strictly off the record — right? I'm an absolute rookie in post, and I've no idea how many toes I'm treading on simply by talking to you."

"You used to be one of Harvey's DSs, didn't you?" he asked, a Lancashire accent made thicker by the phone. "Well, you'd have done it then without blinking, wouldn't you?"

"I'm back in uniform," she said hollowly. "Supposed to be running a nick, not sniffing round detecting."

"Well, you're still supposed to be solving crime. So tell me about this kid."

She did so, winding up with a rueful admission: "There's lots more to her story yet. We've only got her as far as Italy. Or we had when I left this lunchtime. She's not one for terse narratives: she insists we have every gesture, every feeling. And though she prefers a big audience, I simply don't have time to listen to every chapter in her saga as it unwinds."

"Well, you wouldn't. Not if you're running your own nick. Let me have a transcript of the edited highlights as and when you get it, will you, Kate?"

"If you give me your e-mail address, I'll get Meg Walker — she's the sergeant who's talking to her at the moment — to send you the day's transcript when she sends it to me."

"Thanks. If the girl's telling the truth, she's probably been involved with some very nasty people. As far as we can see, the Albanians have their own version of the Mafia in Italy, with resultant turf wars. Murder, drugs, illegal immigration, all funded originally by prostitution and vice rackets, now nicely profitable in their own right. They're infiltrating the States, too, living in places like Arthur Avenue."

"Sorry — that should obviously mean something."

"It's an Italian enclave in the Bronx. The thing is, the Albanians all speak Italian: they pick it up from Italian TV stations back home. And it doesn't go down well with genuine Italians in Italy or the States — all these nasty, vicious bastards outdoing them at their own games. There's a fear they're infiltrating Soho with hordes — if you'll pardon the pun — of cheap prostitutes, doing anything anywhere, no condoms. They'll drum out the local toms in no time."

"We really are talking big-time here."

"Absolutely. So if you go in, Kate, make sure you go mobhanded. They've got a reputation for getting very, very violent."

The next phone call was to Digbeth, where Meg Walker and Madame Constantinou were still working — just.

"Another five minutes and you wouldn't have caught us," Meg announced. "I was just about to take her Christmas shopping with me."

"Before you do, tell me, has she given any intimation that the people who kidnapped her know she's in Birmingham? Any at all?"

"'Any intimation'? Goodness me, Kate, you sound just like an inspector. No, she hasn't."

"Thank you," she said drily. "And now I'm going to sound like an inspector again. I want her moved to another safe-house."

"But —"

"I want her interviewed somewhere different each day, which each of you will get to by a different route. Call me paranoid, Meg, but I want us all to get out of this in one piece."

And then it was on to the computer to e-mail the night relief. No one, repeat no one, was to go alone into the wholesale market.

Kate waited till after supper before she raised the problem of Graham, prefacing it with the information she'd picked up from NCIS.

"This is all looking very serious, isn't it?" Rod agreed. "Pity information like that doesn't percolate down as a matter of course."

"It may well do. There may be a file somewhere in my in-tray. Trouble is, I can't see my in-tray for the mountain of material I should have dealt with yesterday."

"All the latest and greatest Home Office priorities." Perhaps the silence wasn't just because he was preoccupied with the washing-up.

"You really don't mind this lunch business, Rod?" she ventured. "If you don't like it, just say so. I can simply postpone *ad infinitum*."

"That's not a very satisfactory way out. If you don't want to meet Graham, that's a different matter. But you ended the affair very abruptly, from what you said. And he didn't have a chance to talk things through while you were in Devon. Perhaps a few words of explanation would help him to . . . come to terms with his loss."

"You're not just a teeny bit jealous?"

"Quite enough to boost your ego. Kate, whom do you come home to every night?" He turned to her. "Whose arms are you in now? Well, then . . ."

CHAPTER
TWELVE

"This man whose veacle should of . . ." Kate supposed she should be relieved that Wednesday's reports from the night relief demanded nothing more serious than a course in communication skills — better still, basic English. What had happened to the spell-check, for goodness' sake? Even if the perpetrator had been in a frantic hurry to complete his or her paperwork before the end of the shift.

They'd all signed off very promptly — yes, all those counted out had been counted in again — but had obviously decided that they had nothing worth a special report. So she just needed a quick flash through her e-mails for an update. Neither of the two officers patrolling the wholesale market — and this was at four o'clock, when it was at its busiest — had seen or heard anything untoward. The night-security guard, Mick, him of the tightly laced tea, had been too pissed to say anything worthwhile, though the officer who'd accompanied Jill Todd put in a rider that he might, of course, have been scared. The jury was out on that, then.

There was a scratch at the door.

"Helen. How are you?" When Helen made no effort to move, she added, "I was just about to get the kettle on. Care to join me?"

Funny: she could have sworn the young woman was scared. "Don't mind if I do, so long as it's that herbal stuff of yours."

She was still pregnant, then.

"What I was wondering, like," Helen resumed, as Kate returned to the room and handed over her mug, "was whether Mrs Speed was going to be in today."

Kate shook her head. "No idea. But it's a bit early yet, isn't it?" She glanced at her watch. Seven forty-five. She looked sideways at Helen. "A bit early for you, too. The morning sickness is . . .?" she floated.

"Well, I thought I could help out a bit if I came in earlier, like. I know it's a long time ago, but I did shorthand for a bit while I was a nipper. And if her's still bad —"

"That's a brilliant idea." To hell with the fact that Helen's phone skills might not have the clipped grammatical perfection of Mrs Speed's. She was about to say that spending the day sitting still rather than dashing around might be good for an expectant mother, but instead simply waited. If Helen wanted to say something, she didn't want to wrongfoot her. She leant back in her chair, stirring her coffee, and smiled.

Helen managed a smile in return. "This bab of mine, gaffer. Would you mind if I keep it? Really?"

"Helen, what have *I* got to do with it? It's your decision absolutely." She got up and squatted beside her. "You're *entitled* to maternity leave! By law. And by

European law," she added, as if that were somehow conclusive.

"Oh, ah."

Kate had never heard those two syllables used so meaningfully or so flexibly as by Black Country speakers. According to their inflexion and their context, they could mean total agreement or complete opposition — and many other things besides. Helen's clearly signified extreme scepticism.

"The law may say one thing," Helen expounded more fully, "but it's them as you work with as really matters, ay it?"

"Yes and no." Gammy knee protesting, she struggled upright. "As I said, you're legally entitled to paid leave before and after the birth, and you get support afterwards, I think, if the baby's ill and you need time off. I'd have to check on that. And, of course, you can save up your time off in lieu."

"But it ay just that. It's — well, how they treat you. This mate of mine caught for one and her station sergeant put her on nice indoor work."

Kate wasn't quick enough to pick up on the sarcasm. "So he should."

"Oh, ah. Putting on computer details of all the child-abuse cases on file from the year dot."

"I won't ask you to do that, Helen, I promise. And if anyone else tries something similar, you come straight over their head to me. It won't be grassing them up. It'll be obeying a direct order. OK?"

"Well, if you're sure . . ." She buried herself in the mug of tea.

146

Kate stood. "The only people who have to be sure are you and the baby's father."

She was rewarded with a beam, doubtful at first but then expansive. "Oh, ah! The dad's over the fucking moon. Same as I shall be when I stop throwing up, I dare say." She was halfway through the door when she turned back. "And you'll make it all right with the others, gaffer?"

"Of course I will. Now, you phone Personnel and sort out the leave entitlement you can expect."

And leave me one officer short on a long-term basis — and probably with higgledy-piggledy attendance after her maternity leave expires. Great! Still, maybe Personnel will come up with a temporary replacement.

But there was an immediate knock on the door, and Helen, grinning like a gorilla, came in again, waving a couple of flimsy pieces of paper. "Good news, bad news."

"Good first."

"Well, I done me first bit of shorthand and I can read it back."

"Great! And the bad?"

"Message about Phil Bates, like. You asked some folk to see if he was with his family. Out in the wilds, Wales or summat. Well, he's not. And the worst news is they want to know what's being done to find him. His family, that is. And they reckon as how they'll get their chief on to our chief. Sorry."

"Don't worry — I don't shoot messengers." But she tugged her own hair before recalling she was supposed to be radiating managerial calm and efficiency. "Shit,

shit, shit! Look, phone through to the Operational Commander's secretary bang on nine, will you, and tell her?"

"Let her break it to the old bugger, eh?"

"Quite. And hope he doesn't shoot her."

"Nah. Her's a civilian — her'd cost too much."

Today's talks with Natasha were being held, as Kate had directed, at a different police station, Ladywood. This wasn't far from a huge traffic intersection always referred to, mysteriously, as Five Ways Island, though it was the confluence of six, not five, main roads. For some reason, although ten thirty was well past the rush-hour, traffic was solid from Smallbrook Ringway. It would have been far quicker to walk the couple of miles involved. And there was no prospect of it getting better: Hagley Road was solid, too, and whatever was causing the problem had inevitably involved Ladywood Middleway. A tersely phrased enquiry into her radio elicited the news that a lorry had jack-knifed across three lanes of the A38(M) approaching Spaghetti Junction, and all traffic leaving the city that way was caught in the snarl-up. Since the lorry had caught fire, the southbound carriageway had been partially blocked by emergency vehicles. Well, at least she wasn't in Traffic. She wasn't one for minced and sliced bodies, especially those burnt to a frazzle.

By the time Kate had finally got to Ladywood, cursing the total waste of time — why on earth hadn't she had the nous to check on road conditions before she'd set out? — Natasha's narrative had taken her from Naples to Rome, Meg Walker reported, over a restorative coffee in the canteen. Natasha and the interpreter were still in the room they'd been allocated, gossiping nostalgically, according to Meg, about the old country.

"Lots of fatbellies in Rome," Kate ruminated gloomily, thinking of the mounds of male tourist flab, not to mention the homegrown pasta-induced variety.

"On the contrary, who should turn up but Vladi. So no fatbellies, just a wonderful Roman holiday with Vladi, who wined and dined her and bought her lovely clothes."

"Sounds wonderful," Kate prompted. "Why do I think everything's too rosy?"

"Because you're a cynic. He bought her something else, too. False papers. She became an Italian overnight."

"Did she mind? God, this coffee's vile!"

"You should have had the drinking chocolate. No, not if it meant staying with Vladi."

Kate pushed the disposable cup aside. "So she's now officially an EU citizen, entitled to work and to have healthcare and the rest of it. If the papers were legitimate, of course."

"Quite. He assured her that they were the very best forgeries. And the poor little kid's over the moon, because — still in Rome, remember — Vladi says he wants her to meet his family. That's why she needs the papers. To travel."

"I'm sure there's going to be a but."

Meg laughed. "We're just approaching the but stage now, I fancy."

Kate's face stayed dead serious. "I wish she could be more concise. I need hard facts about how she got here. And I need them now. Preferably yesterday."

"Don't think I haven't tried to urge her on. But she simply slows down again and returns to this no-details-spared account."

As the women headed back downstairs, Meg said, "Tell me, gaffer, why all this cloak-and-dagger stuff? Different venues, different routes? A bit OTT, isn't it?"

Kate stopped, shaking her head slowly, as if unable to believe her precautions herself. "I've just got this feeling," she said at last.

Meg nodded, as if she'd had a full and logical explanation. "Copper's instinct? That's a good enough reason for me."

"Where are the loos round here?"

Kate was washing her hands when her mobile rang. A knifing in Hurst Street.

"The big question is, was the incident racially motivated?" she said, back at Scala House, three hours and no lunch later. She'd have murdered for a coffee, but could hardly ask Helen to make her one, not when she was off caffeine at the moment — not to mention on the phone. She rested her bum on her desk, running her fingers through her hair.

"One Chinese waiter stabs one Bangladeshi waiter. It'd be hard to prove racial motivation, not in the accepted sense," Dave Bush said.

150

"But it might be. Oh, it's OK for one waiter to stab another, so long as it's decent, honest, personal needle, but if one of them said anything nasty about the other one's ethnic origin, then books have to be thrown." Kate sighed.

"Actually, what I don't like is their doing it in broad daylight," Dave said.

She looked up, startled. "Is stabbing an after-dark crime, then?"

"Not as far as I know. It's just that if it had been at night, Jill Todd would have had to deal with all the paperwork, not me."

"Such commitment to the process of law and order amazes me. OK, Dave, it's more than time you tasted freedom. Just one thing before you go — have you had a chance to talk to Mr Choi?"

"He's in Manchester till tomorrow afternoon. Won't be free till four-ish. I'll hang about here or pop into town and do some Christmas shopping, then go and see him. I've made an appointment so he'll know it's serious."

"So long as you remember to book it in for TOIL. No, I insist. You never know when you'll need to take it. Hell, make it paid overtime, if you prefer — Christmas is always a good time for a little extra cash, isn't it? Now, if I don't see you tomorrow, remember to press as hard as you can without landing yourself in the shit. I want to know what's happened to Phil Bates, and I'm sure one of Choi's contacts will know something."

"With respect, gaffer, that's a huge assumption to make. Just because he's Mr Big in one of the triads doesn't mean he knows everything that's going on."

"Did you ever know a Mr Big who didn't know far more than he needed to know to maintain power? If there's anything going on in his bailiwick, he'll know. Or know someone who knows."

"Or know someone who can put pressure we can't on someone who knows."

"My God, Dave, I hope I didn't hear you say that. And I don't mean simply because I got lost before the end of your sentence."

"No more you did."

"Go on. I'm going to have to get back to the OC and rattle his cage some more. And if I succeed it won't simply be a field intelligence officer on Choi's case, it'll be a whole pack of CID."

"So long as it doesn't come to the know-all MIT mob — oh, sorry, gaffer. No offence meant."

"None taken. I'm perfectly happy for Rod to come down here to my office as my bloke, but I don't want him sniffing round our patch professionally."

It was only because the problem of Aunt Cassie's finances was urgent that Kate felt able to heed her own advice and take some time off in lieu. Or, more accurately, work only three hours' overtime, unpaid because that was what happened when you were an inspector. She'd been so tied up with paperwork that she was setting out for Kings Heath late, with no time even to change out of her uniform. The solicitor himself must operate on the principle of helping Cassie as a person, not just a client: how many lawyers accepted their last client appointment at five fifteen?

Both kept the preliminaries to a minimum, though, Mr Robson retiring prim and dapper to the far side of his document-laden desk where he opened a file placed ready on his blotter.

"I don't want to move Cassie, Mr Robson. She's happy where she is — the home seems very well run."

"It certainly passes the urine test."

Kate had heard the expression before, long ago, from Graham, but Robson wasn't to know and was embarking on an explanation. "Anyone who spends as much time as I do visiting old people in residential homes learns to apply one swift and infallible test. If the lobby smells of stale urine, you remove the person to a better place at once. If you penetrate to the hinterland before the odour assails you, you can usually improve things by a firm word with management. And in the case of this particular home, there's rarely any smell, even in the rooms of the oldest inhabitants."

"So you rate the place as highly as I do?"

"And agree that your great aunt wouldn't wish to move. But she'll have no option unless the market recovers. Which it assuredly will eventually."

"But it isn't 'eventually' we have to think about. It's soon."

"She still has jewellery to dispose of, but I know she'd rather leave that to you. No, I'm sure you don't need it, but it is her wish that you have it — eventually."

He managed another neat smile. Perhaps he kept his lips closed because his teeth were bad.

"So can I buy the house properly? That should free up —"

"Since you own it, I fail to see how you can buy it again. She transferred the property legally to you, Inspector."

"Sell it? That would free up some cash, and I could buy a much smaller place."

"I hardly think you'd like that. And the house is going up in value all the time. That would be foolish."

"Couldn't I simply put funds into her bank account every month — the equivalent of rent?"

"Don't think I hadn't thought of that. But she still insists on checking her accounts every month, and I can't see that she would miss that."

Kate flung up her hands. "Pay the home directly?"

"The same objection would obtain. I must admit, Ms Power, my own mind is going round in circles at the moment, but now I've put you in the picture and raised some possibilities —"

And shot them all down in flames!

"— I think we should avail ourselves of a period of quiet reflection and reconvene for further discussion next week."

And you'll charge me for another half-hour of your time. "Very well. I'll talk the problem over with one or two of my friends. How long do we have?"

"A few months, I'd have thought. Unless the market becomes even more bearish."

"So there's no panic."

"If you plan to sell the house, Ms Power, you must allow at least six months." He shut his folder and stood up. The appointment was over.

So what was he doing, advising against selling and then implicitly recommending it? In a way, it made brilliant sense: she was hardly ever at the house, and was coming to call Rod's "home". Rod had frequently suggested it, and she'd been on the verge of agreeing. But he would want her there because she wanted to be there, not because he'd discovered that a financial mat was being pulled from under her feet.

There was a piercing whistle. A hand slammed her wind-screen. A cyclist held her wing mirror long enough to yell, face up against the side window, "Look where you're going, you stupid cunt!" before setting off again.

Surely this was a one-way street. Surely she couldn't have been so preoccupied she hadn't noticed a change of use. Gazing into her rear-view mirror she noticed him meting out the same treatment to the car behind.

She was out of the car before she even knew she'd released the seat-belt.

Grabbing him by the seat of his Lycras, she yelled, with more glee than she liked, "You're nicked."

"Get your fucking hands off me. This is assault."

Her fellow motorist staggered out to assist her by propping up the racing bike. "I thought I was seeing things. No lights. And it's a one-way street. Jesus. I thought I'd hit him."

155

"Well, something else has," she declared, dragging a reluctant arm up his back. "The law. What's your name? You — I asked your name?"

"What fucking business is it of yours?"

Perhaps he hadn't noticed the uniform? "None at all. I'd just like to use it when I arrest you and caution you. OK, if you'd give me your name, please . . ."

"So you won't be a great fan of this new Euro-legislation they're talking about that decrees that any accident involving a bike is the fault of the car driver." Guljar Singh grinned, lounging against the custody sergeant's desk in Kings Heath police station, watching the departing back of the errant and abusive cyclist one of his colleagues had just processed. "Oh, I see congratulations are in order." He gave a mock salute, nudging the spotty constable alongside him to do the same. The custody sergeant muttered long and loud about paperwork, and retired to address himself to the computer.

"I've only been in post a week or so," she parried.

"Enjoying it?" he asked with a hint of — doubt? derision, even? — in his voice.

"It's a funny thing, but all the training in the world doesn't prepare you for actually doing the job." In other circumstances she might have enjoyed a confidential natter with Guljar, a supportive colleague when she'd been based in Kings Heath, but she wasn't about to confess any reservations in the presence of an acned kid of eighteen. Surely modern medicine could do something for spots like those.

156

"Budgets? People?" Now Guljar sounded genuinely interested. Perhaps he was due for promotion himself.

"Lack of both," she said firmly. "Plus endless government initiatives."

"Which change as often as I change my socks."

"Not very often, then, Sarge," offered the constable, no doubt expecting the cuff he promptly received. He retired to lick his wounds.

"Time for a cuppa?" Guljar asked.

Kate thought of Rod and the supper she'd promised to cook. "Sure." What else could she say? But she was surprised he led the way unspeaking not to the canteen but to the empty sergeants' office, stopping *en route* to help them both to water from the chiller.

He shut the door carefully. "Tell me if I'm out of order, Kate, but how are you getting on with Phil Bates?"

"Why do you ask?"

He looked taken aback.

"Sorry to snap. It's just that — and this is between the two of us, Guljar, until it becomes horribly public, as I'm afraid it will any day now — he's disappeared."

"Done a runner?"

"Flit the coop. Whatever. No trace of him at his home, or with any of his relatives. So that's why I jumped down your throat — sorry."

He pushed a chair towards her, which she sank into — God, she was tired, wasn't she? "No contact with anyone?"

"Nope. I've told the OC, but he says Phil's a skiver and not to worry."

"He's a skiver all right. Which is why I asked. But I've never known him do anything like that. He usually has an excuse for his skiving. Would it — Kate, I know you said all this was between us — but would it help if I asked about a bit?"

"I can't see it doing any harm. Trouble is, Guljar, I can't see it doing any good either. Not to help us find him alive."

CHAPTER
THIRTEEN

As soon as she'd left Guljar, Kate phoned Rod, to reach only the answering-machine. So he was working late too. Since she was in Kings Heath, should she double back to Worksop Road to check her house? Or go straight into Moseley to see Aunt Cassie? She checked her watch. Nearly eight. Hell, what had happened to her energy? She ought to be able to tackle both. But she didn't want to do either. Not until she'd come to a few decisions. Mr Robson had disturbed her more than she'd realised. No time to repine now, however: what she must do was stop off at Tesco or Safeway for something for supper. Unless that was what Rod was doing at the moment — his mother had done a good job of domesticating him. She tried his mobile number.

Nothing. She left a message saying she'd buy some food and start cooking it. Perhaps tonight was the night to be a bit more adventurous — except that Rod might faint with shock if she were.

Rod sank on to a kitchen chair and, smiling almost absently, reached without comment for the glass of wine she'd poured as soon as she heard his car. There was, however, an alertness about his eyes that told her not to interrupt his thought processes with cooing questions. The smell of the steak would disturb him soon enough anyway. For all she'd hoped to conjure something exotic, all she'd managed was a ready-made sauce to pour over it. OK, she'd added some mushrooms, not quite as an afterthought. And baked a couple of potatoes, on the grounds that salad was a bit miserable on a night when the temperature was already around the –5 degree Celsius mark. But when she triumphed with perfectly steamed broccoli and carrots, she positively preened. She'd have welcomed an official fanfare to bring Rod to the table: she always feared he rated her gastronomic aspirations not much higher than she rated them herself.

"Ta-ra, ta-ra!" She made her own.

"Wow!" he obliged her. "This looks good. And tastes good."

Almost apologetically she said, "I decided to go organic for the meat. And the sauce."

"And it shows. And the wine — hmm. It must have cost you a week's pocket money. Which reminds me, you keep on paying for food and groceries. We ought to have some system, sweetheart. I can't have you paying for everything."

"Come on, since when did you let me pay for a meal out or contribute to your mortgage?" She hoped the tone was jokey, but she wanted to make the point. And a lot of others. But was this the time?

"But you're already maintaining a house. Kate, my lovely Kate, I was wondering —" He took her hand, and smiled into her eyes. "Hell and damnation!"

160

The phone was ringing. And his pager joined it in an infuriating duet. All it needed was for his mobile to ring, too.

Kate took the phone. It was for him.

He raised comic eyebrows and covered the mouthpiece. "So much for the romantic evening."

Was that what he'd been thinking about so deeply? She'd assumed it was work. She waited for him, hoping that the food she'd so anxiously prepared wouldn't congeal on the plate.

He was very brisk, cutting the call with little of his usual politeness. He smiled and picked up his knife and fork. "Goodness knows when I shall eat anything as good as this again, so I'm not hurrying. That call — they've come up with what looks like an interesting job and it was about that. I'm not sure whether it'll involve an MIT at this stage but —"

"So why contact you?"

"Because I asked them to. Sorry. Guilty as charged. Kate, this must sound completely mad. Pat the Path wants me to have a look at a stiff."

It must be serious if Pat was still working at nine at night.

"Pat's a mate of yours, isn't he? Do you want to come too? Not much of a date, but . . ." His eyes said lots of things his mouth didn't.

She hoped hers did. "I'll get my coat."

"No. The stiff won't be going anywhere fast so let's finish this first. Far too good to waste. Thank goodness the wine's got enough character to survive recorking."

I've got the weirdest theory about something," he said, starting the car. "But what I'd really like you to do is bring me up to date on that poor little prostitute you acquired the other day. Didn't you say she'd come up to the market in a lorry? What's the latest in her saga?"

Kate threw her hands in the air. "Saga, indeed! For a start, it took me an hour, literally, to get from Scala House to Ladywood nick —"

"Ladywood? But Pornography and Paedophilia, or whatever they call themselves these days, are based in Digbeth."

She explained about her fears for their safety. "I know it sounds silly but —"

"It doesn't sound silly to me at all. Not if you're up against an international gang of people-traffickers."

"Better traffickers than traffic — at least this morning's. All that time absolutely wasted sitting in a car."

"And all you can think of is the heaving in-tray. Poor you. But I think I may know what caused the jam. That's why I want to talk to Pat Duncan."

"It must be urgent if he's working on it at this time of night."

"Oh, bless him, he's rushed it through as a favour. He's off skiing this weekend and doesn't want a backlog." His voice changed. "I suppose your grotty knee doesn't ski?"

"I've never asked it."

"It might prefer swimming? In a warm blue ocean?" He took advantage of a red light to squeeze her hand.

162

"I could ask it." To think she'd been feeling tired and miserable earlier!

"I thought Christmas somewhere wonderful — two lots of annual leave permitting."

And her heart sank again. "As long as Aunt Cassie's alive, Christmas is a Birmingham event," she said flatly.

"Of course it is. I'd forgotten. Hell — that gravel-spreader's going to spray my nice new bonnet. Let's just pull over until he's gone. We could play courting couples." Stopping illegally in a bus lay-by he kissed her roundly. "What about New Year? Or do you always have to spend that with Cassie, too?"

"No. I always offer, of course, but she's never once let me. She used to worry about messing up my social life. I'm not so sure she's quite so aware of my social life, these days."

"Oh, I wouldn't write her off — she still seems to have a full quota of buttons to me. Usually," he conceded, pulling back on to the main road. "I admit her conversation's not what it was, but that's because she's getting institutionalised. And also because she's more preoccupied with topics most people don't air quite so freely."

"Like bladders, bowels and haemorrhoids," she observed drily.

"Quite. I promised to get stuff off the Internet on all three. I must get round to it."

When had he promised that? Ah, possibly when she was having that skirmish with Graham — another problem to resolve.

The Broad Street traffic was as slow as in the rush-hour, complicated by clubbing pedestrians swarming all over the road.

"What was that you said about this morning's hold-ups?" she asked.

"Ah. A lorry hit the central reservation at speed and jack-knifed, if you recall. It caught fire before the driver could be rescued."

"Witnesses? Quite a major accident, after all."

"Plenty to see what happened but not why, of course. Except for one observant HGV driver who came forward to say that he was sure he saw the passenger running away from the scene. And an equally observant fire-fighter thought the driver looked unnaturally passive — indeed, dead — as they tried to release him. And one of his colleagues detected petrochemical fumes inside the cab."

"Not just from the vehicle itself? Are you talking murder and arson? That this passenger did something to cause the driver to crash?"

"Let's see what Pat the Path has to say."

Kate and Pat the Path, who was known to the rest of the world as Patrick Duncan, had now been friends long enough to have forgotten the little hiccup of a not very romantic interlude in their past. Kate had never mentioned it to anyone, and she was fairly sure Pat wouldn't have, unless he cared to tell stories against himself. Extremely embarrassing stories, too, involving sex and motorcycle leathers.

He usually greeted officers attending post-mortems as if they were honoured houseguests. This time, however, since, as he told them, he'd already given a detailed explanation to the officers currently in charge of the case and he had a new CD of Bach trio sonatas calling him, he was more eager to get to the point than usual.

"But I wasn't expecting to have the pleasure of your company, too, Kate."

"She's working on what I think may turn out to be another aspect of this case."

Kate didn't so much as blink, but still had no idea what the hell he meant.

Pat raised an amused eyebrow. "So there's nothing in the rumours about you two?"

"I didn't say that."

"Are congratulations in order?"

"I didn't say that either. But we're here on duty now."

Whatever Pat meant to say, he merely led the way into his lab and turned to the current occupant of his table. "Which concerns this gentleman."

"Quite."

She was used to the sights and smells of the dead, but had never dealt well with victims of fire. She mustn't gag. She must try to think round the smell and sight of a charred human being, spread out like a three-D jigsaw. Not neatly, this time. The corpse was grotesquely drawn up, the flesh burnt away unevenly. No. Mustn't think about the smell.

Rod made fewer bones about his revulsion, covering his lower face with a clean, neatly-folded handkerchief. After a moment, he passed it to her, producing a less pristine specimen for himself.

"Here. This is the interesting part," Pat announced, gesturing with a scalpel.

"In layman's words, remember, Pat," Rod said. "Kate may still remember her anatomical terms, but I don't."

Pat shook his head. "But the classical languages are so beautiful. OK, mate," he continued, in a false-Brummie accent, "someone slit the poor bleeder's throat, then doused him in petrol and set fire to him. That clear enough for you?"

"I can see the throat wound. And presumably the pattern of burns . . .?" He paused, delicately.

"Most people, if alive, would have made some vain effort to protect the face. So the back of the hands would have been burned more badly than the front. That is not the case with this man."

"Tell me everything you know about him."

"Are we still in a jargon-free zone? Male. About five foot eight. Afro-Caribbean. Late thirties. Good teeth — little dental work needed or carried out. One of the fluoride generation. And slaughtered before roasted. Poor bastard. Or lucky bastard. Seen enough?"

"Enough to make me grateful for having our meal before, not after, this."

"How's your cooking, these days, Kate?" Pat asked, with a slight barb. He himself produced tiny cakes, so

166

immaculate in conception and production that they might even have put Women's Institute prizewinners' to shame.

The evening's culinary triumph under her belt, she managed a cheerful smile. "I could still write a *Which?* guide to local takeaways."

"I'm proud to share my kitchen with her," Rod insisted. "And when you come back from your session on the piste you must come and eat with us."

"It'll be a pleasure."

An attendant knocked on the lab door.

"Ah. We have to vacate our table. The natives are getting restless. Riots in the waiting room. You must excuse me."

Despite Kate's suggestion that she could take a taxi so that he could go straight into work, Rod insisted on running her home. Which home?

"After all," he said, unlocking the car and holding the passenger door for her, "we may not be seeing too much of each other for the next few weeks. We'll both be working flat out, if I'm any judge of things. I want to take advantage of every minute in private." He kissed her.

"In private?" she repeated, as he took his place beside her.

"I think we may be coming across each other at work rather more than usual."

"Hang on. I thought you were saying that for Pat's benefit — to explain my presence."

"In a sense I was. But all sorts of things are circling round my brain at the moment, some so vague I don't want to say them aloud in case they flit away."

"Let me say them, then. You have a murdered HGV driver; I have a missing policeman and a loquacious kid. How can either of my problems tie up with yours? Possibly?"

"I don't know yet. But if there is a connection, I shall find it."

"What sort of connection? She certainly didn't kill your chummy and bolt."

"But she was brought here by someone and escaped from someone."

She tapped lightly on his head. "Come on, Rod, unless your intuition's working overtime —"

"All the best cops have hyperactive intuition. And, as I said, I've no idea what the connection might be."

"Whatever it is, keep your sticky mitts — and your sticky MITs — off my nick. And leave me to find out the rest of Natasha's story."

"Would she talk to anyone else?"

"Not if I asked her not to."

"I didn't hear that."

"No. And you didn't hear me say that with my staffing levels I might almost welcome an incursion of fresh troops. Especially if you ended up leading the charge."

"Things must be serious, then."

They drove in silence. Home. His house, not hers.

Although she had her key ready, he got out with her. "Don't wait up. Promise? We're both going to need our shut-eye when things get moving."

"So long as you promise to let me warm your hands and feet." She reached up to kiss him. And was left in no doubt of his answer.

However much Kate tried to cut it, she made no sense of Rod and his intuition. At last she gave up trying and headed for bed. After all, whatever time Rod got home this morning, she'd better be at work for six thirty. If there were any connections, which she doubted, she intended, however much she loved Rod, to have done her best to wrap everything up by the time an MIT was brought in.

If only she knew what she was wrapping.

CHAPTER
FOURTEEN

"When I say I want you here at six in the evening, I don't mean eight the following morning," Chief Superintendent Oxnard thundered.

"Sir." He hadn't told Kate to sit down, so she was standing at rigid attention. He was, after all, the commander of her operational unit.

"You come here the other day getting your knickers in a twist when there's no reason. When there is, you don't bloody turn up. What's wrong with you, Power?"

Still trying to catch her breath — the city centre was already snarled up and, not wishing to be late, she'd simply thrown her car into the first convenient meter space and legged it as fast as she could — she began, "Sir, when did you —"

"I'm asking the questions, in case you hadn't noticed. I suppose you were lying with your legs apart for that miserable-looking DCI down the corridor? Well, I've got news for you, Power. At this level it isn't who you shag but how well you do your job that matters." He got up and came round his desk to jab at her chest.

She must control her breathing — couldn't risk him making cracks about heaving bosoms. "I came as soon as I heard, sir. Unfortunately we don't have any clerical support at the moment, and messages aren't getting —"

"It wasn't a sodding message, Power, it was a fucking order." His spittle sprayed her face. "You sit on your fanny doing fuck all while we've got some snotty-nosed village bobby in Little Piddle under Muck on the phone telling us how to do our job." He stomped towards the window.

Well, it was one way to describe the chief constable of the West Mercia Constabulary, and who was she to object? Or venture to correct him? On the other hand, people said he preferred his officers to show a bit of spirit, so she'd stop offering explanations or excuses. "With respect, sir, they didn't teach ESP at Bramshill, or I'd have been here before you phoned."

"ESP?" He wheeled round.

"Extra-sensory perception, otherwise known as mind-reading, sir." She took advantage of his momentary recoil to add, more hotly than she'd have preferred, "And I got this promotion because I was on the accelerated-promotion scheme, and working bloody hard." Denying that she'd had sex with Graham was pointless and, in any case, a diversion from what she wanted to say. And the less said about her current relationship the better. "I'm still working bloody hard. I'm starting each morning at six thirty and finishing well after seven in the evening, then working when I get home. And we haven't even got a panic on. Yet," she added, with an ironic smile. "Or is there one now?"

"What have you done about locating Bates? Oh, sit down, woman. Making the place look untidy."

She obeyed. "I've checked with family and friends, none of whom reports seeing him. I've checked his personnel records — as you said the other day, sir, he's never been the most reliable of officers. I was about to ask the Occupational Health people to talk to him."

"You haven't already?"

"No, sir. I wanted to make sure," she said carefully, "that I wasn't just being a hysterical female and 'getting my knickers in a twist' about something no one else saw anything wrong with." Like the superintendent himself, for instance. "Being new in post I — I —"

"If you're trying to protect your predecessor, don't bother. He was a fine officer and more than earned his promotion. And, as a matter of fact, he had contacted Occupational Health."

So Twiss had shared her anxieties. And Oxnard had been sufficiently interested in what she'd said the other day to check.

"It's just that they'd done nothing about his request because they reckon they don't have enough staff." *Surprise, surprise.* "So he was flaky, no doubt about it. But he's also missing. So what are you doing about that?"

"I've already set routine inquiries in train. No response yet. We've already talked to the security guard on the night shift. He's less than forthcoming — we wonder if someone's put the frighteners on him. But he may be plain pissed: that's his usual state. As a precaution, I've told my teams always to patrol in pairs

172

the area where Bates was last seen. I've got a Cantonese-speaking officer interviewing one of the big cheeses in the Chinese community this afternoon. The trouble is, sir, much as I'd like to have preserved the scene, without Bates being officially listed as missing, I don't see how I could have caused what would inevitably be a huge disruption in a very busy area."

Oxnard peered through a gap in his Venetian blinds. The brilliant sun lit his face as if in a *noir* movie. "Like the disruption that RTA at Spaghetti Junction yesterday's still causing. The heat from the lorry fire burnt away half the road surface. Know anything about that, Power?"

Quite a lot, as it happened. But that was between her, Pat and Rod at the moment. "Not on my patch, sir," she said neutrally.

"But the truck was coming from your patch, I should think. He'd been delivering tomatoes or some such. It'd be nice if you could find a bit out before some MIT comes sniffing round. Get on to it, will you, Power?"

"Right away." She looked at him with wide-eyed innocence. "Extra resources, sir?"

He gave a snort of laughter. "You off your head?"

She gave a concise account of her staffing position. "And to make matters even worse, I'm having to keep tabs on an East European child prostitute. In fact, I shall be seeing her in this building in about five minutes."

"Here? Steelhouse Lane? What's wrong with Digbeth? That's where she should be. With the unit there. Why you should be anywhere except at your desk is beyond me. Haven't you got enough work to do?"

Since she couldn't give herself an honest answer to the last of his questions, she replied to the others: "Different venues and different routes each morning, sir. You see, I think we may be talking to a victim of a major people-trafficking ring. According to NCIS —"

"Talked to them already, then?" It sounded like praise.

"Sir. The people most likely to be involved have an international reputation for nastiness. I don't want to expose Natasha or the officer involved in debriefing her — do you know Meg Walker, sir? — exposed to any danger. Or the civilian interpreter for that matter. Wouldn't look good in the media, sir. Which reminds me, have they got wind of Phil Bates's disappearance yet?"

"As soon as he becomes a missing person they'll know." He returned to his desk and collapsed into his chair. "And the press office will make the statement and you will say absolutely nothing, Power — get that? Whatever you think of the official version."

"You'll make sure they bear in mind the family's on the warpath, sir?"

He nodded, allowing a grim smile to flit briefly across his military features. "I shall indeed, Power." His snort wasn't hostile. "They told me you'd tell the chief how to wipe his arse, given half a chance: I reckon they were right."

★ ★ ★

174

Kate made it down to Reception just in time to greet the interpreter, wrapped this time against the weather with much greater style. She'd flung about her the sort of fur stole that would have been at home on a fifties movie star but was these days little short of animal-rights bait. For the first time she realised how glamorous Madame Constantinou must have been. Those cheekbones, that jaw must have been spectacular before jowls sagged and fronds of neck wrinkles arrived. Her legs, with barely a vein showing, were still excellent for a woman in her sixties, ending in neat feet encased in frivolous high-heeled ankle boots with fur cuffs that Kate rather coveted. It would have been good to talk to her about her past and how she came to be here. And to ask what had made her change her image so sharply. But now was not the moment. Meg Walker and Natasha were bustling in, and it was time to embark on the saga once again.

This time, however, Kate had her own agenda. "I want to skip part of your story," she told Natasha. "I'm happy for you to tell it the way you want afterwards, but in the meantime I need some information about your journey here to Birmingham."

Madame Constantinou raised rather over-plucked eyebrows heavenwards, rolling her eyes in amusement. Meg minutely shook her head. So Natasha's reaction to the request didn't altogether come a surprise. Her eyes and teeth and hands and stamped feet and raised voice came together into a magnificent tantrum. After she had ranged round the interview room like a caged animal in pain, she quietened down enough to deliver a few words in a thrilling hoarse whisper.

"Don't tell me, she wants me to go fuck myself," Kate suggested, as Madame Constantinou struggled to frame a translation.

The response was a chilly smile. "You have the gist, Inspector. She says it is her story and she will tell it her way or not at all."

As if in confirmation Natasha, tossing her loosened mane, stomped off to a corner, turning a speaking back on her audience.

"Natasha, I really need to know what happened to you in Birmingham."

She responded with another torrent. Kate thought she might have picked out the word "whore" — though to whom it applied wasn't immediately apparent. Then Natasha returned to the table, in a huge dramatic torrent of tears.

Kate left the room, motioning Meg to follow. They leant, as if exhausted already, against the corridor wall. "Come on, you're the mother of teenage girls. You must know how to handle them better than this."

"I'm afraid mine need wheedling, and often straight bribes. I'll go and have another bash, shall I?"

Loath to hang around in the corridor like a naughty schoolgirl waiting to be admitted to the head's study, Kate headed for the ladies' loo. And found the mirror occupied by her old boss, DI Sue Rowley, peering anxiously at a spot.

"I'm practically begging the doctor for HRT and there I go sprouting teenage zits," she said, as if she and Kate had last seen each other two minutes ago. "Who'd be a woman? Hey, Kate, girl, you look very fine in your formal feathers!" Grinning, she hugged her. "I'll swear you've grown an inch."

"On the contrary, I've just been cut down to size. I've got this teenage tom having a mega-tantrum in Romanian, and I can't deal with her."

"What's upset her?" Sue turned back to the mirror, dabbing extra foundation on the pimple.

Kate explained. "Perhaps the Romanians have arcane rules governing their story-telling and I offended her by asking her to break them."

"Or perhaps she's a stupid drama queen needing a good slap. Which, alas, you're not allowed to give her. Oh, just tell her straight that if she doesn't pull her finger out, you'll have her sent back as an illegal immigrant. She may not have much English but I'll bet my pension she'll know those words. Time for a cuppa before you go back to Scala House? Graham's at the dentist's."

Natasha had responded to the treatment Sue Rowley had suggested with a magnificent sulk but a modicum of co-operation.

"Some time in London you decided you had to escape from — well, whatever you had to escape from?" Kate suggested.

Natasha shrugged. That would emerge only when she was good and ready.

"But you didn't have any money for a train or a coach. What did you decide to do? Did you hitch

177

a lift?" She curled her thumb. "No? OK. Now, you've already told us that you came in the cab of a container lorry. Had you ever met the driver before?"

"No! Never. And I wouldn't know him again, before you ask!" Madame Constantinou translated deadpan.

"'Methinks the lady doth protest too much.' So what did he look like, this kind lorry driver?"

Natasha shrugged. So did Kate, getting ostentatiously to her feet.

"Was he old or young? A fatbelly?"

No, he wasn't a fatbelly, emphatically not. With the hint of irony now becoming familiar, Madame Constantinou suggested that he was neither as young as Kate nor as old as herself.

"About Meg's age, then? About forty?"

Natasha shrugged again, most elaborately. Kate seethed.

"As young as Vladi?"

No response. If she hadn't already had a breather, Kate would have called one. The other women needed a break too. Catching their eyes, she led the way out. But she shook her head when Natasha followed, gesturing her back into the room with the flat of her hand.

"And we, ladies, will have coffee and biscuits, and she, poor dear, will have none." Kate turned in the direction of the canteen.

Meg demurred. "I think it's that she really doesn't want to tell you anything about this man. Not that she's just being awkward."

"You mean she might be trying to protect him?"

178

Madame Constantinou nodded. "She is a very bright child, although her education and upbringing have been deplorable. Recollect those pictures she drew. She has a very good visual memory."

"Should we ask her to draw this man?" Meg asked doubtfully.

Kate shook her head. "That won't do any good if she's protecting him. I wonder why —"

"If he is in danger she will be loyal," Madame Constantinou declared.

"He'd only be in danger if Vladi and Co. knew him and his part in her escape," Meg said slowly.

"You think she wasn't escaping from London, but simply being taken elsewhere? On Vladi's instructions?" Kate asked.

Meg pulled a face. "Could be. But why take her by lorry? Not car or train?"

Madame Constantinou declared, "The sooner we hear the whole story, the sooner such details will emerge."

Kate nodded. Somehow she couldn't dismiss it as a detail. It seemed a vital part of the story. But there was no point in offending someone she depended on utterly. She bit her lip. "This may sound silly . . . Look, what if she thought her saviour was in here? Already in our protection, or under arrest or whatever."

"How could she possibly think that? We could *tell* her — but she's fly enough to know we're lying."

"Quite. But if she *saw* someone like him."

"And how do we know what he looks like?"

"We don't. But — and I have to protect my source here, sorry — I have a clue as to what he might look like. More specifically, and absolutely between ourselves, might have looked like."

"You mean he's dead?"

"Let's just say, Meg, that we have a corpse. A lorry driver's corpse."

"Oh, the poor child! Someone who was kind to her!" Madame Constantinou wailed.

Kate bit her lip. Where had her feelings gone? The way of all police feelings, if they got in the way of an investigation. And Natasha herself was holding things up, quite deliberately. So, was it worth the gamble? Was it unethical? "Look, why don't you two take her down to the canteen for however much food she wants? I'll see if I can put my plan B into operation."

"You're not going to upset her?"

"I want to shock her into saying something — anything, Meg. It's not just Natasha — don't you think Vladi and his mates are treating countless other kids just as they treated her? And the longer she pisses us about the more kids they can abduct and rape." Perhaps she was convinced herself. She headed up to Sue Rowley's office before she could change her mind.

"Black officer? Male, female?" Sue looked puzzled but unfazed. "What do you want to borrow one for, anyway?"

"I want a male, aged just short of forty, about five nine. Plain clothes. And all I want him to do is stand and talk to me in the canteen. With his back to someone."

"This sounds a bit dodgy to me, Kate, and that's a fact. Better tell your Auntie Sue what you're up to."

Kate explained.

Hand on phone, Sue recapped. "You want this guy simply to talk to you, not to pretend to be anyone, not to entrap anyone. Just to jog a teenage girl's memory. So if the chief gets to hear of this he'll simply pat you on the head and congratulate you on using your initiative."

"Hole in one."

Eyebrows raised heavenwards, Sue dialled.

"Didn't you play football or something?" Marcus Ford was asking.

"Play! No, when I came to Brum I got inveigled into coaching a boys' team. I sometimes have a hankering to go to a match, but I rarely give in." Out of the tail of her eye she could see Natasha, shoulder hunched from the others, digging into some of West Midlands Police's less healthy options — cake, a couple of doughnuts and a glass of milk. She was gazing into space, eyes unfocused. She didn't look especially unhappy, though Kate couldn't have blamed her. She simply had the patient, enduring look of a badly beaten donkey. The poor kid needed a hug and a lot of love and all she was going to get was a nasty shock. *What the hell are you doing, playing God like this?*

She drifted Ford in the direction of the servery. "Do you play?"

"Had a trial for West Brom once."

"Premier League! Keep looking towards the food, Marcus, if you wouldn't mind."

"They weren't then. Are you sure this is OK, Inspector Power?"

"In this situation, I'm Kate. It's a short-cut. The girl's got what I think's invaluable information, and I have to make her cough. Oh, she will sooner or later, but I don't have that sort of time. Brace yourself. I'm just going to wave." She did. Natasha registered nothing. "So, what are you working on now?"

"Depends — what's the latest bee in the Home Secretary's bonnet? Well, I'm working on that!"

They'd reached the counter. "What can I get you? I'm going to wave again."

"A bowl of that soup. Then I can work through — Jesus!"

There was a piercing yell — not a scream. "Joe!"

"Better turn round. The poor kid's got to realise sooner or later."

Natasha dashed at Kate, fingernails at the ready. "Not Joe! Not Joe!" she screamed. And then she simply subsided into Kate's arms.

Marcus patted her ineffectually on the shoulder and stood with a bowl of soup in one hand. "You can tell you're a bloody inspector," he grumbled, "leaving me to pay when it was your shout."

Kate hardened her heart again. "This Joe you thought I was talking to, Natasha, who is he?"

No answer.

"And why should you think I might be talking to him?"

No answer.

"Let me tell you what I think. I think Joe was the kind man who drove you to Birmingham. I'd really like to know why he drove you here."

Natasha tossed her head, but less convincingly than usual.

"What happened, Natasha? I really need to know. Because I think that if Joe was kind to you, he might have put himself in danger. Don't you?"

CHAPTER
FIFTEEN

Madame Constantinou translated deadpan.

Natasha gave a repeat performance of her hunched shoulders and sulky silence.

"If it hadn't been for Joe, you'd be stripping in a seedy club, wouldn't you?" Kate insisted, standing. Why not show anger in her body language as well as her voice? She had to know whether Joe had been a lorry driver genuinely responding to a thumb, or if he'd been supposed to take her somewhere, as part of Vladi's gang. If only she could trust Natasha — she had to admit that there was no real reason why she didn't, but she wondered whether the girl might have been telling them what she thought they wanted to hear. Or, if she'd liked Joe so much, that she might have been deliberately misleading them. "Or you'd be having sex with fatbellies again? And now — because he helped you — Joe may be in danger." Then, more in sorrow than in anger, she continued, "Is this the way to help him? You know what Vladi's friends can do when they put their mind to it. Think of Joe being beaten up by a gang of thugs. Apart from anything else," she added drily, when all the pleas failed, "they may make him tell them where you are. If we could protect him, that wouldn't happen."

The policewomen watched the play of emotions as Madame Constantinou translated. At last it seemed that self-interest won the day. Natasha muttered.

"She will tell you after lunch," Madame Constantinou announced, with a sardonic curl of the lip. "Meanwhile, she is so very, very hungry."

"These bloody delaying tactics," Meg Walker muttered.

"Quite. Meg, stay here with her." Kate patted her mobile. "I've got to take some phone calls — I'm supposed to be running a nick, for God's sake — and then we'll have sandwiches in here. Madame Constantinou, tell her she can have a proper meal when we've finished. And not before."

Out in the corridor she learnt that the Scala House world was turning satisfactorily without her, according to Helen Kerr, who didn't seem to have the same reservations about eating on reception duty as Kate had had.

"Now, the good news is that Mrs Speed'll be with us tomorrow, her says. And I had a message for you to ring this sergeant out in Kingstanding or somewhere. Funny sort of name."

"Guljar? And Kings Heath, not Kingstanding?"

"Could be. Me pencil broke while I was doing me shorthand, see, gaffer."

"Any other news? About Phil Bates?"

"Nah. Come on, gaffer, everyone knows he's done a runner, doh they?"

"Remind everyone I want detailed reports on paper or e-mail for when I get back," Kate responded, voice crisp with Natasha-induced anger. "And get Dave Bush to call me as soon as he's finished with Mr Choi. The instant. OK? Though with luck I should be back by then . . ."

Guljar responded second ring. "Yes, I've just picked up this rumour about Phil Bates," he said. "They say he might have won something on the lotto on Saturday."

"Do they indeed? A lot? And who are they?"

"His drinking pals. A couple of lads from this station and a few low-lifes. Boozers, all of them."

"So it'd be worth checking his house to see if he's taken a passport."

"You haven't already?"

"He's not officially a missing person, is he? And everyone told me not to prioritise this, didn't they?"

"I know, I know."

"You weren't the only one, don't worry."

"Sorry, Kate. But I'm thinking —"

"That the OC'll want my head on a plate if I don't get on to it this afternoon."

"Spot on."

"Shit. Would you mind having another word with your lads about this win? Only I don't have a moment."

"Ah. Doesn't time fly when you're enjoying yourself?"

"Natasha, I have precisely five minutes — get that?" She held a hand in the air, fingers spread. "Five minutes before I leave the building. I want to know about Joe now. No messing. Now. Understand?"

Natasha cowered. *Jesus! You're supposed to be caring for this kid, and after all that melodrama in the canteen you're resorting to straight bullying! But it's working . . .*

Joe was a lorry driver, surprise, surprise, who'd been one of the clients at Vladi's club. He'd been a nice, kind man, and she'd asked him to help her. Because she'd asked nicely, which Kate assumed was a euphemism for offering sex, he'd promised to take her to his mum's in Manchester. But Natasha had had enough of men and their promises, so she decided to escape while he was delivering boxes to the market.

"Any idea what was in the boxes?"

A shake of the head. Natasha couldn't have cared less, then or now.

Yes, he had to drive here regularly, Birmingham and this other place. Sometimes he did several places in one day, Joe had said. He was a nice man — so far as men went, one gathered. With slight distaste, Madame Constantinou informed them that, without being asked, he produced a contraceptive. The sex was quite ordinary, nothing kinky, but Natasha had found it hard to . . . Madame Constantinou faltered. Natasha indicated quite clearly giving him a blow-job while he was driving very fast on the motorway and jerking him off at a service station. No, just a technical problem with the blow-job. She hadn't minded. A man liked sex, what was new? But she'd had the chance to slip out of the cab and had hidden and then had run and run and then she'd found Kate, she concluded with a beatific smile.

Despite her irritation, Kate smiled back. To Meg Walker, she said, "I want every scrap of information about this guy. E-mail, OK? By four?" Then she said to them all, "You've worked very hard. Thank you. Have some lunch and come back here. Remember to be very, very careful. We'll meet at Digbeth at nine tomorrow." A thought struck her and she beckoned Meg out of the room. "Natasha's clothes. I take it they were bagged as possible evidence? All that semen flying around: there's just the chance of the Lewinsky syndrome. It'd be nice if we could find some and match any DNA with —"

"The DNA of this corpse of yours? OK, gaffer, I'll get on to it!"

This time she'd get Chief Superintendent Oxnard's views before she dived in, but she would have placed bets on what he'd say.

"Get in there, Kate. What are you waiting for?"

"Do you think we should invite CID to the party?"

"Your old crowd or an MIT?"

"Your shout, gaffer. We'd rather have neither, of course."

"But you're short-staffed and wah, wah, wah . . ." Laughing sardonically, he mimed a record going round. Then he said, dead serious, "Look, just get on and do it, Kate. Take someone — one of your sergeants, if possible — you can trust not to blab. And get on the blower the minute you find anything. Or nothing. Oh, and make sure you get the place locked up right and tight afterwards. We don't want some scrote noticing a broken window and helping himself."

Alan White, the man who'd helped Mrs Speed, was the sergeant on duty. He scratched his head doubtfully. "If it's an order, gaffer, well, I shall have to, shan't I?"

"Who else can I ask?" she demanded.

"OK. Let's hit the road, then." He looked at her sideways. "At least you lead from the front, gaffer."

"Where else is there to lead from?"

He laughed. "That's what the old gaffer used to say."

She let him drive to the road in Erdington she'd been to before. She turned her back as Alan produced a highly illegal set of skeleton keys, bequeathed him by a real pro, he'd said, almost proudly. It beat breaking windows any day, she agreed.

They donned gloves and began their search.

Nothing. The central heating had kept the house warm, but it had also kept it stuffy. With a sense of *déjà vu*, Kate collected the post, dropping it on to the kitchen table, while Alan half-heartedly, it seemed to Kate, turned over the contents of a surprisingly tidy bureau in his search for a passport. Kate stayed in the kitchen. Phil had washed up and stacked the dishes and pans — a bit of a cook, then — but hadn't got all the grease off them. He'd wiped the work-surface, but left a trail of crumbs.

"Gaffer?"

Kate joined him. In his hand was the passport. "So he's still in the country. But that doesn't mean still in Brum. You know what this means?"

"It means we have to check his clothes and stuff. What are you expecting to find?" he added, as he followed her upstairs.

"Not a corpse, at least — we'd have known straight away, in this heat." She turned into the back bedroom. "God, I hate doing this when you know someone's dead. When they're still alive — we hope! — it seems so —"

"Voyeuristic? What Burglar Bill sees all the time, remember, gaffer, people's rooms as they left them when they last walked out. Stuff they forgot to put away, stains they'd rather no one saw . . ."

By common consent, neither spoke much. There were no gaps in his wardrobe, no sign of the holdalls in his boxroom being disturbed. There was no doubting Alan White's relief when, with a jerk of her head, Kate motioned him back to the car.

Dave Bush looked relieved to see her running back up the office stairs. Paid overtime or TOIL was all very well, but not when it landed you in the middle of the Birmingham rush-hour on a very cold evening.

"And it's my Cantonese class, you see," he added. "I don't want to miss that. And the parking up there's dreadful."

"It's a hell of a long day for you, Alan."

"Not much longer than those you're routinely working," he countered. "And inspectors don't even get overtime."

"No more we don't. OK, come in, sit down and tell me what Choi had to say."

He sat crossing and uncrossing his legs like a middle-aged woman nervous of getting varicose veins. "Not a lot. He's seething about something, Kate, and that's the truth, but he's not letting on what."

"Don't tell me he was inscrutable!"

"Well . . . He said he'd heard further disquieting rumours, two of which had really unnerved him. He really does speak like that, Kate," he added, looking up and suddenly letting a grin transform his face.

"I've met him, remember, it's his mugs we're drinking out of. 'Unnerved' — it's an odd word, all the same."

"You know what," Dave began, leaning forward earnestly, "from the expression on his face, I'd say it was dead serious. In fact, come to think of it, he messed round with those very words. 'Why hadn't I said *deadly* serious?' That sort of thing."

"So you think we're talking about, well, literally, a death."

"I'll press him some more tomorrow. I've promised I'd lend him a book about the history of the English language — you know, by that travel-writer guy . . ." As if aware he was gabbling, he added, "Look, mind if I push off? Only I —"

"Not at all. Dave, thanks for all this. No one else could do it, you know."

"Well . . ." He flushed with embarrassment and was gone.

Kate was already reaching for the phone.

★ ★ ★

It was strange meeting Rod officially, inspector to superintendent, but that was what she was doing, openly snatching supper with him in the Lloyd House canteen. Any moment they'd be joined by Chief Superintendent Oxnard, so they had an excuse to be talking shop.

"Poor little Natasha — honestly, Rod, I know I put her through hell this morning, but really I just want to gather her up and hug her better, like Aunt Cassie used to do." She'd had more affection from the old woman during the school holidays than she'd ever had at home.

"Funny. I'd never have seen Aunt Cassie as a hugger-better. More a woman to give a quick dab with the iodine and an injunction to be more careful next time."

"She was. She might have been cavalier about outside knocks but she was very good on inside hurts. The treats I had when this or that spotty teenager broke my heart . . . But we digress."

"I like digressing with you. We'll do a bit more later tonight. Or whenever we next get a moment together. I take it you won't be hugging Natasha?"

"And risk an assault or sexual-harassment charge? But she needs a lot of hugs. Nice asexual ones. I wonder what Social Services will do for her?"

"Whatever their merits, I doubt their efforts will extend to finding her a hugger. We'll buy her a teddy bear when the case is over." Perhaps he stressed the last five words.

Kate took his point and grinned. "As Aunt Cassie says, I'm not so green as I'm cabbage-looking. Anyway, after all the tears and tantrums, she talked about Joe. Here's all Meg Walker could glean about him." She passed across the e-mail she'd printed off. "And we're hoping to find the odd spot of his semen or a few of his hairs on her clothes."

"For DNA checks? Excellent."

"Maybe not just Joe's, either."

"Quite. But what the hell made her hold out so long?"

"To get Madame Constantinou a bigger fee? To irritate the socks off Meg and me? Perhaps she wanted to protect the man she sees as her knight in shining armour. To give him time to get away."

"Away from where or whom?"

"Vladi, presumably."

"Only it doesn't seem to have worked, does it? If indeed it was Joe, Vladi and Co. seem to have worked out quite quickly that he let them down and dealt with him accordingly."

"And now he's very dead in one of Pat's giant filing cabinets." She took another bite of cheese baguette. "I'm glad I didn't have meat."

He indicated his tuna salad. "It was a very public execution."

"Whoever it was, it was pretty public. Trouble is, we can't get her to ID him."

"Not until the facial-reconstruction experts have had a go at him. Meanwhile, thank goodness for dental records — except his teeth were so good he might not have seen a dentist for some time. And in any case we need to have some handle on him before we can embark even on that."

"The lorry? They couldn't have eradicated all traces of ownership."

"No. We're on to that. A London firm. Lots of casual drivers. Ordinary day-to-day police work for someone finding which of the many."

"You've started already. You and an MIT." They were statements — not even accusations.

"It was either that or your friendly local CID, headed up by Graham Harvey. I made a pre-emptive strike. I know I should have discussed it with you first, but you were so lacklustre at the thought of meeting him for lunch —"

"That I certainly wouldn't relish the prospect of regular meetings." She met his eye. "He always tried to put me down, Rod. Always finding fault."

"If he were lying on a couch in my office I'd say he was in denial, sweetheart. A state not unknown to me. Have I ever apologised for treating you so appallingly when your house had been attacked and you'd had acid thrown at you?"

"You've certainly shown —"

"I don't think that's enough. I am sorry. So very sorry." He laid his hand on hers. "What my heart wanted to do was sweep you off your feet and take you home and cherish the pants off you. So my head told me to freeze you out of my life. I always have been nuts about you, you know."

Despite herself, she blushed deeply. And then grinned. "And mc about you."

194

"This isn't the most romantic of settings, Kate, but — sir!"

As one they got to their feet. Oxnard was towering over them . . .

"Oh, finish your food. You can brief me as we eat." He plonked his tray alongside Kate's and sat down. As he unwrapped his cutlery and gave it a polish, he added, "As of about two minutes after your phone call, Kate — good, quick work, by the way — PC Philip Bates is a missing person. Now, you talked about cordoning off part of the wholesale market as a possible crime scene: which bit?"

The only part she'd never seen, of course. Without so much as a blink, she said, "The rubbish crusher, sir. Though I've a terrible feeling it'll be too late."

"Too late?" He held the forkful of chicken casserole two inches from his mouth. "And why have you let it get too late?"

She felt Rod stiffen: no, he mustn't defend her. "Because the market generates so much waste I should imagine the end products of the crusher are disposed of every day."

"Disposed of?" At last he'd started to eat.

"In the big incinerator, sir, I should think. You know, down in Tyseley."

"Find out. Hang on, you're not on this case, are you? Not any more."

"No?"

"You've got a bloody nick to run, woman, in an area of — what do they call it? — racial sensitivity. And this is a job for CID, if ever I knew one. Who's the duty

CID chief inspector tonight? Harvey, is it? You'd better get on to him, sharpish."

Smooth as silk, Rod said, "With due respect, sir, this case seems to me to have some strong ties with another case I've already allocated to an MIT. Could I ask that team to take it on? With officers from Scala House to supplement the team if necessary?"

The Lord giveth, the Lord taketh away, eh? But help came from an unexpected quarter.

"You're not taking anyone from there, Neville. They're so undermanned they can't cover everyday essentials," Oxnard declared.

Undermanned? What had happened to a nice gender-free term like understaffed? Still, there were moments to protest and moments to keep the mouth firmly shut.

"Tell me about this new case of yours, Neville, will you, while I eat?" Oxnard applied himself to his chicken with vigour.

"I've got what looks to me like a punishment or vendetta killing — the one on Spaghetti Junction, sir."

"That caused all the chaos the other morning? The one I told you to have a look at, Power, since the lorry might have been coming from the market."

Kate nodded. How had he known that? Just because he was a fingers-in-every-pie man? "Sorry, sir, I didn't have time to check anything out. As you suggested, we got on to the Bates case as priority. And I seem to have another lead to the lorry, but via a different route."

"Well?" Oxnard ate slowly, methodically.

196

"I believe I've told you about the teenage girl who asked me for help."

"The one you're sending hither and thither for questioning. OK."

"She tells me that she was brought up to Birmingham by a kindly lorry driver who'd promised to take her to his mother's in Manchester."

"Manchester? That was a regular part of our man's schedule," Rod put in. "According to the company logs."

"How would you know?" Oxnard demanded, pausing for a sip of water, which left the top of his glass rimmed with grease.

"Part of this investigation into the lorry fire. We don't know for sure that this driver was the one who was kind to Natasha —"

"There's a hell of a time lag. Friday to Wednesday," Oxnard objected.

"Quite. But we're hoping to run DNA tests on items of Natasha's clothing to see if we can make a connection. Hair, semen, that sort of thing."

"Couldn't she ID him?"

"Believe me, sir, no one could ID him."

"That bad?"

"Worse."

To Kate's amazement Oxnard pushed away his plate uncleared. "One of my nightmares, burning to death," he said, gruffly.

"He didn't burn to death, sir. His throat was cut first. In broad daylight. On the A38(M). By his passenger, whom a witness saw running away. That's why the lorry went out of control. Because the driver was either struggling with his assailant or was already dying."

"And one of our officers working in the market has disappeared?" Oxnard looked at them both, holding the gaze of each, suddenly more a stern father than a senior officer. "You want to remember what that man at NCIS told you, Kate. We're dealing with ruthless people here, whoever they are. I want maximum care. All my officers. At all times. And that includes," he added, with a sudden benevolent smile that knocked Kate backwards, "you two."

CHAPTER
SIXTEEN

Kate flung open the door to one of Scala House's less attractive rooms. "Apparently they intended to convert this into a canteen and gym. Then someone realised how few people would actually be based here so the idea was abandoned. But I'd have thought that it was big enough for your MIT presence." The main body would be back at Steelhouse Lane but it made sense to have a token group there as long as any of Bates's colleagues had to be questioned. "What do you think?"

"An estate agent would say it had potential," DCI Greg Smith said, gloom oozing from every pore. He was head of the MIT working on the case. He stepped forward, his bald patch gleaming through his baby-blond, baby-fine hair and squinted into the light.

Rod stepped in too. "A good clean, a few desks and phone lines, and it'll be home from home. Your people OK with the invasion, Kate?"

"They'll have to be, won't they?" she retorted drily.

"Don't see why there should be a problem," Smith muttered.

"Come on, Greg, you know we'd rather have done this on our own."

"All right by me. Go ahead."

Kate avoided Rod's eye. "We just don't have the bodies. I can't guarantee a full set of duty teams, let alone detail a set of folk to clear up something as important as this."

"And to follow up a lot of other ends, which may or may not tie up," Rod added.

Smith ran a fingertip down a wall, and showed the others the result. "I shall need at least one sergeant with some local knowledge. I know Oxnard's worried about your staffing, but we can't manage without."

"Sergeant Dave Bush, if he's happy with the idea," Kate said. "He's the field intelligence officer here. Speaks Cantonese, so gets on very well with the local community at all levels."

Smith jotted. "Anyone else?"

Kate gritted her teeth. "There's a bright lad called Zayn Ara, but I don't know if it's still Ramadan."

"He's fasting, is he? You can't expect anyone to work the sort of hours I shall demand if they can't eat and drink all day."

Rod said, "I believe even the most devout Muslims can get exemption in special cases."

"In that case I'd like to ask him," Kate said, "rather than make a decision behind his back. And I'll have a couple of fall-back names by nine tomorrow."

"Eight. I'll get the ball rolling here, sir. It's all a matter of routine, these days, isn't it? Ah, what about parking?"

Kate thought of the tiny space her colleagues had virtually to fight for. "You'll have to commandeer some

200

public parking. And you'll notice we don't have drinks facilities. You might want to organise a machine."

"Haven't you got a kettle?"

"If you want to keep us sweet here, you won't touch that kettle. It's OK for seven of us at a time, not for your ravening hordes. You'd better order more loo paper, too."

By now it was so late she might as well stay an extra ten minutes to brief the night shift. Rod set off home to make, he said, their cocoa. She still wasn't sure about such openness — but perhaps it was better to be seen as in a long-established, cosy relationship than as a career-grabbing mistress. Yes. She smiled.

"Is that you, Neil? Come on in here a minute, will you?"

"Evening, gaffer. Why are you burning the old midnight oil?" He sat heavily.

"Three guesses."

"Phil Bates."

"Phil Bates and an MIT. No, keep your hair on, Neil. We can't guarantee any of our teams will be full from one day to the next, and we just don't have enough legs to run a full-scale murder inquiry. Do we?" She looked him straight in the eye.

He sighed. "Only if we reduce the teams to below safety level. Which some of them are now."

"And will be smaller. The MIT — do you know DCI Greg Smith, who'll be leading it?"

It was clear he did. "Idle bugger, by all accounts."

So why had Rod selected that particular team? It wasn't like him to suffer idlers lightly. Perhaps — yes, either he wanted to get involved himself, which he couldn't legitimately with a good MIT, or he wanted Kate's people to have a chance. She sent him a mental kiss.

"They want two local people. I've suggested Dave Bush."

Drew nodded. "Obvious choice."

"What about Zayn Ara?"

He pulled a face. "Only a kid. There are lots more experienced folk."

"On whom we'll be relying to run the rest of things. I had thought of Ronnie Hale."

With an obvious effort, he said, "I suppose you could make her acting sergeant in Dave's place."

"On the grounds that if I don't upgrade her, she'll assume the position anyway?"

"Right. She's ready for it, too. And she's not the greatest of team players: she might not fit into the MIT. But Zayn — well, why not?"

"Quite. And as for why, the little I've seen of him suggests he'll go far — it'd be nice to give him a little push. Provided he's not trying to work MIT hours and fast at the same time. Smith's made it clear he can't risk passengers."

"You can see why. Poor old Phil. Makes you feel bad for carping about him behind his back." Neil rubbed his face. "Tell you what, Kate, I wish I hadn't told you he was only on the skive."

202

"Forget it, Neil. I won't say it's his own fault, but if he hadn't had such a bad reputation, things might have got under way a lot sooner. Now, I'll talk to Zayn first thing."

"I'll tell you something for nothing, gaffer. Jill Todd won't be happy."

"To lose Zayn? Well, we don't know he's going yet." They got to their feet. "Look after yourself, Neil — and make sure everyone else does too. As for the MIT, it'll cause disruption, but I've asked Smith to keep it to a minimum. But remind everyone to be tolerant, eh?"

"On one condition, gaffer. If I know you, you'll be back at pig-squealing time tomorrow —"

"Is that when they rise with the lark?"

"Right?"

"Oink, oink," she agreed.

"Well, push off now. OK?" He grinned with what seemed almost like affection

To think that the first time they'd encountered each other, she'd regarded him as an enemy. Or was it the other way round?

"I shall hate it when you're working nights, you know," Rod murmured, as he wrapped himself round her, tucking the duvet carefully round her neck. "Absolutely hate it."

"Would you rather," she made herself say to the darkness in front of her eyes, "that I slept over at Worksop Road?"

"Why?" He pushed himself clear.

"To save disrupting —"

"Good God, no! Absolutely not." His voice lost confidence. "Unless, that is — I'm sorry, I never thought —"

"I'm never happier than when I'm here, with you," she said, turning to face him, and drawing him back to her. "Never."

"In that case," he said, "do the obvious thing and move in here. Properly. For always. Unless you'd rather we found a house that was ours from the start, not mine." He heaved himself out of her arms, but only for a moment so that he could switch on the bedside light.

She screwed up her eyes and tried to burrow; he held on tight to the duvet, laughing.

At last she consented to open her eyes, blinking hard. "You look like an owl."

"I shall have the RSPB on to you for cruelty. What did you do that for?"

"So I could see what you want to do, not just hear." He took her face between his hands.

"Of course I want to live with you. I love you. I'm afraid you won't like my clutter in your house, though."

"In that case we should think about — hell, who wants plans when — Oh, my Kate."

Despite herself, knowing she ought simply to be happy and fall asleep, her back tucked up to his chest, as always, she was suddenly alert, panicking almost, thinking. Hamster-on-wheel thinking. Silly thinking. Telling Aunt Cassie. Letting the house. Finding the tenants. Telling Aunt Cassie.

"I can tell you're awake," came an accusing murmur. "Just switch off and get some sleep. Now we've got the important decision made, the details can wait. We've got busy times ahead of us. In fact, I might even be out of the house before you tomorrow."

"Want a bet?"

It was only the Radio Four newsreader's announcement that it was Friday that made Kate realise this was the day she was supposed to be meeting Graham for lunch. A break for food! Some hope. For all that others were now investigating Phil Bates's disappearance, she couldn't imagine there'd be anything light about today's load. Apart from the day-to-day running of the nick, there'd be questions to face from Greg Smith's team, for her as for everyone else. And she'd need to fill the gaps left by Dave Bush and Zayn Ara, if he was going to join the MIT.

She'd better deal with Zayn first, so as to clear the ground for anyone else. Or should it be Jill Todd? Zayn: he might not want to be transferred. Or was that cowardly?

Before she could decide, there was a knock at her door, and Thelma, the cleaner, appeared. "You're a hard woman but I know my duty," she announced.

"I'm sure you do, Thelma, and I'm sure you do it, too. Have you got time for a cup of tea? The kettle's still hot."

"It'll eat into me hours, thank you all the same, madam. No, I came with this. Since it's got your name on it I thought as how you'd want it." She plonked a battered envelope on Kate's desk.

"Thank you very much." Before she picked it up, she knew what it was. And knew it would have been opened. "As a matter of interest, where did you find it?"

"I don't want to get anyone into trouble, mind."

Kate smoothed it out. "It's just an empty envelope — why should anyone get into trouble?"

"It depends what they took out of it, doesn't it, madam? And before you ask, it wasn't me."

"I'm sure it wasn't. But where did you find it?"

"Down behind the cistern in one of the lavatories. I knew you wouldn't do a thing like that. You'd have put it in your bin in the proper place. I hate litter, I do so."

Kate nodded.

"So someone else must have put it there. So I say to myself, maybe the inspector doesn't know her letter's not where she thought it was. And I saw it had been opened, and I just wondered . . ." Thelma paused. "That nice inspector before you, lovely man he was, he used to say, 'If something strikes you as odd, it might strike me' — meaning him, madam — 'as odd too.'"

Kate nodded with more conviction than she felt. "So it strikes you as odd that a letter to me appears in the loos you're taking such pride in."

Thelma beamed.

"And you're sure I'll find it odd, too. Well, Thelma, I do."

"You see, if they'd put it in their own bin, whoever it was, I'd have known, because I always check what I'm throwing away."

206

Jesus! She must make more use of the shredder — and remind everyone else to. "I'm sure you're right. Now, come on, have that cuppa, because I want to warn you — your life's just about to get a lot busier, I'm afraid, and . . ."

She was just returning from the still immaculate loos when she almost ran into Zayn, still clipping his tie in place. "Can you spare a moment in my office straight away, please?"

"Ma'am — I mean, gaffer." He followed in her wake, pushing the door half closed behind him.

"Zayn, how soon is Eid?"

He grinned. "You want to come to the party, gaffer? You'd be very welcome."

"Love to, but that's not the point. How much longer will Ramadan last?"

"It's all according to calculations I can't make head or tail of, but probably Sunday or Monday."

"And today's Friday. How would you feel about giving up your fast? Because I've had a request for your services. It's not an empty-stomach job, though."

"With all due respect, you should let me be the judge of that."

"Not you, not me, but the guy who wants you on his team. And while you're absolutely right from one point of view, I can see his, too. We're talking eighteen-hour days, Zayn. And in anyone's book that means regular meals — OK, drinks, at least."

"I could talk to my imam, gaffer."

"He wants an answer by eight, Zayn."

"Who does?" Jill Todd appeared in the half-open door horribly on cue. She stepped inside, pushing it behind her. She stepped towards Zayn. "Well?"

He froze to attention.

Kate said sharply, "Zayn doesn't know, Jill. Now you're here, I can tell the two of you together. Greg Smith. He's heading the MIT investigating Phil Bates's disap —"

"MIT. You mean he's —" Jill's colour drained.

"Officially still no change from yesterday. He's a missing person. But yes, an MIT does suggest —"

"So what's Zayn got to do with the MIT?" She was now as flushed as she'd been white.

"They want two officers from here on the team."

"I can't spare anyone from the early-duty team. No way."

"All the teams are short-handed. Now, it may be that Zayn would rather stay put, the religious situation being what it is. But if Eid is on Sunday, Zayn —"

"Give me five minutes, gaffer, just five." Probably glad to escape the atmosphere steadily thickening in the room, he bolted.

Kate sat down, as if relaxed, registering the envelope half tucked under her phone.

Jill took a couple of steps forward. Legs braced, arms folded across her chest, she personified fury. She uncrossed her arms, the better to jab the air. "You don't take my officers, not without my say-so."

"It isn't me taking your officers, Jill. But if it were me, yes, I'm afraid I could do so without your permission."

208

"What do you mean, it's not you?"

"I thought you'd have worked it out by now. The MIT want him. And Dave Bush, as it happens."

"Oh, no, you don't — not so bloody fast."

"Dave's not negotiable. He's a sergeant, our FIO, Jill, not part of your team except for admin reasons. Zayn, well, I admit he'd be a loss to your duty team, but any good copper would be a loss to any duty team. And I have to say we don't even know what his decision will be."

"Oh, no? That sort'd sell their grandmothers to get promotion."

"Jill, just listen to yourself. Sit down and take a couple of deep breaths. That's an order," Kate added, voice dangerously quiet. "Zayn's a good officer, but he's not the only one in this nick. You're a good officer, too. You'll help your relief cope. Look, the news about Phil seemed to upset you."

Well, it did seem to have done. The changes of colour, the anger over her plans for Zayn: they just might have been a result of that. If she were Jill, she'd certainly want to pounce on it as an excuse, if only to get out of further, possibly more embarrassing, questions. Yes, Jill might have sat down, but her eyes kept drifting to the envelope.

She recognised it, didn't she? Was this the moment to tackle her? No, there were too many other pressing matters. And maybe it would do Jill good to stew a bit. Or were these simply excuses for postponing what would probably be an unpleasant few moments?

Jill said, "I'm fine. Absolutely fine. It's just that even if you don't like someone, it's still a bit of a shock to realise he's probably dead."

"I'm sure that's what we're all finding." Kate stood. "Well, you'll be wanting to go and do the morning briefing. Apologise from me about the disruption having the MIT here will cause. Any problems, get back to me. OK?"

"Zayn —"

"Will no doubt let us know when he's made his decision." *Which had better be bloody soon, hadn't it?*

And was. He popped his head round her door thirty seconds after Jill had left. She'd have liked to have time to check that he really was prepared to do what DCI Smith wanted and break his fast, but raised voices behind him brought her to her feet.

"OK, Zayn, good luck. No need to tell you to work hard."

"No, gaffer." He grinned, then, as the noise got louder, grimaced and fled.

"I never gave you permission —" Kathleen Speed was saying.

"You don't have to give us no permission. The gaffer gave us permission. And I just did the best I could, like. And if my best isn't good enough for you, Lady Muck, then you know what you can do."

Kate emerged. She ought to be laughing at the sight of Helen Kerr going at it hammer and tongs with Mrs Speed, but perhaps her sense of humour wasn't awake yet.

"I have a proper system —"

"Look, I don't know nothing about you and your sodding system."

"That's quite clear!" Mrs Speed flapped ineffectually at the messy desk.

"So I tried to —"

"Make as much chaos as you could, by the look of things."

That was clearly enough. "Someone had to take phone calls, and do what else they could," Kate said. Her legs were at least as braced as Jill's and arms at least as tightly folded. "It's a shame if your system's been messed up, but at least, thanks to Helen, the office kept ticking over and the calls were sorted."

"That's the job of the central switchboard."

"And when did you ever know them do it? Now, Mrs Speed, I'm very grateful to you for coming in so early, because I'm afraid today isn't going to be the easiest of days. As you can hear. And see."

The first cohort of the MIT bundled upstairs, laughing and talking at the tops of their voices. Seeing Kate, they subsided like schoolboys caught in the act.

"Quite," she said, every inch a headmistress. "Let's just remember it's one of our colleagues who's missing, shall we?"

A silence fell, among the newcomers and the regulars, as profound as if none of them had ever spent a whole shift moaning about him.

All this and it still wasn't quite eight. She was dreadfully hungry. It'd be all too easy to send someone out for food. No. She'd slip out herself for a *latte* and croissant. It was a pity the sharp morning air was already thick with fumes: one deep breath, and you could almost count the particulates leaping into your lungs.

Mrs Speed rose to intercept her as she ran back up the stairs. "Inspector —"

More complaints about Helen? Kate forced a patient smile into place. "Mrs Speed."

Mrs Speed leant towards her, conspiratorial finger towards, but not touching, her lips. "You may want to leave those with me, Inspector. You have a visitor."

CHAPTER
SEVENTEEN

A visitor important enough to deserve special treatment? Senior enough not to have to kick their heels in the corridor but to be admitted to her sanctum? The only person she could think of was Oxnard, checking up on the case so far. He hadn't given her much time, had he? That was bosses for you: snarl when you request action, and then, when they get interested, expect everything done yesterday. He might moan, but he'd secretly be pleased to see Kate eating on the hoof. So despite Mrs Speed's advice, the *latte* and croissant went with her.

The man standing peering through the blinds at her dubious view wasn't Oxnard but Graham Harvey. How long was it since she'd seen him in that position? His stoop was more pronounced, his hair greyer than she remembered. He'd always looked like a tired schoolteacher; now he looked like an exhausted one. And he was only a year or so older than Rod. What had caused this slither into middle age? Was it the job, or his miserable marriage? Or even the part she'd played in his life? She'd been the personification of temptation — the wicked siren. His Church had the same unforgiving attitude to sexual trespass as the most celibate Catholic priest's. Every moment he'd spent with her, therefore, had been sinful. Even if they were no longer together, the very fact that he might still lust after her was just as much a danger to his immortal soul.

Although she closed the door quite firmly — this was one conversation that shouldn't be casually overheard — he didn't look round immediately. She crossed to her desk, parking the coffee.

"Graham?"

He flung round. "What the hell are you doing," he demanded, his face ugly with anger, "going over my head? This should be a straightforward CID job, and you invite an MIT in!"

She mustn't apologise. "Not my decision," she said, as crisply as she could. "It was made over *my* head. I'm answerable to Oxnard, as operational commander. Talk to him about it, if you've got a problem."

"You had no right to discuss it with him without seeing me first."

"I had every right to tell him that one of my officers is missing. Every right and every duty."

"You should have told me."

She said nothing.

"I never thought you'd be so disloyal."

"It's a matter of hierarchy, not loyalty."

He stepped towards her, eyes like ice. She hoped hers were equally cold.

"You knew this would reflect badly on me — humiliate me. But you chose to go ahead. And then to invite an MIT in. The clear implication is that you didn't trust me and my colleagues — *your* colleagues,

214

Kate, *your* colleagues, until a few days ago — to do a decent job."

"That's not true." Perhaps it would sound less defensive if she added, "And you know it. I didn't make the decision. Indeed, I had no part in it. The only part I've played was to recommend which two of my officers should be seconded on to the MIT. And even," she continued, suddenly more fired up than she'd expected, "yes, even if I had had sole responsibility for the whole thing, do you think I'd have asked you to come and sort out my problems? Think of it, Graham. Working in the same building every day again. Having regular meetings and consultations. No, I don't think so." She added, more gently, "There's no point in opening old wounds."

"I hoped we could be friends," he muttered.

"I hoped we could. I hope we can. But you have to — *we* have to get used to each other's change of circumstances."

"In other words, I have to accept your having a lover. No, a mere DCI wasn't good enough for you, was it, Kate? You wanted a superintendent. I'm surprised you didn't go for an ACC."

She could have slapped his face. "So I could fuck my way to the top? Grow up, Graham. I slept with you because . . ." She tailed off. She didn't want to remind him and his conscience about their first sexual encounter. He'd come to visit her at home when she'd been on sick leave and had forced himself on her. That she'd been too in love with him to protest was irrelevant.

He dropped his eyes. "You could have reported me for rape."

She savoured the words, but said nothing. He wouldn't understand, would he?

"That was between you and me. The whole of our relationship should be between you and me."

"I'll bet you've told Rod Neville all about it."

"Why should I? Oh, he knows we were lovers, but only because when any other man dared talk to me you strutted round like a cock on a dunghill. He didn't have to be a great detective to work things out." Neither did a lot of other people, of course.

She glanced at her watch: she seemed to have spent too long already this morning having rows or adjudicating them. "Tell me," she said, changing the subject, if not enough, "this letter of yours — is this it?" She passed him the envelope.

"You know it is," he said, his voice hoarse.

"The cleaner found it tucked behind a loo and gave it to me this morning. I believe her when she tells me that it had already been opened."

"So the letter . . .?"

"Whatever you wrote is now in someone else's hands."

"What possessed you —"

"We've been over this, Graham. I thought my question more pertinent. What possessed you to write to me? What did you say, anyway?" She regretted the question as soon as it was uttered. And she wished she'd sounded less interested.

"My wife . . . suspects. She may contact you. I wanted you to — deny everything."

So he hadn't got round to separating from her, much less divorcing her. What a surprise.

"I would have done anyway. What made her suspicious?"

"Something Aunt Cassie said to Mrs Nelmes."

She suppressed a smile. So Aunt Cassie was still Aunt Cassie in his mind, while he always referred to his mother-in-law as Mrs Nelmes. And Flavia was still "my wife". Had he whipped himself up into that quite spurious rage about the MIT just so he'd have the courage — or was it even to have a motive — to come and talk to her? When she had so much, so very much, to do. And she ought to be on her way to Ladywood for another quick talk to Natasha. It was quite clear that she didn't have time to continue these regular conversations, and she ought to break it to the girl in person that she wouldn't be seeing so much of her.

"Did you come in your car?"

He looked completely nonplussed, as well he might. She couldn't explain that all he was today was an interruption in more important business.

"Could you give me a lift? I'm due at Ladywood in about fifteen minutes and, believe me, it'd be useful."

"What about getting back?" he objected.

"I'll hitch a lift from someone there. Or walk. It looks like a beautiful day." She picked up her jacket.

"It gives a very bad impression, that sort of thing," he said, pointing at her coffee and the unopened croissant bag.

"Thanks, Graham. That would have been my breakfast," she said drily, locking the door behind her. "I'm just off to Ladywood," she told Mrs Speed. "I should be back within the hour. If not, send out a search party for me."

At least they had something to talk about in the car.

"A tom. You're going to all this trouble for a tom!"

What had happened to his Christian forgiveness? "She's a little girl who was kidnapped and forced into the profession," she said quietly.

"All the same."

"She ought to be at school, preparing for her GCSEs. Except I think she's too young for them. That's how much of a tom she is." *Think about casting the first stone, Graham.*

She was just about to get out of the car when he said, suddenly humble, "I suppose it's off, then — lunch?"

"I shall be eating that croissant, I should think. I'll call you when all this is sorted, Graham. I can't see my feet touching the ground till then. In any case, I go on nights this weekend."

"I'd talk to Oxnard about that," he said. "I'd have thought you'd be more useful on duty during the day, when the MIT's going flat out."

She glanced at him. Yes, he meant it, and it was good, dispassionate advice. "I might just do that," she said. For old times' sake, she dabbed a kiss on his cheek, and was off, running up the steps just as Meg Walker and Natasha arrived. She turned to wave. A grey, metallic-finish Audi had slowed right down as it passed

218

the station. Perhaps it was just to let Graham pull back into the traffic. Perhaps it wasn't.

"Inside! Quick!" she shouted. She got most of the registration number before the car accelerated hard down the Middleway. Enough for the computer, she hoped. First she'd better check all her flock were together. Yes, Madame Constantinou was waiting with distinct disdain by a reception desk manned — there was no other word — by a huge man with the most tattooed hands she'd ever seen. Beside him Mick of the market would have looked a mere amateur.

"Take them through. I want to check a car reg."

Meg looked at her hard, but did as she was told. She returned almost immediately. "Do you want to check another one while you're at it? Madame Constantinou reckons her taxi was tailed. And she had the nous to take the number."

"So despite your precautions, you think someone is on to you?" DCI Smith reflected.

He'd joined Meg and Kate in the small interview room their Ladywood colleagues had provided, having come, as he grumbled, to the mountain, rather than waiting for the mountain to come to him. Kate would rather he hadn't come at all, but when she'd phoned Oxnard with the news — it was serious enough for her to refer it upwards — he'd told her he'd despatch Smith on the grounds that it looked as if Rod was right and everything would tie up somehow. "And," he'd added parenthetically, "it's always good to keep a man on his toes."

"According to my contact at NCIS, the gang is likely to be big and efficient," Kate told Smith, watching the light glint on his scalp. "They must be even bigger and more efficient than we thought." She poured coffee and handed it to her colleagues. This wasn't a moment to worry about falling into female roles.

"The cars?" DCI Smith prompted.

"Both stolen from suburban London drives last night," Kate said.

"So they may even have a profitable little sideline in the auto trade," Meg put in.

"Quite." It was clear Smith wasn't interested.

"So what now?" Kate asked. "We obviously need another safehouse for Natasha. But now we have to worry about Madame Constantinou's safety. Can Witness Protection take a hand?"

"You've got to persuade her of the need, first of all. It seems she disobeyed your instructions to vary her route: same minicab company, same driver, same car each day. 'Because he drove so smoothly'," Meg explained drily.

"I'll work on her," Kate said. "How do you think we should pursue this from now on, Greg? If the rotating-venue option hasn't worked, how can we all get together from now on?"

"Do you have to be involved at all?" he asked. "You've got the essentials and you'd be more use to me at Scala House. No, I know you're not part of the MIT, but you've worked with one in the past, I gather, and you'd still be in CID if it weren't for this daft rule that every promotion means a return to uniform."

Kate stroked her chin. Giving up this responsibility would certainly make life easier.

"It's true that what Natasha and Meg really need to do now is go through the story to make it into a formal statement — I don't envy you that, Meg. But even if I'm not involved, the basic question remains, how can the women get together safely?"

"Dead easy. We move the whole lot to a safe-house. No travelling involved, then."

"But my kids' exams!" Meg wailed. "No, I really don't want to go anywhere. Not that I think you'd get Madame Constantinou to go anyway. She's very attached to that flat of hers."

"Twenty-four-hour protection for her there?" Kate suggested, without conviction.

"And for Natasha, and Meg, and for whoever types everything up? Think budgets, woman."

"You wouldn't need a typist," Meg declared, "provided I could have a nice little laptop with a delete button. Then I could e-mail everything I got. But I'm not going anywhere," she repeated, belatedly.

"Sooner it's done, the sooner you won't need to," Smith said obscurely. "Come on, Walker, you're an experienced sergeant, not just in CID in general but Paedophilia. The kid likes you. Madame Whatsername knows you. It's obvious."

"It's not obvious at all. I've all my Christmas shopping to do — I haven't even bought any cards. There's the Christmas exams and then the school carol concerts — no, I really don't want to."

Smith sighed. "If you got cracking today, you'd likely be finished by Monday night. I can't order you to, but it'd make sense."

"I'll have to talk to my husband. But there's no point until we hear what Madame Constantinou has to say."

What Madame Constantinou had to say turned out to be a great deal. She said it with considerable drama, as if she'd been taking lessons from Natasha, her usually impeccable accent thickening with every paragraph. Her very hands expostulated that such a venture was completely and entirely out of the question.

Until Smith introduced the question of her fee. She would pack a case immediately.

It transpired that Madame Constantinou lived in a flat in a very pleasant development on Bristol Road. There would be at least two cars accompanying the one in which she'd be travelling, and the armed-response unit was going to rendezvous there — just in case, Smith added.

"In case of what?"

"Unwelcome attentions, Madame Constantinou," Smith said brusquely.

"In that case, I would like Kate to sit beside me. She is a very reliable officer, Chief Inspector Smith."

"Of course I'll go with you," Kate agreed, heart sinking at the waste of time. But she had an idea. "Then when we've got your things, the driver can drop me off at Scala House, where I normally work, and take you on to the safe-house."

222

"That's settled, then," Smith snapped. "Get your arse back ASAP, Power — OK?"

Bristol Road, more formally the A38, was one of the main arteries of the city, taking traffic from Spaghetti Junction through industrial Longbridge and then to the M5. Although for much of its length it was a dual carriageway, not all of it was, and those sections could clog with traffic very easily.

The traffic heading south was solid. The driver did an illegal U-turn, heading back through some of Birmingham's oldest and most distinguished residential roads to turn north up the A38 instead. That, too, was solid. But the police car, and its escorts, pushed its way through, Madame Constantinou making admiring remarks about the Red Sea.

"It must give you such a sense of power, officer — oh, Inspector, I do so apologise."

"That's OK," Kate began easily. Then she saw the expression on the older woman's face, and followed the line of her widening eyes. She grasped her hand, putting an arm round her shoulder. They were pulling into Viceroy Close just behind a flotilla of fire appliances.

"That is my apartment," Madame Constantinou croaked, pointing with a shaking index finger. "My apartment. Inspector, it is my apartment that is on fire. My little dog! My paintings! My furniture! My clothes!" She scrabbled for the door.

Kate pulled her back, but opened her own door. "I'll see what's going on," she told the driver. "Get her out of here — fast."

CHAPTER
EIGHTEEN

"It's not as bad as it could have been," the senior fire officer, a grizzled man called Jenks, told Kate. "Flats as upmarket as this have very efficient alarm systems. And one of the neighbours heard the smoke alarm and found the front door open and had a damn good go at fighting the blaze with his kitchen extinguisher. Hospital now, of course — smoke inhalation."

"The door was open?" She was still breathless from her run up the stairs.

"Yes. And before you ask, I'd say — off the record, for the time being — that it was arson. Look."

He wasn't taking much of a risk. The door had been jemmied open, and the centre of the fire was obvious even to Kate. "What's that stain?" She pointed.

"Blood. From that."

A terrier lay half out of the kitchen, its throat cut. It was clear Kate wasn't going to be back at Scala House for a while. She'd better let Smith know.

He wasn't pleased, interrupting before she could explain. "Busy? What sort of busy?"

"Busy with another arson attack and another slit throat."

224

"Shit! Have you got the fire-service people there? Put me on to whoever's in charge."

She held out the handset. "This is Detective Chief Inspector Smith, sir, in charge of the team looking into the Spaghetti Junction lorry fire, which," she added, "involved a remarkably similar *modus operandi*."

Jenks drummed his fingers with obvious irritation as he listened to Smith. At last he said, "OK, I'll see you later at the fire station, shall I? I just thought you'd want to see the scene first hand and fresh."

"'Course I bloody do. Jesus. OK." He cut the call.

From the expression on Jenks's face, it was a pity Smith didn't run to such expressions as "thank you" and "I'm on my way".

What she still wanted to do, of course, was phone Rod. She gave her conscience a quick check: yes, it was definitely for his professional input. Meanwhile, she made herself invisible while the fire-fighters went through what looked like a well-rehearsed routine of stowing equipment.

At last — no, it wasn't very long, considering the traffic: Smith must have put his foot down hard on the accelerator — she heard his voice on the stairs. He was with a plain-clothes officer she didn't know and Zayn Ara. Well, progress on one front, at least, even if it didn't need three guesses as to who'd end up doing the routine work.

"No dead humans here, at least," Jenks greeted him. "Just the old lady's little dog. Nasty yappy things — I'm surprised she was allowed to keep one."

She took a pace backwards. She didn't want to look at the dog again. Not for its own sake, but for Madame Constantinou's. She had been sucked into something very nasty through no fault of her own. It would be bad enough having to tell her about the smoke and water damage.

"Maybe a neighbour trying to shut it up," a passing fire-fighter suggested. So it wasn't just the police who used ghoulish humour to relieve strain.

"Chummy's trademark," Kate murmured, among the laughter.

Smith shot her a sideways glance. "You're sure this place belongs to —"

"Madam Somethingorother," Jenks supplied.

"Madame Constantinou. Yes, she said it was hers."

"Does she know about the dog?"

She shook her head. Perhaps Smith had a human side.

"I'd like you to be able to tell her any good news first."

You. Obviously a man for delegation.

"Now, would it be possible to see the state of the flat, Jenks?"

"You off your head, man? Got to get the investigation team in first. Most of her stuff's salvageable, I'd have thought. The bedrooms are virtually undamaged. Not like the flat down below, I should add." He sighed, as if ashamed of his own human feeling. "Lot of water damage there."

Kate said, "She said something about paintings."

226

"What's insurance for? Look, miss, we're lucky the whole block didn't go up — don't you start belly-aching about some old trout's pictures."

She turned to Smith. "When I phone, I shall be as upbeat as I can. But the little dog —"

"Come on," Jenks said. "It could have been her, couldn't it? Perhaps that's why that old codger went risking his life."

"As a matter of interest," Zayn asked, "how did they get as far as here? There's a security lock on the main door."

Jenks shrugged. "Who knows? Pushed their way in when someone was coming out? Or did the usual thing of pressing a few flat numbers at random till someone let them in?"

"I'll get on to it, shall I, sir? See if I can get any sort of description?"

Smith nodded, with something like approval. "You'll need help. You go too, Eliot. Get some more uniforms in if you need them."

Zayn took to his heels. Eliot followed silently.

The two men agreed to meet again later, when their respective forensic teams had finished.

Smith started down the stairs with Kate. "Miserable bugger," he observed, rather too loudly, given the acoustics.

It took one to know one.

"Most of the morning bloody gone and for what?" he demanded.

"Quite a lot, I'd have thought."

"All bloody negative, though. Things getting worse, not better. I joined to make things better — didn't you?" He let her into his car. "Not to start a case and find we're making things worse."

"Not us, sir. The villains. Thanks to a bit of stupidity from Madame Constantinou."

"Someone ought to get on to that taxi firm of hers. See if the driver's noticed anything before today. I suppose you haven't got time?" One look at Kate's expression and he continued, "OK. Any other ideas?"

"The only person I can think who might be worth talking to is the first interpreter we tried. Natasha took a real dislike to him. I thought it was just because he was male, and she's had enough to put her off men for life."

"Seems reasonable. Especially if she's got to talk about, well, women's problems."

"Like fellatio and anal sex and things like that," Kate agreed smoothly.

Smith shot her a sideways look. "Any other reason why she might have taken against him?"

"I should have asked. Meg should be able to find out."

"What did you make of him?"

"Nothing much. I only spoke to him for about a minute, and not in the easiest of circumstances. Mihail something, as I recall. Very bad skin. Otherwise terribly handsome, in a matinée idol sort of way. Mihail Antonescu."

Smith made a note. "He'll be in the list of accredited interpreters?"

"That's where Meg got him from, anyway. I'll get her to ask Natasha why she reacted as she did." She fished out her mobile. The number was denied. Security had stepped in already. Another job for later. "The problem, of course," she added, "is that in a sense you're absolutely right. You're supposed to be finding out what happened to Phil Bates, aren't you?"

He said nothing, concentrating on parking his car. "I could do with your company at the market. I always think better aloud."

Kate thought of her own schedules. But it was another glorious day and it would be good to get the smell of the fire out of her nostrils. "Fine."

They nodded at the daytime security guard, a youth so thin Kate wanted to press chocolate bars into his hands, and strolled in, not, Kate sensed, at random. By this time of day there was little activity. The dried-flower and florists'-equipment stall was still busy, but there was no one outside the coffee bar. Some overalled men were giving gutters a desultory sweep; further away a mechanical sweeper was doing the same thing more efficiently.

"There you are," Smith said, pointing.

They were still forty yards from the mechanical crusher but the smell was strong enough to turn Kate's stomach. Not for the first time she thanked goodness she wasn't in a forensic-science team, one of which was swarming around the taped-off crime scene.

"I'd say that's Bates's last resting-place," Smith said grimly. "Only hope he was dead when they put him in it."

Kate looked at the machinery, oozing with crushed vegetation: she couldn't see a cat's chance of getting evidence from it.

By now they'd reached the tape. A SOCO whom Kate didn't recognise approached them. Smith didn't introduce him.

"They empty it every working day," the young man said, pushing the hood of his white suit back to reveal improbably orange hair, "and burn everything within forty-eight hours at Tyseley. So if there was a corpse in there, he'll already have done his bit for the national grid."

"He what?"

"All the energy generated by that particular waste-disposal plant is converted to electricity and sold on. The ash goes to road-building and breeze-blocks, that sort of thing. Ever so useful."

Smith's face hardened. It was clear he didn't approve of the young man's levity. "So there's no chance of finding his warrant card? Or his epaulettes?"

"Not so much as a rusty button, mate. No, what we're hoping is that he was killed before he was put in. That way we might get a few blood-spatters for you."

Kate had barely skimmed through the first of her messages when Dave Bush appeared at her door. "Remind me never to join CID," he said, taking a seat with what sounded like a grateful sigh.

"You're too valuable here," she said. "But you'll want promotion when the time comes, uniform, CID, whatever."

230

"I don't know about that. No, I really don't. I'm happy as I am, gaffer."

"How did you get on yesterday with Mr Choi? Hell, I see I'm down for a meeting this afternoon I'd forgotten all about: CCTV."

"Me too — at Cherish House." He grinned. "Would you mind if I brought my sarnies through and ate while we talked?"

"Go and get them now. I'll brew some coffee."

"Would you mind using mine, gaffer? Only it's Fair Trade coffee. And I like to do my bit, if you see what I mean." Still talking, as she followed him out of the office to the kettle, he added, "You pay that much for a jar, whatever it is, these days, but less than a tenth goes to the poor buggers producing it. So I buy Fair Trade stuff whenever I can."

"Like Neil and being Green," she said.

"Neil? Never knew that. I'll have to get him on to this." He spooned granules and poured. "Now, try that, and tell me it isn't as good as your average brew."

God, all this fuss over a drink! Shop. They ought to be talking shop. But having someone volunteer to eat with her — what had happened to her resolution to take everyone in rotation out to lunch? — felt like such a breakthrough she should let him natter away. And the coffee wasn't at all bad, either.

"Mr Choi now reckons," Dave began, through a mouthful of egg and cress, "that something's happening, not here but in Manchester. Look, have one of these — my wife always makes too many. He's got a lot of mates up there — well, there's a proper Chinese

Quarter, much bigger than ours. There's also a red-light district."

"Thanks." Kate nodded. "Yes. Between the gay village and Piccadilly."

"And Mr Choi reckons that there's a flood of toms. Very cheap. Do-anything-anywhere toms. No condoms, that sort of thing."

"And they're very young and don't speak a lot of English," Kate prompted.

"Quite. So they can't complain if they get beaten up, either by their pimps or by their clients. Poor kids. I know they're toms, but Mr Choi says some of them are only twelve or thirteen."

Kate swallowed before she spoke. "So why is Choi so concerned? I don't altogether buy his reputation as a bastion of public morality and friend of the British bobby."

"Nor should you. I'm sure of that. At least, I'm sure he's both as far as it suits him. And he keeps any dodgy dealing quite separate from his civic life, I'm sure of that, too. But in his other life, I reckon he's into prostitution himself, gaffer, only at such a far remove no one could possibly associate him with it."

"So it'd really suit him if we could take out a rival organisation."

"Absolutely. He assures me he'll feed us any information he gets."

"After he's acted on it first?"

"Not if we can do it more publicly and at no cost to him." Dave dusted the last crumbs from his fingers and closed his sandwich box.

232

"You're very well organised," Kate said.

"That's my wife. She's a teacher. Very disciplined. She prepares all our lunchboxes the night before. Sometimes the system goes wrong and I get weird-flavoured crisps or whatever instead of my apple, but we never starve. And my eldest's started to cook the occasional meal. Seems really funny, a lad taking that sort of interest."

Kate smiled. "Rod's a much better cook than I am." There. It was out. A nice casual reference to him.

"Would that be Superintendent Neville, gaffer? The one young Jill Todd carried a torch for?"

"The same." She mustn't encourage him to gossip, but wouldn't have minded his take on the situation, all the same.

There was a token knock at the door, and DCI Smith's head appeared. "I need a formal update on — What the fuck are you doing here, Bush?"

"He's been briefing me about Mr Choi. As I asked."

"All very cosy, I must say. Well, shift your arse, Bush, and treat us to the same briefing. It'd have saved time if you'd done both at once. Why don't you come along, Power?"

"Good idea. Thanks for the invitation." She thought he might have missed the irony, however. "But I've got to be at Lloyd House in twenty minutes."

"Power!" Chief Superintendent Oxnard's voice rang down the corridor. "In my office. Now!"

The old bugger. He must have known she was trying to sneak home unnoticed. After all, it was well after five, and any decent human being would hear the call of the weekend echoing along the Victorian corridors.

"Sir?"

"Come along in. I want to hear what's going on. Your young man's here, too."

Jesus, not Graham. He was the last man of hers Oxnard had referred to. And Graham might have appeared to simmer down, but residual grievance could have festered enough for him to go steaming along to seek redress. Trying to appear as nonchalant as anyone could after two hours of bitterly inconclusive policy discussion, she smiled and followed him into his office.

To find not Graham but Rod sitting in a visitor's chair. He winked with the eye further from Oxnard.

"I believe you know Superintendent Neville," Oxnard said, with belated heavy irony.

"Indeed I do, sir. But that shouldn't stop you bollocking me if needs be. It wouldn't stop him."

Oxnard gave an appreciative bark. "Deserve a bollocking, do you?" He waved her to a chair.

She nodded. "There's a very important phone call I haven't had time to make. And the problem is, I don't even know the number to call, since it's one for a safe-house."

"Which safe-house? I thought Natasha was safe and sound," Rod observed

"She was. Until Madame Constantinou — she was the interpreter we used to interview the Albanian child — got too clever for her own good and led Chummy to Ladywood, where he got a nice clear view of all of us on the station steps. So now Meg, Natasha and

234

Madame Constantinou are all closeted together in another safe-house, and I need to tell Madame C that her flat was probably torched — yes, she knew it was on fire — by someone who also slit her dog's throat."

"So I told her to involve Smith," Oxnard said. "Power!" He suddenly fixed her. Surely he'd told her to sit? "Tell me, Power, what time did you start work?"

"Six thirty."

"OK. Well, the sun's well and truly over the yardarm. Here." He produced a bottle of Bell's and tipped a good couple of drams into a mug. Before Rod could argue, he repeated the process with two other mugs. "Well?"

"Hits the spot nicely, sir. Thank you." She beamed.

Rod's smile was rather thinner, but he sipped his too. "Could you give us a slightly more detailed briefing, Kate?" He listened carefully, making several notes. Once or twice he frowned. But he waited for Oxnard to speak first.

"Who are you supposed to be working for, Kate?" Oxnard asked at last.

"Sir?"

"Me or DCI Smith?"

She flushed. "You, sir. I'm sorry, sir." She wouldn't allow herself to look at Rod.

"It sounds to me as if DCI Smith hasn't quite realised that you've got other responsibilities."

"I didn't make all that much effort to remind him, sir. I like to get to the bottom of a case."

"Two cases, by the sound of it. And I know that Bates was one of your officers and you feel a responsibility there. But you don't have to be a dogsbody, Kate. It's not your job to trot round finding phone numbers and phoning people. You're a manager."

"And a very good detective," Rod put in.

Oxnard grunted. "Well, the station's been known to run itself quite well without an inspector. A lot of good experienced officers there. Do you want to continue riding two horses?"

"As long as I can, sir. So long as I have your authority to draw lines."

"You do, you do. Do you have any problem with that, Neville?"

"Only one. Let me take you back, Kate, to that point in your account where you said Chummy arrived outside Ladywood nick. Two Chummies, I think you said in your more detailed account?"

"Yes. We checked the vehicle registration numbers: both cars were stolen."

"And you were clearly visible on the steps with Meg Walker and Natasha."

"Yes."

"In that case, sir, I think we do have a problem. If Meg, Natasha and Madame Constantinou are at risk, I have a terrible feeling that Kate is too."

CHAPTER
NINETEEN

Kate took a deep breath. "I was in uniform at the time, just like now, complete with hat. I don't think they'd have seen enough of me to recognise me, or to see my number. The person who may be at risk is the person whose car I was travelling in," she added, with a fleeting glance at Rod: although he'd been relaxed enough about the missing letter and the lunch invitation, he wouldn't necessarily like the news. Whatever his feelings, he'd give nothing away to Oxnard. "They'd almost certainly have got his number: they definitely slowed down long enough to. DCI Graham Harvey, gaffer." She addressed Oxnard, not Rod.

Oxnard blushed. "I — I . . ." He glanced sideways at Rod, who looked in turn at Kate, a certain amount of dour enjoyment lurking in his eyes.

"DCI Harvey thought a personal disagreement between us had prevented me simply asking CID for help. He took some convincing that the decision was yours, gaffer. By then I was late for Natasha's debriefing at Ladywood, so I asked for a lift."

Oxnard reached for the internal phone. "Is he still in the building?"

"No idea, gaffer." Though if he'd been duty officer yesterday evening he probably was. What excuse had he given his wife for such an early start this morning?

"Only one way to find out," he grunted. "You wouldn't know his extension number?"

He'd been her boss long enough when she'd been in CID. She rattled it off. Part of her was as amused as Rod apparently was. Rod and she knew the truth of the situation, but Graham would no doubt be at such pains to show there was no basis for the rumours that he would simply make Oxnard more suspicious. And embarrassed.

But not as embarrassed as he was himself when he opened Oxnard's door to find the three of them.

Without preamble, Oxnard said, "Power thinks you're in some danger, Harvey."

He looked at her coldly. "Indeed?"

"Yes, you explain, Power," Oxnard said. "Sit down, Harvey, for God's sake. Bugger it, not God. You don't like me bothering him, do you?"

Kate gave him a succinct account of the morning's events. "And your contact at NCIS said they were ruthless enough to have the Mafia running scared. They've killed, we suspect, a man whom we know helped Natasha. They've killed the dog —"

"A dog! In any case, most criminals simply try to stay away from us — they don't actively go around killing people for revenge."

"These appear to. Or why target Madame Constantinou?"

"I still don't see the problem," Graham said. "To identify my car, they'd have to have access to the PNC or the DVLA computer."

"And you don't think they're powerful enough to get hold of either?" Kate enquired. "There are such things as bent cops, Graham. Or terrified computer operators."

"You're talking as if Birmingham's some Hollywood movie," he said dismissively.

"Or they could simply have hung around here and kill you when you reach your car. Or they may prefer to trail you home, of course," Rod observed, his voice devoid of expression.

Graham looked straight at Oxnard. "Will that be all, sir?"

"Graham, the people running this operation have a propensity for slitting throats and torching things," Kate persisted. If only she could shake some sense into him. "They've got an international reputation for major violence. Your mate at NCIS was very anxious to be kept informed — and equally anxious that we should watch our backs."

His jaw set.

Smacking his silly head was an attractive prospect, too. She looked hopefully at Oxnard.

"It's not just you, Harvey, that's at risk. It's anyone likely to drive that car."

"Or anyone who might be at the address to which the car is registered," Rod said, very formally, as if at last irritated. "Your wife, Chief Inspector, for instance."

Very huffily, Graham said, "I'll take on board what you say, sir."

"You'll do more than that," Oxnard said, his face reddening. "You'll get one of our security buffs around to your house first thing tomorrow. And meanwhile, you and your — you have got . . . got . . . a wife? Well, you'll move out for a bit. Take her away for a quiet romantic weekend. And that's an order." The more embarrassed he got, the louder he barked. And there was no doubt that he was very embarrassed indeed.

As was everyone.

"Why don't you leave your car here?" Rod suggested. "Pick up one from the pool?"

"That surely can't be necessary."

"Put it another way," Oxnard chimed in, "you're not even touching the bloody car till it's been checked over. Unless by any chance you left it in the secure parking area?"

"It was full by the time I got in. I parked in Steelhouse Lane. Nice and public — far too public for anyone to tamper with it."

Oxnard stood up, shaking his head. "Laddie, I've seen what they can do to a car in two minutes in Northern Ireland. Give me the registration number so I can get the boffins to look it over, and get yourself a cab home at the end of your shift. Understood?"

Graham stood, face red with baffled fury. "Sir."

"Keys?"

He fumbled them out of his pocket, then nodded to Oxnard and Rod, studiously ignoring Kate as he slammed out.

240

After a moment, during which he might have been suppressing amusement or indignation, Oxnard looked straight at Kate. "And you, young lady, how do we look after you? Because I honestly don't see how we can send you on compassionate leave or whatever when you've got yourself two jobs to do."

"Always assuming she'd consent to go," Rod put in. "Well, Kate?"

"Oh, yes! Leave everyone else to look for one of my own team? But I know I've got to take a few precautions. For one thing, perhaps I should wear everyday clothes, and fairly pretty ones at that," she added, "something as unlike blue serge as possible."

"But baggy enough to wear body armour underneath," Oxnard said. "Remember that."

"And I have been known to wear a wig, if absolutely necessary. Nasty itchy thing it was too," she recollected, ready to giggle — with reaction, she supposed.

"I'd have thought night duty was off," Rod said, absolutely not meeting her eye.

"You'll certainly be more use to the MIT during the day," Oxnard mused. "But look here, Power, I'm not having you act as some dolly-bird secretary to Smith. He's got a whole team there, and you're still responsible for a raft of everyday policing activities."

"Including wall-to-wall policy meetings," she agreed, with a sigh. "Look, gaffer, I could simply travel backwards and forwards in ordinary gear. It might be better for morale if I wore uniform once I was safely inside."

"I'm not sure. Let me think about it. Look, it's the weekend tomorrow. You wouldn't normally be going in, would you?"

"With a murder investigation going on? With due respect, you've got to be joking, gaffer. I'll be in by seven."

He ran his hands through his hair. "It's not as if there are lots of different routes you can take to Scala House. And you certainly aren't taking your own car and leaving it in its usual spot."

"So how do I get to all my meetings, sir?"

"I think the taxpayers'll have to run to having you ferried around as and when necessary. Did you ever go on one of our advanced driving courses, Rod? You know, the sort they send you on if you're having to protect diplomats and so on?"

Rod shook his head. "Not as advanced as that. But I drove on motorway patrol for a couple of months."

Oxnard looked at him shrewdly. "I wonder why you stopped. Anyway, Kate, if you want to work tomorrow you'll do it from home."

"Sorry, sir. My place is with my team. Perhaps Superintendent Neville would be kind enough to drive me in."

Rod responded with a gracious inclination of the head worthy of royalty. He also raised two fingers of the hand Oxnard couldn't see.

Oxnard shrugged. "Very well. But I'd much rather you both came into town on the bus and did your Christmas shopping with everyone else." He stood up, indicating with a somewhat absent smile that the interview was over. As they reached the door, he called, "Where's your car now?"

"Steelhouse Lane — on a meter."

He considered. "You'll be running her home, I take it, Rod? Well, since we're getting the boffins out anyway, it might just as well stay there. Keys, please, Kate."

"How are you off for clothes?" Rod asked, as he unlocked his car. "And when did you last collect the post?"

"Seems like a year ago. Have we time?"

"Well, I'm not going back to work tonight, and I truly hope you're not, now you've done your duty by Madame Constantinou —"

"Eventually! Rod, I feel so ashamed —"

"— and you know she's in safe hands," he overrode her. "I must say, by the way, I think Oxnard's right to worry about you being a dogsbody for Smith. The man could delegate for Europe. Now, you deserve a decent meal and some decent wine." He fastened his seat-belt.

"Trouble is, if we're in the Moseley area I rather think I ought to pop in to see Aunt Cassie," she ventured. If he was anything like as tired as she was, this wouldn't be the best suggestion.

"Are you going to tell her about us? About your moving in?" He gripped her hands with boyish enthusiasm.

"Oh, I'd love to! Yes!" And then she reflected, all the dead-of-night worries flooding back. "But I'm not quite sure how to. She may not be very happy about it."

"Why on earth not?"

"Because — shall I talk while we drive?"

"Let's see how she is before we make any decisions, shall we?" Rod suggested, pulling up neatly half-way down Worksop Road — not because he had any obvious fear of an attack but because there was nowhere else to park.

Kate nodded. "The important decision's been taken, after all," she said, slipping her hand into his. "Ours. My God, it's colder than ever tonight. I'd better notch the central heating up."

She left Rod gathering up post and sorting it while she took a couple of bin-liners upstairs for more clothes. On impulse, she threw in all of her jewellery, even the items she rarely wore, and some favourite books, too. She came downstairs to find Rod on a similar mission. From time to time he'd bought items of glass and china for her, and now he was wrapping them in tea-towels. He popped them into the bin-liners letting the clothes pad them further.

"You're afraid they'll get on to this place, aren't you?"

"My love, I hope not. And lightning isn't supposed to strike twice." He gathered her to him, a tacit apology for letting her down the last time she had been at risk like this, when her house had been torched. "Anyway," he said positively, "you ought to have your things around: it's your home, now. You must decide what to do about furniture."

"It'd be nice if there was room for this." She stroked the dining-table. It was George II, not in perfect condition but she loved it. Whether she let the house furnished or unfurnished, this ought to live with her.

"Thank goodness it's so small. It'll fit into the back of the car now, if you want. You'll need a study table. I'll go and fold down the seats. Whatever did we do before we had hatchbacks?"

Aunt Cassie was bursting with news. Mrs Nelmes's daughter and son-in-law — Flavia and Graham Harvey — had had a row while they were supposed to be visiting her. "On and on it went, according to Mrs Nelmes. She says — Mrs Nelmes, that is — her daughter says young Graham has a fancy woman. Not those words, of course, far too mealy-mouthed for that, both of them. She's got a mouth like a hen's backside, Rod, Mrs Nelmes has. And her daughter — only hers is a hen's with piles!"

Kate gripped Rod's fingers till both sets of knuckles were white. Swiftly he laid his other hand on hers. It was all right: she mustn't panic, the hand said. His mouth said, "Hen with haemorrhoids would sound even better!"

Kate giggled, but not as loudly as the old lady. She must make an effort. "Let me freshen that drink for you, Aunt Cassie. Is there enough for Rod and me? It's been a long, hard day."

"In that case you ought to go and get yourselves a decent meal. Why not treat her, Rod? You both work hard — she shouldn't have to cook every night."

Kate took one look at Rod and collapsed into giggles again. "Oh, Aunt Cassie, it's Rod who's the cook. I can barely boil an egg."

"That's not true, and you know it," Aunt Cassie said sharply. "You were a good little cook when you were a girl. Come on, Rod, you make her do her fair share. She'll forget how if you're not careful. And that'd be a shame."

"I'll let her off tonight, though — as she said, today's been a bit hectic."

"In that case you should get her to take you out. Fair's fair, you know. Off you go. No, I've got my television programme to watch and there's talk of a bit of whist later. Go on, be off with you. Tell you what, you can give me a hand down to the TV lounge."

"She's such a good sort, Aunt Cassie," Kate said, as soon as they'd delivered her. "She usually watches TV in her room, so this business of our escorting her was just an excuse to get rid of us."

"Quite. But I'm not arguing. I can't wait to get home, have a very quick shower and something to eat."

He drove home, glancing at her from time to time. She knew she had to say something about Graham.

"The Graham business didn't exactly help, did it?" she began. "He was at Scala House before eight, on his high horse about who should be looking into Bates's disappearance. The only sensible thing he said was what you said later: that I'd be better value working days, not nights."

"He wants you back, does he?"

"You know what Aunt Cassie would say: 'I want doesn't get.' Apparently the missing letter was to warn me that his wife was suspicious and to deny everything if she phoned. As if I were likely to confess all. Except to you. You can have chapter and verse, if you want."

"Sweetheart, we both come with a sexual history. I'm not at all sure that confession of such matters is good for the soul. Especially the soul of the person being confessed to. Would it make you any happier to know exactly what I said and did to Jill Todd? Well, then."

"Mrs Harvey might phone you to warn you against me."

"How on earth would she know anything about me?"

"Knowing Graham, he'll have said that I was with someone else. And knowing her, she'd worm your name out of him. And then she'd phone you at work and — oh, I don't know."

"Stop demonising her. She's probably just a very unhappy woman in a bad marriage. You know there are rumours about him with other women? Romantic entanglements, if not full-blown affairs."

"Even I know someone who certainly carried a torch for him. I must say, when I met Mrs Harvey, long before — before I even fancied Graham — I didn't take to her at all. I had to go round to their house once, when he had a sickie, and I was about as welcome as a cat at a canary show."

"Why 'Mrs Harvey' all the time? Doesn't she have a name?"

"Not one Graham uses. He always calls her 'my wife'. But then, with her first name, I might prefer to be called 'Mrs Harvey' or 'my wife'."

"What the hell's her name, then? Lucretia or something?"

"Joke not. Flavia."

He shook his head. "Parents have a lot to answer for, don't they? Come on, no more wasting your breath on her." He turned the car neatly into his drive — their drive — and parked. "Let's not bother sorting all that stuff out tonight. We'll just dump it in the hall and deal with it tomorrow. We need to eat."

She heaved the bin-liners into the house. "It'll be hard getting in anywhere at this time of night."

"That's why, my love, I booked this morning. We weren't going to celebrate the first night of the rest of our lives here with a bag of chips in front of the TV." He kissed her. "Now, give me a hand with this table, will you? I don't want to knock it. There. And lest you're about to worry over how much champagne I can consume without risking my licence, I've got a cab booked too. We've got about twenty minutes before it arrives. Last one in the shower," he added, flying upstairs, "is a ninny!"

CHAPTER
TWENTY

Rod extended a hand to silence the alarm. "I could wish," he said mildly, "that Bob Oxnard had actually ordered you to go Christmas shopping this morning." He switched on the bedside light, burrowing back to pull the duvet over his eyes.

"You could go shopping without me," she pointed out, rubbing her face. "We ought to get some Christmas cards, charity for preference."

"You're rather missing the point."

"Am I?" She sat up. "My God, whose idea was it to have a whole bottle of fizz?"

"Not to mention that very elegant Burgundy." He emerged again. "Shall I make coffee while you shower or vice versa?"

"Honestly, there's really no need for you to get up. I can take a cab into work." It was a very feeble protest. Reaching for her dressing-gown, she felt for her slippers. "Hell, the central heating hasn't come on yet."

"Of course you could. But it would be much more entertaining for me to drive you in and go and irritate Greg Smith for a few hours." He pushed back the duvet decisively.

"He ought to be at Steelhouse Lane today. Scala House is only an outpost of his empire."

"If past form's anything to go by, Mr Smith will be at the place of least activity. He's not a man for epicentres at all. All in all it's ironic that it should be he who's looking into Bates's disappearance — I suppose it takes one skiver to know another."

Kate had a suspicion that Rod wouldn't want to know that, rather than improving her vocabulary, he'd started to use her clichés. But she had to ask, "Why put him in charge of an MIT, then?"

"Not guilty. I just inherited him. And would love to get rid of him."

"But did you have to allocate him to Scala House?"

"I'm afraid so. What with on-going cases, annual leave and a couple of victims of that stomach bug, there was no one else to choose from. And much as I'd have liked to don my pants over my trousers, and fly in to your rescue . . ."

Rod might not have taken the most advanced driving course available to police officers, but he drove very well. This time he'd set himself the task of eluding an imaginary tail, not hard, he confessed, before seven on a Saturday morning.

"I must say, I've never come such a bizarre way to Scala House." Kate laughed, as they approached from Bristol Road, having briskly taken in many of the lesser sights of Edgbaston en route.

"This is the last time you'll be travelling in this car for a while," Rod said, going all the way round the

250

Holloway Head island as if retracing his steps. He pulled into a bus stop. "Scarper. I'll be with you as soon as I've parked."

The early-duty team were clearly surprised to see her in mufti. Her brief explanation, given in her flattest, driest voice, brought gratifying expressions of concern to most faces. But there was no doubt that she was right to be there: her absence would have been deeply resented, when many of the day shift had come in early, and even one or two of the late shift had slipped into the back of the room. A long day for them. Almost as long as hers was likely to be. Warning everyone to be extra vigilant, she retired to her office to check her e-mails.

There was one from Meg Walker: yes, that was where she'd start. As she brought it on to the screen, Rod popped his head round the door to tell her he'd parked in the Arcadian complex car park, which had the reputation of being safe. He'd be reviewing any progress Smith had made — he winked at this point — and would no doubt see her later when the whole team had a meeting.

Meg reported that all the women had been rattled by the events of the previous day.

Natasha's suddenly into co-operation, Kate, pouring stuff out, but poor Mme C is terribly hesitant with her translation. Can hardly blame her, I suppose — fancy seeing your flat on fire and not being able to check it out. Then when the news came about her dog . . . Well, the funny

thing is, Natasha came up with the goods, and started singing this Albanian lullaby — sounded a real dirge to me, but they ended up with their arms round each other sobbing their hearts out. Fortunately as soon as they'd arrived, they'd sent one of the constables on guard out with an enormous shopping list — real specialist stuff — so they could cook their favourite food. Had it for supper. Tasted OK if you like that sort of thing. Give me a decent British curry any day. (Joke!) Anyway, the good news is they're both determined to bring this Vladi to book, so we're due for an early start tomorrow. Talk to you then.
    Meg XX

Kate put her head into her hands: she'd joined the police, like Smith, to make things better, yet she hadn't spared time to make a simple phone call reassuring an anxious woman about her property until five or six hours after she should have done. She hadn't even thought of sending her some flowers. Admittedly that would have been hard, since she wasn't supposed to know the safe-house address, but it wouldn't have been impossible. Not if she'd thought about it. A job for today. If she had time.

She heard footsteps outside her office. It was time to look alert, in control of the job. One of them at least. Perhaps for the time being it should be the official one, being in charge at Scala House. And what was better evidence of being in charge than opening the post, a waste-bin conveniently to hand? The fact that it was the best part of a week's post was best ignored.

She had the paperknife already poised when the footsteps stopped. Before whoever it was could even tap, she called, "Come in." And then was on her feet, arms outstretched. "Helen, what's the matter? Come and sit down!"

"It's the bab. I think I might be losing the bab. I've got this fucking awful pain — Christ, there it goes again!"

"Like contractions?"

"Yes. Like period pains, like." Helen clung to her hand.

Kate returned the pressure. She made a quick decision. "Look, you're going to sit here very quietly and I'm going to call an ambulance."

"Shouldn't it be a first-aider?"

"What do you think?" She was already dialling.

The worst part was when the paramedics were ready to take Helen off. She'd responded to each wave of pain with a convulsive clasp of Kate's hand. Now the grip tightened again. "Gaffer — you couldn't see your way to coming with me in the ambulance, like? Only I'm bloody scared."

"You don't need me, you need the baby's dad," Kate said gently. She felt sick: she simply didn't have time, but how could she deny a request from the heart like that? "Is his number on your file?"

"Ah. Only he's somewhere on the M5 in his HGV, isn't he? Kate —"

There was another tap on the door. All she needed was an audience when she had to behave like a louse.

"Mrs Speed!" Heavens, it wasn't yet eight, and in any case Mrs Speed didn't work at weekends.

"What with the Phil Bates business and all the extra work from the MIT, I thought . . ."

Kate smiled. "You shouldn't have, but I'm very grateful all the same."

"I've a mound of filing. But what I'd like to do, Inspector, if I may, is go with Helen. As a woman. And, I hope, a friend."

Helen's eyes filled.

Was Mrs Speed sincere or was she just giving a wonderful impression of sincerity? After all, it seemed only minutes ago that Kate had been adjudicating a stand-up row between the two. And did Kate care? Only inasmuch as her conscience was horrified at the relief swamping her.

"You see, Chief Superintendent Oxnard's just arrived and is asking for you, Inspector. I thought you'd want to know."

"Thank you. Very much." Terrified of changing her mind and insisting on doing her duty to Helen, however much it might conflict with all the other duties, Kate bent and kissed her cheek. "Best be going, now." She squeezed her hand and passed it to Mrs Speed's.

Shoulders braced, she led the little procession from her room. There was no sign of Oxnard. And, indeed, why should there be? The investigation was the MIT's

254

job, not his. Mrs Speed gave what might have been a wink as she left.

Back in her office, the least Kate could do was bring up Helen's file on her screen and make the call to her partner. Even as she was doing that, however, Smith pushed open her door. "Got a few minutes?"

"Not until I've made this phone call. Sit down, it won't take long." It didn't. Helen would have her bloke with her in a couple of hours.

But Smith didn't sit. He leant across her desk. "Putting personal calls before official business? What sort of cop are you?"

"The sort who cares for her colleagues. Which reminds me, I heard a rumour that the MIT was making extra work for our clerical worker. I hope it was mistaken."

He shifted. "If the stupid cow's bellyaching about making a few extra cups of tea —"

"She's not. But she's so behind in her real work — and making tea is *not* part of her job description — that she came in before eight. On a Saturday. Unpaid overtime, I need hardly point out. I thought you were going to get in your own facilities."

"For God's sake!"

"No. For everyone's sake. I take it you didn't requisition extra loo paper? What a good job I did."

The bastard muttered something about women's work.

Before she could erupt, the door opened further. Oxnard, very red in the face, though perhaps that was as a result of a brisk climb up the stairs, glared at him with the sort of ferocity that had made Kate wince before now. "I hope I didn't hear that, DCI Smith." His index finger was an inch from Smith's chest. "Because if I did, I shall have to recommend that you be put back into uniform and sent on some more equal-opps training. A lot more. Get your fucking arse into the MIT room, man. Inspector Power, we've just had some news. There are a lot of Scala House people around so I've asked them too. Would you care to join us?"

Sarcasm? No, she didn't think so. She thought it was Oxnard's not very subtle way of showing how you should treat a colleague — the way he was now holding the door open for her. Despite the urgency, she remembered to lock it.

Ears still red from Oxnard's scorn, Smith took his place in the room now the territory of the MIT. He stood in front of a whiteboard they'd conjured from somewhere.

"As you can see, we've been joined by Chief Superintendent Oxnard —"

"One of my own people, damn it," he snarled. "Of course I want to be here."

"— and Detective Superintendent Neville, who as you know is in overall charge of all the MITs."

"Like Chief Superintendent Oxnard," Rod said, "when one of our own is involved, we all want to get stuck in. It's good to see so many of you Scala House people here today, by the way, on what I'm sure is a rest day for many of you. When stall-to-stall enquiries and fingertip searches are involved, the more the better."

256

Not, as they all knew, that there was much hope they would find anything interesting. But they couldn't not try.

"We're also here because we want to reassure you that although you'll all be questioned till you're sick of it over the next few days, this is simply routine. It's not, repeat not, because any of you are under suspicion." He seemed to Kate to look particularly at Neil Drew. There might even be a hint of a reassuring smile. Jesus, she'd never even thought of offering Neil that sort of reassurance — what had she been playing at?

"We've also got a bit of a problem concerning Inspector Power," Oxnard said. "I don't know how much she's told you about yesterday's events. As most of you know, Inspector Power's involved with the investigation into how an Albanian child forced into prostitution was brought over here illegally. It seems that some of the people we're investigating may have clocked her. Since we've already had one lorry driver's throat cut and lorry torched, we're anxious about her safety — especially when we suspect that they may have killed the interpreter's dog and set fire to her flat. We're talking about unpleasant people — even the Mafia don't like them. Hence, as she may have told some of you, I've asked her not to wear uniform and to vary her appearance as much as possible. So no sniggers if she turns up in a wig, eh, Power?"

"You can snigger all you like so long as we nail the people involved. Who may or may not be involved in Phil Bates's disappearance?" She ended on a question. It was time to leave the limelight to the senior officers.

"More than disappearance, I'm afraid." Oxnard stepped forward again. "The SOCO team have found evidence of a crime involving the loss of blood. We're awaiting the results of DNA tests. But from the pattern of the blood, it looks very much as though the crime was violent. And it took place a matter of yards from the rubbish crusher in the wholesale market." By now his voice was very gruff.

"Before we continue, sir," Kate found herself saying, "could we have a minute's silence for Phil?"

"Good thinking," Oxnard said, adding piously, "We all need a moment to reflect and remember."

Despite the sentimentality — perhaps because of it — the whole room stood.

She hoped she didn't have to end it: she wouldn't know how. At last, it seemed to end itself, and Rod gestured to Smith to continue.

"Trouble is, we may never find — anything. The crusher's emptied regularly, and the contents taken for immediate incineration, at temperatures that preclude the identification of anything, animal, vegetable or mineral. The blood-splatter is all we have to go on."

"No witnesses?" Rod asked.

Smith shrugged. "Folks in the market are a fucking load of Trappist monks."

Someone Kate didn't know raised his hand. "Isn't Sunday a pretty quiet night down there?"

Neil Drew replied: "Not as quiet as it used to be. Folk have got used to having their fresh veg and stuff every day of the week, thanks to the supermarkets. So there are quite a few folk around."

"So someone could have come along expecting it either to be seething so he wouldn't be noticed or dead quiet so there'd be no one to notice what he was doing," Zayn said

"Good point." Rod nodded.

"Only he found Phil was there and . . ." Zayn spread his hands.

"Neil," Kate began, "you were hoping to sort out a Sarbut. Sorry, official informer. Did you have any joy?"

"None at all. I haven't seen him for a bit. I thought he'd maybe got the stomach bug. Oh, my God — you mean he could . . ." He mimed throat-slitting.

Kate leaned forward. "It's OK, Neil. He may well have the bug. But have you any idea how to get hold of him? Just to make sure?"

"I'll be on my way now, if it's OK by you, gaffer."

She looked at her watch. "You can spend one hour checking for an address. You phone it in. And then you go straight home to bed. Is that clear?"

"Hang on," Smith interrupted. "We need to talk to you again, Drew. You were the last person to see him alive, remember."

"OK. Come back here for half an hour — that's thirty minutes, right? — and then go straight home to bed. That all right by you, sir?" She spoke to Smith, but she knew that she'd have Rod's and Oxnard's support.

"Gaffer." Neil lifted a hand in valediction to the room as a whole and left.

"We can rise to some overtime," Smith said huffily.

"So I should hope. Three-quarters of the room will be claiming." She looked around, catching eyes. "But

Neil's —" She bit back an observation about his home problems. "Neil's got a lot of responsibilities here. I want him to have something in reserve. The same applies to all of the Scala House team," she added. "We're here to help the MIT, not to make things worse by working when we're overtired. And we all still have our normal duties, apart from Dave Bush and Zayn Ara, who've been seconded full-time. By the way, I'll let you all have news of Helen as soon as I have any."

Kate knew she needed a break when she deleted an e-mail she meant to keep and tried to forward another to herself. When she got to the kettle, it wasn't, of course, there. Neither were the mugs. And the milk container was empty, with a fag end drifting enticingly inside.

All the senior staff had abandoned the Scala House annexe of the MIT, Rod included. She wasn't surprised or disappointed that he'd left without saying goodbye. He'd no doubt have been deep in conversation with Oxnard and Smith, doing his job just as he assumed she'd be doing hers. Which she could do as soon as she'd had a coffee.

Hell. There was certainly no possibility of nipping out casually to get one today.

She pushed open the door to the incident room. It would have been nice to find it seething with activity, but she hadn't expected it to be deserted but for a couple of young men hunched over a computer. It'd better be Holmes or some similar database they had on screen. Especially as they were drinking milky coffee from Mr Choi's mugs. The rest were scattered around various desks, to a greater or lesser extent revolting with dried-on dregs. She tossed a mental coin: she was damned if, in a horribly gender-programmed way, she cleared them up; she was damned if she left them where they were, because she wouldn't get a drink.

If she looked over the young men's shoulders she could see what they were up to and treat them accordingly.

"Yes? What do you want?" one asked, not taking his eyes off the screen, which did seem to be throwing up criminal records.

"Your attention for a couple of minutes." Surely she'd never been so rude when she'd been their age.

"Can't you see we're busy?" he replied.

"Yes. It's a good job for you that you are."

He froze in a most gratifying way. But his mate continued to scroll down the screen, making occasional grunts.

"I'm afraid I don't know your names." Her voice chilled to sub-zero.

"Al. He's Mike," said the grunter.

"Good morning, Al. Good morning, Mike." She didn't move.

They turned as one.

"I," she said, saying what, deep down, she'd wanted to say for several weeks, "am Inspector Power."

CHAPTER
TWENTY-ONE

Kate surveyed the clean mugs and fresh milk with pleasure. Al had shown a real gift for washing-up, while Mike had not only brought in milk, he'd also replenished the biscuit and sugar tins. It was a shame that her first serious pulling of rank had resulted in nothing more beneficial to the world. But at least she could console herself with the knowledge that when Mrs Speed reappeared she'd not feel she ought to turn to menial tasks before she started on whatever it was that had originally brought her into work.

Now Scala House was satisfactorily quiet: the two trainee detective constables — that was what they'd proved to be — had settled back to their work scanning the Holmes database for possible links with other, similar crimes. Occasionally their phone rang, and Kate would hear the murmur of an earnest voice. Yes, it was very rewarding to make young pillocks sound earnest. Meanwhile she could wade through the mound of paperwork that Helen's arrival had interrupted. Hell, she'd rather be out there with her MIT colleagues, but since they'd need to protect her she'd be more a liability than an asset. She'd be much more useful doing the routine work, which had suffered recently.

She even made time to contact her Witness Protection colleagues, who promised to organise some flowers in her name. There was no question of inviting Interflora to deliver a tasteful bouquet.

The only fly in Kate's ointment was that Jill Todd hadn't been at either briefing meeting — the Scala House people's or the general one. She should have been: according to the computer, she was due in at eight. But that was certainly her voice out in the corridor. Should Kate talk to her now? Challenge her — and maybe discuss the missing letter? Or, on the grounds that poor Jill was well and truly having her nose rubbed in the present situation by Rod's intermittent presence, should she leave well alone?

She'd finish the post first.

"Inspector?" It was Mrs Speed.

"Oh, Kathleen! I was miles away." She came round the desk and took the mug she was offered. "Thanks."

"So I could see — buried deep in government directives. Now, do you want the good news or the bad?"

"About Helen? I hope the good outweighs the bad. Do sit down. Better still, go and get your own mug and sit down. Really, you deserve a break. It must have been a very harrowing couple of hours."

"If you're sure . . ." She scuttled off, to return with her hands clamped round a mug of something that smelt like Ribena. "A Blackcurrant Bracer, according to the label," she said, in response to Kate's interrogatory sniff. "It's so cold out there. A lazy wind, my father used to call it —"

"Because it doesn't bother going round you —" Kate began.

"It goes straight through you!" the woman chanted together.

"We must have similar fathers." Kate grinned. "Now, tell me about Helen."

"The good news is that the baby's still there, safe and sound. The bad is that they're going to keep her in for observation."

"Well, we expected that. Did you get any idea how long it might be?"

"Well, I wasn't supposed to hear, of course, but several days. Then maybe sick leave, and only light duties when she gets back."

"What's that?" Jill put her head round the door.

"Come on in, Jill," Kate said. "Mrs Speed was wonderful this morning: she took Helen into hospital when it looked as if she was going to lose the baby."

"I thought that was what she wanted. To get rid of it."

"You're a couple of days out of date, Sergeant," Mrs Speed said, with a smile that interested Kate and seemed to irritate Jill.

"But why *you*, for Christ's sake?" Returning irritation with insult, no doubt.

It was time to step in. "Mrs Speed came in early to shift some work. And when she heard Helen had to go into hospital she kindly offered to go with her."

"And why wasn't I informed I was an officer down?"

"You'll find an e-mail," Kate said. "You weren't around first thing, as far as I could see."

"I took some TOIL."

Mrs Speed drank the rest of her Bracer and rose swiftly to her feet: a tactical withdrawal if ever Kate had seen one.

"I didn't notice it logged on the attendance chart," Kate said.

"I couldn't get into the system."

"No. You couldn't. Because the system's geared for me to make all the changes so I know what's going on. You'll have had one of my very first e-mails to that effect."

"But us sergeants have always used our discretion. Always. Twiss never objected."

"I'm not objecting." Except to "us sergeants". "Take your TOIL to suit you. But I need to know. Heavens, our teams are all over the place. There are still some officers I've never even met."

Jill smiled seraphically. "You *have* been out of the building quite a lot."

"If you'd been at this morning's briefings — yes, you missed two — you'd have heard why. You'll find an e-mail outlining the proceedings. Everyone will. Now, when Helen's fit to return to work, we'll have to work out the best way of employing her. We can't ask Kathleen Speed to take extended sick leave just to give Helen the chance to polish her clerical skills."

"I should hope not. She made a right pig's ear of it, from what I heard. No wonder Speed hates her guts. Did you hear —"

"Then it was all the kinder of her," Kate overrode her, "to stay with Helen till her partner could get there. Yes?"

A middle-aged man she didn't know had appeared at her door.

Her adrenaline surged: had they tracked her here? And then she saw that he was holding up some sort of ID. "Got to fit a lock for you, miss," he said to Jill.

One up for those in uniform.

Kate smiled, and stepped forward. "Is this something authorised by Chief Superintendent Oxnard?"

"That's right, miss." The poor man looked from one to the other. He still wanted to talk to the serge and silver buttons. "Here's the paperwork." He held it somewhere between them. Kate took it.

"Great. Oxnard's asked for a number code door lock so we don't get any strays —"

"Such as me, like," the workman said helpfully.

"— wandering in unannounced. Thanks. I'm sure Mrs Speed will make you a cuppa when you've finished. You'll need to thaw your fingers."

"Thanks, miss." And off he toddled.

"About time. I've always thought we were a bit vulnerable up here," Kate said, smiling to indicate that the bollocking was over and they could resume normal relations. But what about that letter?

"It'll be a terrible pain letting people in who haven't been told the code," Jill said, still sour.

"I shall e-mail everyone already in. And we can phone people still at home — it shouldn't take two people long. Get someone to help you, will you?"

Mistake. She knew it was a mistake. She'd been too offhand. No wonder Jill's hackles had risen.

No, it couldn't be very nice, being taken for the boss-woman and then being usurped by the real one. In fact, Kate's entire incumbency must be extremely unpleasant for an ambitious woman like Jill, especially given the Rod situation. That was something she could spare her, at least.

"Jill, you'll hear this on the grapevine soon enough, but I thought you might prefer to hear it straight from me. I'm actually living with Rod now. This can't be easy for you, especially as we have to work together. I know you cared for him."

"Oh, don't give me any crocodile tears! He's a shit, as you'll soon find out. A hand-in-knickers man, your precious Rod. A word to the wise: don't sell your house. You'll be moving back in soon enough."

"Thank you for your advice, Jill. Now, we've both got work to do."

"You mean that now you're gracing us with your presence —"

"Go and read your e-mails, Sergeant. And take this bit of advice with you. Don't try to make capital out of any letters that may have come your way recently. Don't even think of trying. Because that sort of publicity will hurt other people — innocent people — far more than it hurts me. You may go now." There. It was out. And to hell with the fact that she had sounded like a desiccated headmistress chewing the ears off a silly teenager. She was actually more tense than when the workman had appeared. And jumped so much when the phone rang she was afraid that the person at the other end would hear her heart beating.

"Power?" It was Oxnard.

"Yes, sir."

"Can you abandon your ship for a bit? I've got a job down here for you, if it's not a problem."

"Not at all. I can almost see the bottom of my in-tray."

"That bloody Home Office bumf. OK. One of my lads'll come and collect you. And, unlike your young man, he did pass that course."

She laughed. "One thing, sir, thanks for the security lock. Someone's fixing it now."

"Can't think why it was never done before. I know you're really just an admin outpost but you can't take risks, these days. Shouldn't have, in the past. Anyway, young Henry will be along shortly. What's the code, so he can let himself in? Just for the record, he's twenty-eight, six foot six and a fine fast bowler."

She'd skim-read another document when she heard Mrs Speed getting on her high horse. Not a row with Jill Todd, please. She'd better sort it whatever it was before it grew unmanageable.

But it wasn't Jill Mrs Speed was bridling at. It was a young black man toting more Rasta dreadlocks than she'd seen for a long time. Gold chains, gold rings. The coolest suit. Did this guy have street cred.

"It's all right, Kathleen, this is my chauffeur for the day."

Kathleen's eyes widened. "He hasn't even produced his ID!"

268

"But he fits Mr Oxnard's description — six foot six, twenty-eight and a brilliant fast bowler. That's right, isn't it?"

Henry shook his head. "Got it wrong there, man. Leg spin."

"I know it's only a computer version, not one of those fully realised reconstructions that those characters in Manchester do, but I thought it was pretty good," Rod said. He moved the mouse, making the head turn to different angles. "It's very clever. Look, we can make his hair recede — so. Or give him a little moustache. What do you think?"

"I'm impressed. But I have a nasty sneaking suspicion that I know what's going to happen to it next. It's going on a journey. You're going to equip me with a disk and a laptop and send me out to wherever Natasha is lurking. Right? Yes?"

"Right in concept, wrong in detail. But first we'll have some lunch. Breakfast was a long time ago. And supper may not be all that soon. Come on, let's sample the delights of the canteen. No, on the other hand, let's sample the delights of a quiet pub. But we'll leave via the car park."

They walked so briskly she was afraid of losing her breath, the cold air cramming into her lungs. They flashed down underpasses, wheeled round corners.

"Hey," she gasped, "have you taken some advanced-walking qualification?"

Grinning — perhaps he didn't have any spare breath either — he grabbed her hand and walked even faster.

"A *Bible*? Why should I be carrying a *Bible*? Gaffer," she added belatedly.

"Because we want you to look like a God-botherer — the sort that ring people's front doors just as they're enjoying a good f —" Much to her amusement, Oxnard blushed. "Henry here will drop you some way down the street. You'll consult a piece of paper, as if you're checking for a particular house. And, of course, you'll find it, greeting the person opening the door like a long-lost cousin."

She flashed an underlash glance at Rod: it wasn't so very long ago, when they'd been undercover briefly together, that he'd had to masquerade as her cousin. He flickered a glance back. So he remembered his extremely uncousinly behaviour too.

She and Henry set off as instructed, this time in a beat-up old Metro with a Christian fish on the back. "Where did you get this poor old thing?"

"It like de wan my ol' granny, she drive, and she go to de meeting hall every day de wik."

"Poor Granny. Does hers pong of dog?"

"Loathes the things. Point is, you can't have Christians who tithe their incomes driving latest-reg Vectras — not if you wish to be convincing." His accent had disappeared wherever it had sprung from.

They'd sent down line the software needed to run the clever three-D visuals, so all Kate had to do was bring it up on Meg's laptop to show the three women in the safe-house. There was no doubt about it: the face was sufficiently like Natasha's putative rescuer for her to dissolve into fresh tears. Kate e-mailed her colleagues the news so that they could narrow their London-based search. What taxed everyone most was how many other drivers might still be involved. A watch was already set at Manchester market, and the National Crime Squad were rumoured to be interesting themselves in the case.

"We shall get them," she told Natasha reassuringly. "And the people who attacked your flat," she added to Madame Constantinou, who looked every one of her years, and perhaps a few more.

"Have you seen it yet?"

Kate shook her head. "Only what I saw yesterday. But I —"

"Mr Bassett, how is he?"

Kate flushed: something else she'd failed to follow up. "I'll get the very latest news for you," she prevaricated, fishing out her mobile.

At least other people had been more on the ball. They not only had news of Mr Bassett, they had good news: he'd been allowed to go home. Did Kate want his home phone number? Kate did. Madame Constantinou fairly snatched the phone from her hand and dialled.

Kate left her to it, slipping into the kitchen where Meg was filling the kettle. "How are things with you? I can see that Madame C needs a break."

"They have been better. I've got a family to run, Kate. I know this is all for the best but —"

"Bloody right it's for the best. You don't want to lead them to your family." She put her arm round Meg's shoulders. The tension practically radiated out of them.

At last, with a sigh, Meg straightened. She switched on the kettle. "I shall be all right after a cuppa."

Kate wasn't so sure. "If we don't run this gang to earth quickly, what are you going to do when you're finished here? Go back into uniform? Throw them off the scent that way? Like I'm back in civvies?"

"Suppose so. Not that I'm keen. I enjoyed my job — no way you can do it looking like a policewoman: the kids wouldn't relate to you."

"Only for a bit, anyway. Till we've nailed everyone."

"Better get nailing, hadn't we?"

"Quite. Tell me, Meg — and goodness knows why I didn't ask you about this before —"

"Because you're trying to do two jobs at once, I should imagine!"

"You do that all the time if you're a working mother. Actually, it was because your phone was off yesterday. Look, do you remember how badly Natasha reacted to the first interpreter?"

"Mihail?"

"That's it. Did you ever find out why?"

"Kate!" Madame Constantinou's voice rang down the hall. "Ah, there you are. A phone call for you."

Kate smiled her thanks, shrugging at Meg who offered a rueful smile in return. It was Smith. He'd got hold of a load of mug-shots from Interpol and had sent them down line so Kate and her team could go through them with Natasha. Well, it made sense. All delegation made sense. But just now Kate wouldn't try delegating, tempted though she was. Madame

Constantinou and Meg could have competed for a prize in fatigue: it would be touch and go who won.

By the end of an hour, Kate would have come a challenging third. She was positive that Natasha had no difficulties at all in understanding what she said. And she could communicate easily enough when she wanted to. It was all the drama, the hand-wringing and the pacing round the room uttering what sounded like imprecations that wearied her. How did teachers manage? Parents? Meg and Madame Constantinou, for that matter? She'd have loved to grasp her by the scruff of her neck — noticeably cleaner and plumper than when she'd arrived — and force her to look at the screen.

At last, Natasha seemed to return to the computer of her own accord, but didn't grant it the favour of her concentration. Doggedly Kate brought up image after image of possible Vladis. "This one? Is this Vladi? Or is this one of Vladi's friends?" She was just about to scroll through the lot one more time when Natasha pointed and squeaked.

"Yes? Natasha, is that Vladi?"

If only it had been possible to read the thoughts obviously pounding through Natasha's brain. Within a moment, however, she lowered her lids, and her face became a mask.

Kate insisted: "Natasha, is that Vladi? Look at me, Natasha, tell me — is that Vladi?"

CHAPTER
TWENTY-TWO

"'Quite like Vladi but not so handsome.' What kind of answer is that?" Oxnard demanded.

No one in the still busy incident room pointed out that there was no need for him to be there on a Saturday, that it wasn't his case. Since he'd come in with a thin-faced man called Howard Betts, rather younger than Rod and already a detective superintendent with the National Crime Squad, it was tacitly assumed that this was now everyone's case.

"I suspect she may have equivocal feelings towards Vladi," Kate said, suppressing a yawn. It wasn't so much the lateness of the hour — though it was almost ten o'clock — as the result of a further hour's tussling with the recalcitrant Natasha. "Recalcitrant": a dreg of GCSE Latin floated to the surface to remind her that "recalcitrant" meant sitting on your heels. It seemed a singularly appropriate term for the wretched child — except when she was leaping round the room like a female Nureyev. At least some good had come out of her session, not all to do with Vladi — or quite-like-Vladi. Both Meg and Madame Constantinou admitted to having collapsed on their beds and slept solidly while she was doing battle.

274

" 'Equivocal'? Surely she should be hating the man's guts!" Smith snorted.

"He's the only man who's ever shown her an iota of kindness, dubious though that might have been in our eyes. Perhaps she hopes that it wasn't really he who was responsible — that as her poor subconscious tries to bury the appalling things that have befallen her she's convinced herself that he's a fundamentally good man, but with a rotten choice of friends."

Smith flicked through a sheaf of notes. "Talking of young men, Power, how have you got on with the translator guy?"

"Mihail?" she asked stupidly. "What about him?"

"You're supposed to have been talking to him."

She prevaricated. "I've asked Meg Walker to talk to Natasha about him — why he gave her the wobblies."

"I told you to talk to him."

"Not me." She spoke with more conviction than she felt. Was it supposed to be her job? The fifteen-hour day was beginning to take its toll. She simply couldn't remember. But Oxnard had reminded her that she wasn't Smith's assistant. She was supposed to be running a nick — in her spare time, it rather seemed. Smith had a whole team of minions, two of them hers. No. She wouldn't have taken it on.

"Get it sorted tomorrow first thing. OK?"

"Not me, sir, I'm afraid. I'm already committed to a meeting at Scala House." If it was urgent, he'd have to find someone else. All the same, she made a note to contact Meg about Mihail, as early as was decent.

★ ★ ★

Rod led the way into the car park, heading towards a black and yellow apparition.

"What the hell is this?"

"This, my darling Kate, is your transport of delight."

"If you say so." She peered more closely at the Smart car. "I must admit I've never been in anything quite like this."

"I thought it would be a special treat. Seriously," he added, as he let her in, "I thought it was just the thing."

"Oh, it is. Absolutely." She was failing to suppress her giggles. "But for you?"

"Perfect cover, I should say." His focus shifted to over her shoulder. The thin-faced detective was approaching them. "Howard!"

"Jesus, these fucking meetings. Tell you what, Rod, you couldn't tell me where to get a decent curry, could you? I mean, at this time of night the restaurants'll be full of half-naked kids swilling too many alcopops, won't they?"

"I've ordered a takeaway," Rod said. "I'm sure we can make it enough for three. Have you booked in anywhere yet?"

"Booked but not checked in. Somewhere in Digbeth."

"You'd be far better off staying with us," Rod declared firmly. "Kate, Howard and I go back years. Howard, this is Kate, the love of my life, whose only fault is an incorrigible habit of getting up at an unconscionably early hour. You remember where I live?"

276

"Vaguely — but are you sure?" He looked from one to the other.

"Rod's only fault is to keep people standing around on bloody freezing evenings talking details. Rod, give me the keys to this thing and you go with Howard and navigate for him."

"Wouldn't you rather be driven? You could navigate and get to know Howard."

Kate caught his eye, guiding it in the direction of a straggle of men and women who'd been at the same meeting. "On the whole," she said, not altogether joking, "it might be better if I weren't seen alone in the company of yet another senior officer."

"Particularly if you're going to be sleeping under the same roof, if not the same duvet," Rod agreed. "OK. First one in boosts the heating and puts the plates to warm."

It transpired that Howard had known Rod when he was a first-year undergraduate and Rod a lordly postgraduate. It wasn't clear which particular interests they shared: they seemed to have quite incompatible views on every topic they touched on. There was only one thing on which they all agreed: that much as they'd like to drink their way through every bottle on the table and talk till the small hours got bigger, they were all summoned by their beds. Kate found towels while the men made up the spare bed. She could quite warm to Howard, not only as a working-class lad with a mordant sense of humour but also as their first guest. Another time she was sure she'd have been worrying about laying out fresh soap in the guest bathroom and whether the loo was clean. As it was, it was more important to set the central heating to come on shortly after six so they could all rise to a warm house.

So how come, after a couple of hours' routine but urgent work at Scala House, she got back to Steelhouse Lane to find her name on the incident-room whiteboard alongside Mihail's? Arms akimbo, she stared as if it would rematerialise somewhere else.

"No need to say anything," Oxnard murmured in her irate ear. "I know, Neville knows, you know it's not your job. You shouldn't be doing routine work any half-way sensible DC could do. You should be doing specialist stuff. But in fact it makes sense for you to talk to him since you've met him before. We can bring him in here so you don't have to venture out again. After all, you came in for protection — safer than hanging around on your own."

"I suppose so." Something told her very strongly that it didn't, but on the amount of sleep she'd had, she couldn't remember what. In any case, the only excuse she could think of was that she'd meant to catch up on her official reading. Not the best one. "Where am I seeing him?"

"Mr Oxnard! Phone for you, sir!"

"Good girl. We'll sort the details out in two minutes." He scuttled off.

Before she could move from the whiteboard, Smith muscled in. "Go and pick him up, will you?"

Kate raised an ironic eyebrow. "Pick him up from where he lives?"

"No. From the top of the Rotunda. Of course from his home. What are you talking about, woman?"

The man shouldn't have spoken to a rookie like that. She asked coldly, "Do we know whom he lives with? Who his associates are?"

"The general idea," he said slowly and clearly, his words no doubt reaching the ears of the youngest, greenest kid at the furthest end of the room, "is that you find out all of those things when you interview him. That's what interviewing is, Power. Asking people questions."

"I see." Anger fizzed but she tried irony again. "I drive out there in daylight and sit him in the front of the car with me and remind him of what I look like so that if he does turn out to be one of the child-prostitute smugglers he'll be able to compare notes with his mates? With all due respect, I don't think so. Not after all the trouble everyone's been going to to make sure I'm not seen by anyone who might conceivably recognise me."

"Fuck it, woman."

"Chief Inspector, couldn't an ordinary uniformed constable go and get him? There are other things a more experienced officer like me can be doing. Even," she added, with an attempt to joke the atmosphere clear, "preparing for tomorrow's youth-crime initiative meeting with the ACC."

"You should do that sort of thing on your rest day."

She smiled sweetly. "Today is my rest day. Yesterday was my rest day. Tomorrow I have to be fully briefed for a meeting at Lloyd House at nine sharp with Them

Upstairs. And before you suggest I prepare tomorrow morning, don't forget I'm trying to run Scala House nick and need to be there giving orders at the crack of dawn, just as I've already done today. Is that OK, sir? Because if it is, I could go and phone Sergeant Walker and ask her if she's found out why Natasha didn't want Mihail to interpret."

She didn't give him time to reply. Turning on her heel, she made for the temporary haven of the ladies' lavatory. Hell, why did such silly encounters still irritate her so much? Why did she have to rise to the bait every time? She hadn't needed to justify herself like that: she could simply have said it was Oxnard's instruction that she stay in the building. Or was that simply hiding behind an authority figure? A male authority figure at that!

She hadn't even had the sense to bring her bag with her to repair her makeup. Hell and hell and hell. And Meg's new phone was engaged. She left a terse message.

She peered at herself in the mirror. OK, so she had no camouflage to hide the still angry flush: she'd better simply stride out with her head held high.

When she slipped back into the incident room, there was a full-scale argument going with her two lads at the heart of it. Dave Bush, all his anxiety gestures a-flourish, was yelling at DCI Smith, not, Kate was sure, a good career move. When he paused for breath, Zayn Ara chimed in: "It's not right, putting her at risk.

You heard what Dave said. If Mr Choi's given us a warning —"

"The man's a gangster. Triad boss. And you want to act on his say-so?"

"That's what we do with Sarb — with official informers, sir. We use the information of scrotes to catch other scrotes. And if a man like Choi goes to the trouble of contacting Dave at home —"

Smith smiled, a smile so infinitely charming and tender that Kate wanted to leap across the room and tell Zayn not to trust him. "If you say so," he said, suddenly quiet. He turned to the water-chiller and poured two cups. "Come on, let's drink to a truce."

The mean bastard! What a petty piece of revenge for Zayn's loyalty. He was going to see whether Zayn was still fasting, against the terms he'd set for joining the MIT. And Kate didn't know Zayn well enough to know whether he'd kept his word to her and given up. She didn't want him to lie: she didn't want him to be bollocked if he wouldn't.

Yes, she'd done this once at school in a critical moment before a history test: she could do it again now, whatever it did to her dignity. Leaping on to a chair, she screamed, "There! There!" She pointed to an invisible rodent, tracing its journey with a shaking finger.

Yes. Quite a lot of other folk saw it too. There was much moving of furniture. And then — truly the gods of justice must have been on her side today — someone pointed to a so far vacant mouse-trap under a cupboard.

By now she was at Zayn's side. "Just get the fuck out of here. And you too, Dave. Wait for me in the first interview room on the right." They moved.

"I'd rather not have had to pull the hysterical-woman trick," she admitted with a grin, a couple of minutes later, "but I reckon I owed you both — standing up to Smith like that. What exactly did Sarbut say, Dave?"

"Not much. He was obviously talking from his casino. Just that he was concerned that not everyone was as they appeared to be on the surface."

"I'm sure the oracle at Delphi might have come up with something just as useful," she said. "He didn't amplify, I suppose?"

Dave shrugged. "Ever tried pressing Mr Choi for details?"

"So you and Zayn see this as a hint that someone we're working with isn't kosher?"

Zayn grinned. "Or, indeed, halal."

"And since Jews and Muslims aren't the only ones keen on throat-cutting," Dave said, "you can see why we don't want people from this Albanian mob — Mihail or anyone else — to see you."

"Thanks, both of you. It's not easy standing up to Smith. God, what a pillock! Trouble is, I don't know how long his memory is."

"I'd rather he bore me a permanent grudge than got your throat sliced for you, gaffer."

Zayn nodded in solemn agreement. The room was suddenly full of emotion.

If she couldn't deal with it, how could she expect them to? She managed a wicked grin. "Even if that would be halal —"

"Or kosher!" Zayn flung back.

"I'll talk to Oxnard," she said. "Off you go. Oh, Zayn! Hang on!"

Hand on door, he turned back.

"Got time for a cuppa?" she risked.

"Love one," he said. "But I hear they've got rodents in the canteen, and I'd scream if I saw one." He smiled again, as if they were mates. Then, his face serious, he added, "Eid started a few hours back, gaffer. I wouldn't let you down."

"It's already started? Shouldn't you be with your family? It's like us working on Christmas Day!"

"And have you never worked on Christmas Day? Course you have. There'll still be some food waiting when I get home. My mum'll see to that."

"I'm sure she will. Has she seen to anything else, by the way?"

"Funny thing. The other day I met this cracking young Asian DC just as I came in. She says she's from your old CID section. I'll have to get our mums to introduce us properly!" He smiled and was gone.

That was a nice thought, him and Fatima, who was bright and Muslim and nice.

But she didn't have long to indulge it. As she emerged, she heard her name bellowed down the corridor. It was Oxnard in full throat, and it was impossible, as always, to gauge his mood.

"I wouldn't have put you down for a woman scared of a mouse, Power."

"I'm certainly scared of maggots. You may have heard the story."

"I have. And heard the rumour that you went and got everything sorted and won some bloke's fishing contest for him by warming his maggots in his mouth."

"The last bit's pure fantasy," she admitted. "Anyway, what can I do for you, gaffer?"

"We're putting that Mihail character in an interview room with a two-way mirror. Your lads making that fuss, Kate: nice to see they're so loyal when they've hardly met you."

She ignored the barb — if barb it was. "It's a good team down at Scala House. I shall be glad when I can stop hiding from Albanians. It'd be nice to work there full-time and do it justice."

"Anyway, someone'll give you a bell and you can go and watch if you want. And listen in, of course."

She thought of her lads' loyalty. Keeping an eye on them wasn't the best way to inspire their trust. She shook her head. "They're good officers. They'll know where to find me if they need me. I'd do better to read what else Meg's got out of Natasha."

"But you were with her only yesterday."

"It took all my time and effort to get that ID out of her. If ID it was. I didn't make any progress with her peregrinations round Europe."

"There are times, young Kate," Oxnard admitted, "when I can see why Neville thinks the sun shines out of your arse."

284

It was a long e-mail. Goodness knew what time Meg and Madame Constantinou had finished work last night, and when Meg had managed to transcribe the results of their interview. She printed it off and walked slowly back to the incident room, reading as she went.

The last part of Natasha's narrative that Kate recalled was that the child was in Rome, reunited with Vladi, who had obtained illegal papers so that she could meet his family in London. He'd driven her himself (Meg had added, in parenthesis, that Natasha seemed to think this a great privilege, and perhaps it was, compared with being shoved on board an inflatable boat) as far as Brussels. He'd toyed with taking her to Bruges, but some phone call had upset him, and instead he'd taken her shopping for a suitcase, which she'd hoped he'd fill with expensive clothes. He hadn't. He'd taken her to one of the poorer suburbs and bought cheap stuff from shops run by black people. Not much, just enough to fill the case, which was very small.

Just enough to convince Immigration she was a *bona fide* visitor, Kate thought. She realised she'd stopped walking. She might as well stand where she was and read the rest.

Then Vladi'd had another phone call, and he'd taken her to the station and put her straight on a train to Ostend. He'd written the phrases she needed to use and the words she was to look for on pieces of paper. She was very frightened. He'd given her a ticket for a ferry and a train ticket to London.

Travelling all that way on her own! The poor kid. And what was there when she got to London?

A man called Haxhi, who was Vladi's brother, had met her at the appointed place in Victoria station, but he was very cross because she was late. But it was the train's fault, not hers. She had sat for hours on it, knowing she'd get into trouble, but it truly wasn't her fault.

He'd taken her to London, but it wasn't a fine city, not like they'd promised. There were rows and rows of houses all joined together and very few English people. They were all mixed up, white and black and brown, and she was very scared and very angry.

Hmm. Didn't Kate recollect racist abuse for black footballers playing in Eastern Europe? Presumably Natasha hadn't seen non-white faces before.

But at least Haxhi, Vladi's brother, didn't hit her. He didn't punish her at all. But that was because he wanted her to have a nice body so she could work straight away in a strip bar. She had to earn her keep till Vladi arrived.

Surprise, surprise.

It was at this bar that she had met Joe and fixed her escape.

And that was it. No doubt hysterics or sleep had stopped the tale. Haxhi. Well, it didn't sound a common name, but who was she to judge? Sadly, slowly, she returned to the incident room. It was time to do a little delegation on her own account. Whoever was chasing up the Vladi lookalike with Interpol might as well look up friend Haxhi, too.

286

So far, so good. She'd try phoning Meg again. The phone was still taking messages.

Kate really was half-way through the reading matter for the following morning's meeting when the news came through. They'd got a positive ID for the body in the lorry: Joseph Gardner, a man with a slightly dodgy past, according to the Met. He'd been moderately kind and generous once, and he'd paid the price.

"If the Albanians can track him down and deal with him like that, they must have pretty efficient communications. Looks as if NCIS was right about them being a vicious load of bastards, too," Kate observed, glancing up from her pile of bumf.

"Oh, you *are* part of the meeting, are you, Inspector Power?" DCI Smith enquired. "I thought you were reading the Sunday sups."

"I thought I might as well," she retorted, "but now I've read my horoscope I can give you my full attention." Since she was holding the official papers at an angle where most of the room could identify them at a glance, she earned a general guffaw. "Anyway, this firm that Joe was working for: weren't they rather alarmed about the loss of a lorry? After all, it's not like someone nicking an old Mini. Why didn't they report it, rather than waiting for us to tell them where it had gone?"

"Funny you should ask that," Rod's friend Howard said, "but the forensic team — both ours and the fire service's — have always insisted that the lorry was normal, with no hidden places for tucking in half a dozen poor buggers who want to get from A to B."

"They do admit it's theirs?"

"Oh, yes, and they want a crime number so they can claim on their insurance. We've now spoken to quite a few of their casual drivers, and each and every one denies operating any sort of taxi service for potential prostitutes. I think we can accept Natasha's story. But we do have leads on a number of other petty crimes, so we're keeping an open mind. Meanwhile, our Manchester colleagues are simply keeping an eye open for an influx of Eastern European tarts. And will be interested to see how they get there."

"If their papers are as good as Natasha's, by Virgin train," someone said.

There was a guffaw. And a response: "No, they want to get them there on time."

A movement at the back of the room turned heads. Zayn and Dave appeared.

"Well?" Smith demanded.

"Nothing to report so far, gaffer." Dave stepped forward. "All we've managed is a nice friendly chat about why he's here, how he passes his time and so on. He's a postgraduate student at Birmingham University. Linguistics. So he earns a bit on the side as an interpreter — does a lot of work for the Chamber of Commerce, too."

"What do the university people say about him?"

"We've only spoken to one of them so far — his PhD supervisor — and he says he's an excellent student."

"Well, what are you waiting for? Get on to the others."

"It's Sunday, sir."

"So bloody what if it's Sunday?"

"All the admin people are at home, sir. We can't get at any information about phone numbers or addresses till tomorrow."

Kate's mobile rang.

"Oh, switch the fucking thing off!" Smith snapped.

"I'll take it outside." She was already half-way to the door.

"You're in an important meeting, Inspector."

She thrust the mobile at Zayn. "Go and take the call, will you? And yell if it's Meg." What was in this man's head?

The scent of victory, perhaps. "OK, ladies and gentlemen, that's it for now. Unless anyone has any problems."

His tone didn't exactly invite questions, but she'd raise one, all the same, and not out of malice. "Sorry, sir, but the child-prostitute case seems to be hi-jacking our inquiry. Is there as yet any real connection with Phil Bates's death?"

CHAPTER
TWENTY-THREE

"I do so like it when people ask Emperor's New Clothes questions," Howard said, leaning back expansively after a canteen lunch. "And that was a beaut. You should have been there, Rod. I thought Smith'd have apoplexy."

Rod grinned. "I'd have given my teeth, but there was a load of paperwork on my desk and I don't want to cramp anyone's style, yours, Kate's or Smith's. Now —"

His mobile chirruped discreetly. He turned away to take the message. His face tightened as it always did when he heard stomach-churning news. "I'll have to love you and leave you," he said, standing. "I've got to set up another team straight away. No, nothing to do with our present inquiry, I'd say. Bad enough in its own right. Asian man about Zayn's age — and what a nice lad you've got there, Kate — goes home for Eid to find his wife and two children stabbed to death."

"Racist?"

"I'm keeping the proverbial open mind, Howard." He must have realised how prim he sounded. "Ready to nail the bastard whatever the motive," he added, with a grim, apologetic smile. "So expect me whatever time you see me tonight, both. Leave me the Smart, Kate, and treat Howard as an armed escort. If anyone starts spreading rumours, ask them how many fingers they can count."

"The rumours'll be seething already," she said, with a rueful laugh. "Smith made a fuss about my taking a call so I got Zayn to take it. It was Graham on the line."

"Kate's ex," Rod explained parenthetically. "I must dash. I'll phone about a meal. If I don't, make her cook, Howard — she's far better than she admits."

"As you saw from last night's takeaway." Kate grinned. "Tell me, though, Howard, since Smith couldn't, how much of this is about a prostitution racket and how much about my missing constable? You see, I'd love them to be connected but there's these time gaps. There's about four hours between Natasha escaping from Joe and finding me. And —"

"What does she say about them?"

"You know, we still haven't bloody well tied her down. She will only tell her story in chronological order, detailed chronological order at that. I was hoping that call I told Rod about was from the sergeant trying to deal with her. I wanted information on the interpreter my two lads interviewed this morning."

"Hmm. Smith was jumping the gun a bit there, wasn't he?"

"Possibly. But maybe we all are. Phil Bates gets killed some time during his Sunday-night shift. Joe's murder and the lorry fire aren't until days later. Are we sure there's a connection?"

"We don't know that there isn't one, that's for sure. What's your gut feeling? Connection or no connection?"

"Connection. I'd say that the gang tracked Joe through the club, if he was a regular, found out his route and killed him very publicly as a warning to others. But we have to keep an open mind or we'll miss things. We all know that. I mean, we're busy sniffing round Mihail but he may be a perfectly decent ordinary student."

"You'd prefer it to be the other interpreter? Madame Thingy?"

"Well, it was only her dog's throat that was cut, not hers. And it wasn't a major fire. And she now knows an awful lot. I don't want it to be her — but . . ." She shrugged. "Another coffee?"

"No, thanks. I'm up to my caffeine level. And I'd say you were, too." He leant forward, putting his hand on the back of her chair. "You may hate me for saying this, but I'll say it anyway. Rod's a mate of mine. I rate him. I want him to be happy. Now, not a lot of police relationships survive. Tension, stress, ill-health. One thing that reduces stress in one partner is to have someone loving and supportive at home cooking healthy meals. OK, Rod is paid a lot of money to risk having a coronary. I'll grant you that. But I suppose you couldn't . . .?"

"I may cook better than I admit," she said, smiling down her anger and outrage, "but not well enough to be a wifey sort of partner."

292

He nodded. "And it was a fucking cheek of me to suggest it — I know! But I am going to suggest something else. This is the second rest day in a row you've missed — right? — and you're supposed to be running a nick the remainder of the week. Most people would regard that as a full-time job. Do yourself a favour and work out how many hours' kip you've had this week. If you start breaking up, what'll that do to Rod?"

"Who said anything about breaking up? Or down or whatever?" She found it hard not to yell at him.

"No one. But a week of Smith playing silly buggers on top of a week's work doesn't sound a prescription for health and happiness to me."

"And in a murder inquiry health and happiness are important?" She was on her feet, still managing — just — to keep her voice in check.

He produced a disarming smile. But his voice and eyes were completely serious as he said, "Of paramount importance. After all, Phil Bates is dead and you, Kate, and my old mate Rod are still alive. Think about that." He turned on his heel and strode briskly from the canteen.

She was baffled. Should she run after him and yell? What for? Stating the obvious? No, she'd better leave him with his exit line and admit the sense behind it. Tired? She was knackered. Absolutely knackered. And now she had to face cooking a meal for a stranger who'd known Rod for ages. She didn't even know what Rod had in the freezer. If she wasn't careful she'd bloody weep.

She breathed out carefully. That was how the shrinks said you dealt with stress, not by deep breaths in but by strong breaths out, relaxing. Relaxing toes, hands, face — until the damned mobile goes off.

"Kate? It's Meg here."

At this point what appeared to be a coachload of rowdy young men erupted into the canteen. "Hang on. I need to go somewhere quieter."

"I'll ring back, shall I?"

"No. Just hang on. Keep talking — think of a recipe for three for tonight. Anything. There. I'm just leaving the canteen now and — ah! Blessed silence. Now, young Natasha and her aversion to Mihail. Shoot."

"Ready? She recognised him, Kate. No, no, not as one of the gang. As one of her clients, if that's the term. That beautiful young man is into S and M big-time, partner willing or unwilling. One of the worst she ever had, she says."

"And when was this?" Her pulses might be racing but she had to ask the right questions and get accurate answers.

"In London. Three weeks ago. You remember those awful bruises she showed us? She claims he inflicted them. But, of course, you can't be sure."

"Get what's left of them photographed as evidence. Find out if she told him how old she was. Find out if she said no. Beautiful or not, I'd like him sent down for sex with a minor."

"Very well," Meg said, her voice clipped.

294

A penny dropped. "Jesus, Meg, this is your area, isn't it? Not mine at all. You're the expert. I'm so sorry. I really am."

Meg's voice lightened a mite. "That's OK. Nice to know I can set everything in train, anyway."

"Meg, you're the bloody expert. I've no idea of the procedures. Please, please, forgive me. I'm such a control freak."

"Time you had a rest, then. Got things back into perspective."

"That's just what this friend of Rod's said. And now I've got to cook him tea and I've no idea . . ."

"A nice Sunday roast," Meg said crisply. "You've got time to go to Tesco or somewhere. And you'll find the cooking instructions on the Cellophane wrapper."

"You've saved my life. Now, Meg, I'm really sorry but I need one more bit of info from Natasha. I need to know what she was doing between the time she escaped from the lorry till the time she asked me for help."

"Oh, I can tell you that. She was busy earning money the only way she knows. And deciding, by the way, that she doesn't like Birmingham men."

"That's not a fat lot of use, is it?" Smith demanded, as Kate regaled the team with the news of Mihail's sexual practices. "We've wasted a whole morning following up this suspicion of yours."

"With respect, gaffer, just because Natasha recognises him as a punter doesn't mean he's not involved with the gang as a whole. And I'd have thought a brief discussion about paid sex with a minor would be a useful lead-in. It's not many students who can afford a weekend down in London picking up toms."

He stared at her without speaking for a long moment, then turned to Zayn and Dave. "OK. That's your Sunday afternoon buggered for you, lads. Go and talk to him again."

Eid. How could she wangle it that Zayn could get home in time for some of his family celebrations? "Good officers as they are, gaffer, would we do better to ask one of Meg Walker's colleagues from Paedophilia and Pornography to sit in with one of them? They've got the experience and —"

"Where do you get experience from if you don't practise, eh, Power? I can see you're practising to take over my job. Or are you after your sugar-daddy's?"

"I'm after nailing a pervert. That's all." She picked up her folders again and returned to her reading. Only when he grabbed his coat and headed out of the room did she make a move. Catching up with him a few yards down the corridor, she said, "Sir, you can be as rude as you like to me, but leave my partner out of it."

"Your partner, now, is he? Partners are what people have in the lower ranks, Power. I thought Mr Neville was a detective superintendent. People at his level don't have partners, do they?"

"I'm not talking about sharing a rapid-response vehicle. I'm talking about sharing a home."

"Oh, you mean he's fucking you. There you are. A sugar-daddy. Now, what does having a sugar-daddy make you, Power?"

296

"A bloody fine cop, with or without Neville," Oxnard bellowed, emerging from the men's loos still doing up his flies. "Power, you've worked eight hours already on your rest day. Get your stuff and go home. That's an order."

And one she was glad to accept. She'd been aware of tears of rage and frustration pricking her eyes, and no way could she let herself down by sobbing. The fact that Oxnard was ordering Smith into his office was a bonus.

All she had to do now was get home, with or without Howard as armed escort. Curiously, dressed for the outside, he was lounging against the office door as she turned towards it, jangling a set of car keys.

"Thanks. I'm afraid I've got to stop off at Tesco for some food."

"There's nothing I like better than trolley-pushing." He grinned.

He certainly seemed happy to park their trolley at the end of aisles while Kate made swift diving forays for whatever she needed. She was just reaching for a packet of breakfast cereal — they ought to offer a visitor some choice, after all — when her mobile rang. She jumped so hard the whole lot toppled around her. But it would have been worth a veritable avalanche.

"That you, gaffer? PC Kerr here — I mean, Helen. The one with the bab." She sounded perky enough but, knowing Helen, that might be the result of some mistaken desire to please.

"How are you, Helen?" She bobbed here and there, trying to rescue the cereal packets.

"I'm fine, gaffer. They've let me come home, like."

"The baby?"

"Looking good, thanks. You know, they even let me see it, on this scan thing. Any road, all the pains stopped, so they said as how I could come home, so long as I promised to take it easy. So if you wouldn't mind me doing light duties —"

"Helen, I shall mind very much indeed if you don't take at least three days' sick leave. Helen, can you hear me?"

"You're breaking up a bit, but I can still hear, gaffer. OK. I'll do what you say 'cos that's what the doctor said too. Ta-ra a bit. See you Thursday."

"Only if you're well enough." But Helen had cut the connection. And there were still a dozen or more packets to retrieve.

The evening was calm, relaxing, even. The lamb was cooked perfectly, crisp on the outside and pink within, the potatoes equally crisp and just as succulent, and the vegetables *al dente*, as Rod preferred them. She'd even dredged up a memory of some of Aunt Cassie's Sunday stand-bys, onion sauce and then, for pudding, apples stuffed with mincemeat and baked. Howard proclaimed himself a custard-maker beyond compare, and Rod — back well in time — opened the wine and carved. It would have been, as Kate wryly observed, a perfect evening had not the host, the hostess and even the guest not fallen asleep in turn.

CHAPTER
TWENTY-FOUR

Howard insisted that there was nothing he wanted to see more than the MIT's outpost in Scala House, and that seven in the morning was an ideal time. He was also positive that by eight thirty he'd seen enough, and that Kate's team had seen enough of her to know that she was still in charge. When she opened her mouth to argue, he added, "And it wouldn't do any harm to show your face to Smith before you go off to Lloyd House for that meeting of yours."

"To provide him with another opportunity for rearranging it by biting off my nose," Kate said bitterly, gathering up the sheets of statistics she'd just printed off.

"Well, in his terms you do shove it in," he said mildly. "Though not in anyone else's," he added quickly. "He's just a lazy sod who's been promoted beyond his ability. In an ideal world Rod could quietly arrange to have him moved back to normal CID duties, but now, of course, doing anything like that would be seen as dodgy."

"Sugar-daddy defending his tart."

He looked at her sharply.

"That's how he described us."

"Jesus."

"But I think Chief Superintendent Oxnard, who overheard him, may have said something," she added, managing a smile. "Which won't, alas, help my relationship with Smith."

"Just go in there and do your job," Howard said. "The sooner it's all sorted, the sooner you'll be out of each other's hair."

She contributed very little to the briefing meeting, having nothing new to report.

Zayn, looking distinctly jaded, asked for permission to involve one of Meg's colleagues with a further questioning of Mihail, managing to phrase the request as if Smith hadn't gone off at the deep end the previous day when faced with Kate's suggestion. Kate awarded him bonus points for his tact.

She was setting off for her Lloyd House meeting, avoiding the issue of who should escort her by telling no one she was leaving, when she ran into Graham. Had he been less busy, she'd have suspected him of lying in wait. But grown men didn't do things like that. Even when they greeted their former lovers with the words, "I have to see you. Urgently."

"I can't stop, Graham. I'm due for a meeting with the ACC in seven minutes. Unless you want to walk with me?" Perhaps she wasn't as brave as she'd thought.

"I — no, I've got a meeting myself in a few moments. What time are you free?"

"Twelve-ish, I suppose — I can't see us getting away with much less since the home secretary's got a finger in the pie. I must dash." She turned and strode away. As she ran down the stairs, she realised it wasn't the best of endings for their conversation: she ought to have told him simply that she didn't know when the meeting would end, which was at least as close to the truth as the answer she'd given. No time to worry about that now. She ought to be arranging in her head the answers to the questions she was expecting.

As it was, her guess wasn't far out. They'd finished by eleven forty-five, gathering like children round the window to watch wet snow falling. Kate fought down a rush of panic: what if they didn't get the case sorted quickly? What if she couldn't shop for Rod and buy him the best presents ever? And all the Christmas trimmings? Their first one together ought to be special.

Did she dare nip off to the shops before returning to Steelhouse Lane? It would only take half an hour or so to nip into Rackham's and melt some plastic — that was what Oxnard had advised for her weekend, after all. And she'd seen nothing untoward so far: the world hadn't ended because she'd walked a couple of hundred yards on her own this morning. Bidding her colleagues a cordial goodbye, she headed for the foyer.

"Kate! Kate Power!"

"Graham!" Her astonishment was genuine. He had never risked pursuing her like this when they were together: why should he draw attention to himself now it was over?

He was inches from her, his face as anxious as she'd ever seen it.

"Whatever's the matter?"

"I just want you to come and have a drink with me, that's all."

"I'm not supposed to stray — I'm at risk, remember. Like you. Neither of us is supposed to be wandering round unaccompanied." She got no response, so added, "Did they find anything under or in your car?"

"Nothing." Somehow, hunching into his raincoat and gripping his briefcase, he had propelled them both into motion. "Waste of time."

Letting her exasperation show, she asked, "You didn't go away for the weekend?"

"We had an important event at the church — we were even on TV."

"You or the church? My God, Graham, and you were supposed to be keeping a low profile: did they actually show you?"

"I can't imagine that people like that would be watching TV." Which implied that he'd been on camera. "They gave us quite a lot of footage, actually, with shots from several angles. It was an important event, after all. The dedication of an extension into the old car park, with a full-size carillon."

The car park. Pray God the camera hadn't loved his car! She took a deep breath. "That's those bells you play using a keyboard?"

He managed a self-deprecating smile. "Not quite as hard as playing the organ. Do you ever play these days?"

She shook her head. "But everyone would hear you, not just the congregation. Oh, I'd love to have a go! Hang on, we're heading away from Steelhouse Lane."

"I told you. I just want you to join me for a drink. For auld lang syne, if you like."

She wasn't sure she did like. But she had to eat somewhere, and the longer she was out of Smith's hair the better. "Got anywhere in mind?"

"There's a place in St Paul's Square. Quiet."

She'd eaten there often when she'd been in Fraud. There were plenty of individual eating areas, made semi-private by little balustrades and sets of steps.

She huddled into her rain-jacket, pulling the hood up tight. Why hadn't she had the sense to bring an umbrella and gloves? Because she hadn't intended to come this far, that was why, having spent so much of the weekend being rushed from car to entrance to car again. At least he was setting a cracking pace: perhaps he was afraid his wife would spot them from the top of a bus.

So early in the lunch hour the pub was a haven of quiet and warmth. He established them at a table to the left of the door, claiming with his case and coat the seat facing into the room. She'd known other officers do that — some sort of instinct she didn't seem to have inherited — so she was happy to sit with her back to the bar. But he seemed inseparable from that case: there were so many stories of officers leaving sensitive stuff around that she simply picked up her bag and asked him what he wanted.

He flushed. "But I asked you."

"You can get the next one. Lager? And what'll you eat?" There was a wide choice from a separate counter.

He tucked his case under his coat. "I'll get the drinks. An egg sandwich for me."

She had a vivid memory of the tidy, underfilled sandwiches his wife provided: failure to eat them no doubt resulted in some terrible punishment, as he hardly ever forwent them to eat or drink with his colleagues. Had she really once tipped them into his bin?

They'd scarcely made the merest gestures with their glasses when he put his down and burrowed for his case. Opening it he produced a handful of familiar items: books and tapes she'd given him.

"What are those?" she asked stupidly.

"I want to give them back," he said, his face falling into its most stubborn lines.

"I don't want them back! For God's sake, Graham, why not take them to a charity shop if you don't want them?"

"Because I want you to know that I don't want you to contact me again," he said, wooden as if over-rehearsed. His eyes slipped from her face to some point over her shoulder.

So this was all for someone else's benefit, was it? For his sake — he had to go on living with his wife and a silent lie would cost her nothing — she said quietly, "I won't contact you again, Graham. In fact, it'd be better if I went now, wouldn't it?" She picked up her bag and got to her feet. Yes, she was face to face with an older, tighter-lipped version of herself. Flavia.

304

"Giving him all these things! How dare you? You whore!" Flavia reached past her, grabbing a tape and tearing it from its case. She tugged at the brown plastic, looping it out and cascading it on to the table. "There!" She plunged the rest into Kate's glass. "That's what happens to anything else you give him."

How did the woman manage to keep her voice so low? Kate was sure no one else had an inkling of what was going on. What next? For everyone's sake she mustn't let rip with the tirade that was bubbling up inside her.

"Have you returned everything?"

Graham pointed dumbly to the pathetic little heap.

"As for you, Miss Power, you will make no attempt to take your relationship with my husband beyond the purely professional." Flavia gathered herself together and headed for the door. She turned to look at them, and took a pace back. She had to raise her voice this time. "And I've no idea why you should choose to put a tail on me, Miss Power — I believe that's the correct term, isn't it? — but I'd be very glad if you told him this instant to desist and leave me alone." She turned and marched out.

There was an instant's perfect silence. The whole pub had listened to her last lines. Kate turned to Graham, all her fury that he should expose her to this flaring to the surface. But even as she opened her mouth to berate him, she registered Flavia's words. A tail?

She was on her feet and out of the door. A tail could mean only one thing. And might end in a horribly predictable way — with a slit throat and a car in flames — if the Albanians really thought Flavia was Kate. She'd no idea if Graham was following her. Digging for her radio she switched it to alarm mode: it would convey to the control centre every sound she made — at the moment flying feet and screams of "Flavia! Stop! You're in danger! Great danger!"

Flavia must have heard. In fact, she turned and shrugged a middle-class equivalent of two fingers before resuming her walk to the family car, the one that Vladi's people had seen outside Ladywood nick. Kate sprinted, her elegant civilian shoes slipping and sliding on the slushy pavement. Even her skirt was too tight for a proper running pace.

Flavia had reached the car. There was a man the far side, apparently reading the parking regulations. If Flavia pressed her zapper, all the doors would be unlocked.

"Flavia! Stop! Listen to me!"

Flavia stopped a foot from the car, her hand behind her, thumb already on the zapper, no doubt.

"Please — I beg you — come back and talk to me. To us."

The man reading the notice had a hand in his pocket. He looked along the street. Checking that an accomplice was ready? Another man was sliding towards him, and there was certainly the sound of an engine being gunned.

Kate wasted a valuable second. Yes, Graham was there. "Get some back-up. For God's sake, man!"

Fatal. Flavia had bent to open the door. The man darted up to the passenger door, forcing his way in. Kate ran. She found herself in front of the car, hands on its bonnet. A knife was already at Flavia's throat, exposed by a vicious tug on her hair.

"It's not her! It's me you want. Me! Not her." She ran to the driver's door, dragging it open. "It's me," she yelled again.

There was no way she could grab that knife. One tiny error and she herself would drive it into Flavia's throat.

"Vladi," she tried, "I'm the one who has Natasha. I'm the one you saw. I'm Inspector Kate Power." She fumbled out her ID. "Let this woman go and take me instead."

Yes, he was interested. His eyes left Flavia and focused on her. But the knife still hovered just a millimetre from the vulnerable flesh. By now another man was wrestling with something on the rear wing. She saw a lighter at the ready.

"Tell him, Flavia. For God's sake tell him." Surely there'd be help soon? The pounding in her ears cut out all other noise. She dared not turn to see. She had to keep her eyes locked into this man's. Mustn't flinch. Mustn't drop them.

At last he spoke. "Open the tank. Open the petrol tank, woman!"

Jesus, his mate was going to torch the car and take them all up?

"I don't know how! I don't know how!" Flavia wailed. "My husband always —"

The knife nicked her throat. "Do it!"

"I can't! My husband always —"

Vladi pressed the knife harder. "You do it," he told Kate.

She took a deep breath. She'd no idea either — was it the ignition keys he needed or an internal release catch? — but wasn't about to tell him that. Her boot lock was down by the handbrake. Perhaps the release catch might be there. She must act as if it were. Leaning in, so close to Flavia she could smell fresh urine, she pointed. "There. Down by your knee." And she grabbed the wrist with the knife.

CHAPTER
TWENTY-FIVE

To everyone else it must have seemed quite reasonable to put rescuer and rescued into the same ambulance. Kate would probably have done the same. She certainly wouldn't argue that she should be there: there was suspiciously little movement in a couple of the fingers on her left hand. She hadn't been quite quick enough. The knife had probably sliced a tendon or two: yes, she could say it to herself quite calmly. They'd be able to operate, wouldn't they? And it wasn't as though she was afraid of anaesthesia or a bit of post-operative pain. Her two knee operations had proved that.

As for Flavia, she'd been shocked at first into silence, but had now hitched herself up on to her elbow, telling all who might be interested — and there was no doubt that both paramedics were — that Kate's injuries were the wrath of a just God, who had punished an adulterous sinner. It might have been nice to engage her in a theological discussion as to whether Kate was in fact an adulteress, since she wasn't married, but that would have pointed out quite clearly the extent of Graham's sins. Graham, in an agony of self-reproach, would probably have taken Flavia's side, wouldn't he? Had he been capable of self-reproach: imagine a grown man agreeing to act as he had done — to invite his ex-mistress out so that his wife could publicly humiliate her.

So she lay quietly, watching the blood seep through the dressing and imagining what they'd be doing back in St Paul's Square. She'd heard the armed-response unit arrive, and had seen Vladi taken rather breathlessly into custody by Graham Harvey. Well, let him take the glory for the collar: it might make up for some of the domestic stick he would have to endure for many weeks yet. She'd no idea how many accomplices they'd picked up, though there'd definitely been the crash of metal against metal — someone's attempt at a getaway foiled, she hoped. Well, she'd heard the car start, and she'd seen the man by the petrol tank and —

"Next time you set your sights on a married man . . ." Flavia began again.

Perhaps it was reaction that made her so garrulous: even when she was safely separated from Kate, though in an adjacent curtained cubicle, Flavia kept up her chorus of abuse. At last the young registrar treating Kate — was she Malaysian? — touched her lips and ducked her head round the curtain.

"Madam," Kate heard, "do you not realise that you owe your life to this lady whom you are abusing? Please be quiet, or I shall have you moved back to the waiting room."

She ducked back. "There. This is a bad injury, Inspector. At least two tendons severed, and some other tissue damage."

310

"I thought as much," she said, as phlegmatically as she could. "What's the prognosis?"

Dr Chin avoided her eye. "There are two schools of thought. The one this hospital favours is to wait for the residual damage to heal, in the hope that the tendons — it's a clean cut, after all — will reattach themselves."

"And the other?"

"Immediate surgery. But we —"

A quick footstep outside brought a silly grin to Kate's face. He was here at last.

"Doctor," Rod said, "forgive my interruption, but I had to see my officer." He flipped open his ID. "Superintendent Rod Neville. Do you know a Mr Rhodes?"

Dr Chin looked as taken aback as Kate felt. But, then, she hadn't been expecting endearments and tender words. "The best orthopaedic surgeon in the Midlands for hand injuries."

"He's a personal friend of mine. If you're in any doubt, any at all, phone him and ask for his opinion."

"I think it will coincide with mine, Superintendent. That immediate surgery is the best option. And if he is available, I would suggest you ask him to do it. Otherwise, your officer may lose the use of those fingers for ever."

"Is this Rhodes guy really a personal friend?" Kate enquired, interested despite the pre-med. She'd been transferred by ambulance, complete, to her chagrin, with flashing light, to another NHS hospital and was awaiting the great man's attentions.

"Not yet. But a buddy of Pat the Path — it was he who said whom to mention. You know you're likely to get a commendation, don't you?"

"So long as I'm home for Christmas, you can give it to Flavia. It was she who flushed Chummy out, after all."

"Pity Harvey's likely to face a disciplinary — apparently that bloody TV programme included panoramic shots that took in his car. After all Oxnard said about going away! And he lets his bloody car appear on TV! Stupid bugger."

It took a lot to rattle Rod into swearing. She squeezed his hand.

"As for being home for Christmas, young lady, the NHS is short of beds. You'll probably be out in time for dinner tonight and back to work tomorrow. No! I'm joking! Ah, it looks as if they're coming to take you down to theatre . . ."

Though she had been home for dinner — how had Rod wangled time off to cook it? — she wasn't back at work on Tuesday: even she could see that in her unaccountably wobbly state she wouldn't be any use. In any case, she had to be debriefed both by her colleagues from the Police Complaints Authority, should Flavia wish to moan about the scratch on her neck, and by a psychotherapist, to make sure the chances of post-traumatic stress were limited. She was happy with that: after all, she'd experienced, both at first hand and in others, the effects that untreated stress could have. But as soon as she learnt that there was some trouble at Scala House she declared that an immediate return to health was called for and was up and about on Thursday ready — ish — for action.

"You can't drive, Kate, and that's flat," Rod declared, as he eased a sleeve over the boxing glove of dressing for her. "And until we sort this Asian stabbing I can't always be around to chauffeur you."

"That woman in *Pygmalion*, what did she say? I'll take a bloody cab? Well, then."

"That's possible. Now things are getting tidied up. But there are still people out there whom we've not mopped up yet — and you made no secret of who and what you were and what your involvement was. So I'd say that visiting Worksop Road was out and Scala House personnel ought to come to you, not vice versa. There. Is that comfortable?"

"Fine." Even if she'd be glad of the morning's painkillers now the ordeal of dressing was over.

He looked at her sternly. "How fine?"

"Fine."

"You're entitled to be weepy, sweetheart."

"I don't want to be weepy. Not with Howard waiting for his breakfast." She headed for the bedroom door.

He didn't move. "Dusty Rhodes is absolutely positive everything will heal properly. Positive, Kate."

"So long as I'm a good girl and rest it now and do my physio as and when." Despite herself, her voice still wasn't as steady as she'd have liked.

"What's really worrying you?" He abandoned bracing for tender, reducing her instantly to tears.

"Christmas and shopping and cards and everything. And it was meant to be our first Christmas together."

"Without a single sprig of mistletoe, it'll still be our first Christmas. And not — I know what you're afraid of — at my mother's, because I know how helpless she makes you feel. She knows herself. That's why she hasn't been round this week. But she wants to take you out: there's an antiques fair at Stafford starting tomorrow and continuing over the weekend. Would you like to go?"

"If you're not going to be around . . ." She hated weekends on her own, always had. "If she can put up with an invalid." She sat down on the bed, as if her knees wanted to show just how useless she was.

"I'm sure she can. But not for Christmas. I have plans for Christmas, which I shall keep to myself for a while."

Her stomach somersaulted. "But we agreed — Aunt Cassie."

"Will be visited as usual. Bet you can't make porridge one-handed."

"Of course I can. Though why you won't buy sliced bread for our morning toast I'll never know." Yes, grumpy was better than tearful, as she was sure Rod had predicted. "And while the damned toast burns you and Howard can tell me what Vladi's been saying."

"The only reason I've not told you anything is because there's nothing to damn well tell. He's still silent. Schtum. Not talking. After all this time . . ."

★   ★   ★

314

Her first visitor that morning was Dave Bush, lurking behind a huge bunch of flowers set in a basket. "So you don't have to worry about trimming stems or vases or anything," he said. "Jill Todd insisted. We all signed the note, but she put an extra one in. Here."

Kate removed both notes, but could open neither.

"Can I help?"

She passed him the tiny florist's envelope: she had a feeling that Jill's might refer to the missing letter and possibly a phone call to Flavia. Whatever she'd said, it could wait.

"What's the news from the nick?" she asked, filling the kettle and swearing when she couldn't turn off the tap.

"Oh, Ronnie's totally pissed off because the paperwork still hasn't come through for her to be acting sergeant."

"That's disgusting. She's doing the work, she deserves the pay — not to mention the line on her CV. I'll get on the phone as soon as you've gone — which is not an invitation for you to leave now."

"Are you sure?"

"Absolutely — who'd carry the tray through into the living-room?"

"If you're sure . . ."

"Dave, just relax. You're as jumpy as when we met over the photocopier. Just because I've got a mitt like a melon doesn't mean I'm not me."

Still awkward, he followed her through, setting the tray on the table she pointed to.

"I bet the place is awash with gossip about how we picked up Vladi," she said, with spurious casualness. "It's no secret that Graham Harvey's wife's a bit of an oddball, Dave — and she got it into her head that I was leading her husband from the paths of righteousness. We did — once — have feelings for each other but, believe me, they're all in the past. Anyway, she attracted the attentions of Vladi, the pimp of that poor girl we rescued —"

"I still don't understand how he should get on to her. Or you, to be honest."

"Remember when Graham gave me a lift to Ladywood nick? They must have got some sort of line on me when they started tailing Madame Constantinou. I'd been careful, Meg had been careful, but Madame C uses the same taxi service every day. So they get a tail on her, and see who she's meeting. It looks horribly as though they got on to me —"

"Despite all your cloak-and-dagger stuff?"

"Quite. They're good, these bastards. Very good. No wonder half the police forces in the western world are worried about them. So they see me leave Scala House with a man and they tail him. I thought they hadn't seen me properly, and perhaps they hadn't, if they thought Flavia was me. Or maybe they simply thought that since Flavia was driving Graham's car they might as well take her out anyway."

"In any case, they'd logged the DCI's car reg. And then, of course, there was all that stuff on TV about that weird church of theirs and their new bells and they took those shots of the car park. They must have seen his car and — Jesus!"

"Not very bright of DCI Harvey, I agree, not to take official advice and make himself scarce to invisible, in whichever order. But all's well that ends well, Dave. We've got the prime movers in a very nasty ring." It took her a second to work out why he groaned. She pulled a face. "Bringing children into the country and —"

"But with due respect, ma —"

"Kate in my own living-room, if you don't mind."

"Kate. But with due respect, all isn't well. The word is that Vladi's still not talking. And look at you." He nodded at her hand.

"That'll be OK. We all have to take risks, Dave, you know that as well as I do." She was about to point out that Neil Drew had taken a knife off a lout the night Phil Bates had disappeared but before she could speak he said, "And the other thing — and this is what's really getting to everyone, I have to tell you, Kate — is that we had all this top brass swanning around after a load of whores and the first sign they've got that the end is in sight they all bugger off. But the end isn't in sight. No one seems any closer to pinning Phil's murder on Vladi. Do they? You know he's categorically denied it? The only thing he's said."

"I didn't."

"I thought not. Well, they wouldn't want to worry you while you were sick."

"Anything else I should know?"

317

He grimaced. "DCI Smith's been making Madame Thingy's life hell. He's positive she's the mole."

"Mole? Oh, Mr Choi's person who isn't what he seems! Why the wretched man pretends to be an oracle and won't spell things out . . . Presumably you've tried to ask him what he meant?"

Dave nodded.

She thought again of the comparative lightness of the damage Madame Constantinou had suffered compared with that inflicted on Joe. Best say nothing.

"And I've been stood down — back to normal duties."

She shook her head. "Why? I thought there was something odd about your bringing the flowers — I'm just so dim ideas come and go without giving me time to make sense of them."

"That'll be the shock and the anaesthetic," he said kindly. "They say it's at least a week before it's clear of the system. No, we're so short at Scala House that Oxnard said Zayn and I ought to be released to normal duties if Smith was so sure everything was sorted."

"Sorted? Like hell it's sorted! They're supposed to be investigating Phil Bates's death, and I haven't heard anything that ties it in with the Albanians, nothing that's not circumstantial at best." She took a breath. "Anything else I should know about?"

"Neil Drew's got his knickers in a twist over his Christmas childcare. Seems he'd done some sort of a deal with Phil about swapping shifts, and now there's no Phil . . ."

318

"Tell Neil I'll sort it the moment I get back. Under a lot of pressure, isn't he? But, then, we all are. How's your Chinese classes?"

"I've got an exam tonight — oh, nothing serious. Just a Christmas test. But that reminds me. Mr Choi's been on about coming to see you. I said protocol didn't allow him to make a home visit, so he gave me this for you." He produced an expensive envelope.

She could make out her name in beautiful tiny letters. "Could you do the honours, Dave? And then pour the coffee, for goodness' sake — it'll be stewed to death."

As he poured, she read. Mr Choi would be enchanted if she would join him for lunch as soon as she was well enough. If Dave couldn't extract from him a meaning to his gnomic call about not all being what it seemed, perhaps it was time for her to press him for elucidation. To see what a few feminine wiles could do. Always assuming she could dredge up a few.

Lunch was fixed for the following day. Enlightenment could wait till she'd had her hair done.

"Are you sure you need me, gaffer?" Dave obviously felt safer with a title now he'd left her home and was driving her in a quasi-official capacity.

"Absolutely. And Mr Choi seemed pleased that you'd be accompanying me. Tell me, Dave, does etiquette demand that we offer him a gift to thank him for his hospitality?"

"It's on the back seat, gaffer, gift-wrapped. A dictionary of slang and idiom."

"You'll take the money out of petty cash?"

"I already have."

"Thank God for that."

"For what?"

"A sign of feet of clay. I was afraid you were turning into Jeeves."

"I like a little politeness myself," he conceded. "I don't have to eat with you, you know."

"Oh, yes, you do. But at one point, Dave, I want you to go and powder your nose, in case there's anything he'll only say to me alone. And I shall return the compliment, in case he'd rather impart material to someone he knows and trusts."

"Sounds good to me, gaffer. Goodness, looks as if we're about to be valet-parked."

"At this time of year, I wouldn't look a parking spot in the mouth."

Mr Choi himself was present to hand her carefully out of the car and to escort her through his restaurant to a private room. Mr Smooth. Mr Cunning. And maybe — though a title was never used — Mr Sarbut.

Beside him, dapper in what was clearly a very expensive suit, she felt ugly, bulky. It didn't help having to wear a jacket draped across her shoulders. Why could Frenchmen do it as a mark of supreme style? All she looked like was a refugee from a charity shop. She also felt clumsy: how on earth could she manage lunch without knocking something over, or dropping food down her top — not even her best top, since she couldn't get it over her hand.

320

In fact, lunch rattled along, if such a formal little meal could rattle. Choi produced an astounding range of food, none of it in large portions. He quickly realised that however adept she might be at using chopsticks — and the truth was, not very — she found it hard to stop her little rice bowl whizzing round the plate it was standing on. At a nod from him, all the bowls disappeared, and everyone ate off a plate, with a fork or spoon.

If only etiquette permitted a post-prandial zizz. But despite the extensive discussion of English idioms and homonyms and antonyms and then, as a little respite, place names, she had to stay on her toes. And, since Dave was now excusing himself, on her toes meant alert, wide-awake, on the *qui vive*, and any other synonymous idioms.

She leant forward, attractive woman talking to interesting man. She smiled. "Mr Choi, a few days ago you passed some information to Dave which neither of us — well, I appreciate your tact and diplomacy, but could you spell it out? You see, I'm afraid my boss may be about to pursue someone entirely innocent."

He pursed his lips. "I could hardly spell it out to one of the perpetrator's colleagues."

Dear God! Her hand flew to her mouth.

"I thought you might make the appropriate deductions, dear Inspector. Let me give you chapter and verse. I have a witness to the murder in the wholesale market. There are — very pressing — reasons why he didn't come forward. To cut a long story short,

Inspector, the man who killed your colleague was a police officer himself. He did the deed —"

"How?"

"According to the witness, there was a fierce argument. The officer struck his colleague very hard, and as he fell he hit his head. At first it seemed as if he'd try to administer first aid. But suddenly he gave up, and loaded the corpse without let or hindrance into the crusher. He switched it on. Then he proceeded on his way."

The blood on Neil's cuff the morning he'd reported a knife attack! Oh, God.

"There, you have it in a nutshell."

She could feel the colour coming and going in her face. Making a huge effort, she said, "This witness, would he be in the country illegally?"

"That is a fair deduction. I think if you wanted him to testify officially he would demand indemnity."

"I'll have to talk to my superiors." And to the people at Digbeth, where Neil claimed he'd taken the youth who'd tried to knife him. Please, God, let their records show he had.

"This has been a great shock, Inspector, and you are very far from well." He put his hand under the table. The waitress appeared with a selection of brandies and liqueurs. He took the brandy and waved away the others, pouring three small tots into huge glasses. "Medicinal, Inspector."

She waved the bandaged hand as if it were a comic appendage, not really part of her. "I shouldn't."

"Medicinal. I insist."

322

She succumbed. It was the sort even Rod kept for special occasions only. She told herself that she wasn't really on duty.

Dave returned as unobtrusively as he'd left. He had no hesitation about the brandy either. "My day off," he announced, smiling equally to both.

Kate thought of TOIL and Dave's post-exam celebrations and the job ahead of her. Dave looked at her hard. Did he think she was pissed or something? She smiled and touched her watch. Let him initiate what she suspected would be a long and complex series of farewells and thanks. He did. It was.

"Thought you were going to pass out back there, Kate," Dave observed, pulling the car into the traffic. It had been valeted.

"I nearly did. The heat. The food. The brandy. Especially the brandy." She let her eyelids droop. She didn't want him to ask about her conversation with Choi.

"Still not over that anaesthetic, see?"

Anaesthetic? That was what she needed. She was in a haze of pain. Nothing to do with her hand. The agony of knowing she had to investigate an officer she'd come to regard as a friend.

CHAPTER
TWENTY-SIX

"No record at all of a knife attack that night? You've checked and double-checked?" Kate's knuckles were white on the phone.

"Yes, ma'am." The Digbeth sergeant to whom she was speaking was clearly offended.

"I'm sorry, it's just I know how chaotic paperwork can get if you're pressed for time. Thanks, Sergeant Field."

She replaced the handset as if it were fine china she was afraid of breaking. She was certainly afraid of breaking Neil Drew's career, not to mention his family life. Damn it, the man's whole life. And all on the say-so of an illegal immigrant who might be making the whole thing up to get an excuse to stay here by invitation. Please God his allegations wouldn't square with what the forensic team had found and Neil would be in the clear.

She made herself another black coffee, turned up the central heating in an effort to stop dithering with cold, and dialled Oxnard's number. As he picked it up, she remembered that the man she should have called was Smith: it was his case, after all. Too late. This conversational wheel was now in motion, just as the legal ones soon would be.

"This bloodstain you saw when you were debriefing Drew —"

"Was on his shirt-cuff, gaffer. And I should imagine the shirt is long since gone. Wouldn't you?"

Oxnard sighed heavily, not just because he was clearly uneasy in Rod's easiest of chairs. He looked at Smith, equally tense, trying not to fiddle with ornaments as he ricocheted round the room. "It's going to be a very messy business. We'll have to ask all sorts of questions about Drew's relationship with Bates. Apart from this sodding illegal, it's all a matter of circumstantial evidence and —"

"There's a possibility of a confession," Kate put in. "I'm sure Neil's an honest man at heart."

"He hasn't shown any signs of confessing so far?" Oxnard asked Smith. "When you spoke to him the day we brought the MIT in?"

"And I told you to go easy on him because he was always tired out." Kate buried her face in her hands. The texture and smell of the bandaging were so alien she pulled back immediately. "If it is him I reckon it'll be to do with his kids. Dave Bush said he was frantic about getting cover for Christmas. Maybe Phil reneged on a deal they'd made and Neil just flipped."

"It'll be over to Forensics, anyway." Oxnard sighed. "Even if he's thrown away a shirt, he'll have spatter marks on his jacket or whatever he was wearing.

Sponging won't have shifted them. Thank God for science."

Or not.

At last Kate had to break the silence. "There's another problem about our witness. The immigrant or refugee or asylum-seeker or whatever. There are strong suspicions that Mr Choi is involved in a number of illegal rackets . . ."

His eyebrows rose. Smith was more interested in a framed Saxton map in the far corner.

"You ought to talk to Sergeant Bush, our field intelligence officer. He's just been stood down from the MIT and is back on regular duties. I believe Sergeant Todd may have some information, too."

"'Believe'!" Smith whipped round. "You should *know*, Inspector!"

Oxnard, purple with embarrassment, muttered something.

"It's not Sergeant Todd's relationship with Rod that's prevented me speaking to her, Chief Inspector. It's the fact I've hardly been at Scala House."

"E-mail? Never heard of e-mail?"

"The woman's on sick leave, Smith."

"But he's right, gaffer. Either I'm working with the MIT or I'm running a nick." That was right: strong and assertive. So why did she have to add, "At the moment I don't seem to be able to do either very well." And why, for God's sake, did she have to burst into tears?

Oxnard patted her shoulder awkwardly. "It's the anaesthetic, Power."

Bloody anaesthetic!

326

Oxnard sent Smith off to make tea for them all, and came to sit beside Kate. "How far do you want to be involved with talking to Drew?"

"Not at all, the way I feel now. On the other hand, he might find it easier to talk to me. And a confession might stand him in better stead than having MIT thumbscrews applied. But it's not easy. I can't just drive over and ask to meet his kids and say to them, 'By the way, I might have to arrest your dad.'" Any moment now she'd weep again.

"Your office would be better. A simple end-of-shift debriefing. We'd be in the incident room there, ready to take over."

Was that someone at the front door? No? And if it had been, whoever it was had gone away.

"That's a hell of a risk, if I may say so," Smith declared, slopping tea from the fistful of mugs he'd brought through on to Rod's carpet.

"You mean he might attack me?" Perhaps there was some warmth in his heart, after all.

"I meant you might start snivelling and blow everything." He plonked the mugs on to an occasional table, slopping even more.

Kate got to her feet and, without speaking, headed for the kitchen. She returned with a wet cloth. She slung it on to the floor. "Give the spots a scrub before they stain, will you? And the table. You'll leave white rings otherwise." She found some mats. She glanced up under her lashes. Yes, he was certainly thrown by her sudden rush of domesticity. And it was always good to have a senior officer brought to his knees.

As Smith dabbed at the table, she said, "You see, we all do things we wouldn't dream of doing outside our own home. When do we start, gaffer?"

"You don't, Kate, I'm afraid."

They all swung round. More tea landed on the floor. Smith bent with the cloth.

Rod shook his head. "Sorry. I've just had Personnel on the phone. They say that she cannot and must not work while she's officially unfit to work. And there'd be nothing like her name on a record of someone's arrest to prove she was breaking the law, would there?"

Furious, Kate turned on him. "And why, may I ask, should they phone you?"

"Because you'd left the answerphones on — yes, here and in Kings Heath — and your mobile was switched off, so they couldn't get through to you. It seems your friend Mr Choi grassed you up."

"Mr Choi? But I thought we were getting on so well," she said stupidly.

"So you were. So well that he phones the chief, no less, to see if he could give you a present as a sign of his appreciation for what you're doing to clean up prostitution in the area."

"Bollocks he does!"

"No, honestly, Smith, that's what he said. The chief said it wasn't a good idea till the case was over. Sorry, Kate, no present and no more work, not until you're signed off." He wandered out, returning with a mug of coffee.

"There's got to be a way round this," Smith said.

"Why should there be? You've got a whole MIT raring to go. And, as you said, Kate might lose her cool and cry."

Despite the heat erupting from the radiators, the atmosphere fell to sub-zero. At least she could do something about the central heating. She stepped into the hall and tweaked the thermostat. Leaning against the doorjamb, she said, "I suppose the chief wouldn't know if I shoved my three-penn'orth in now? Right," she continued, addressing Smith, "I'd like your assurance, that you won't indulge in a home arrest. It sounds as if Drew's kids have had enough without seeing their dad arrested in a dawn raid. And make sure you've got Social Services alerted before you even try passing the time of day with him at Scala House: they'll need to be collected from school or put to bed or whatever. And can we get the pressure off Madame Constantinou? If I were her I'd be putting the words 'lawyer', 'sue' and 'West Midlands Police' together in the same sentence. Oh, and one more thing. The price of my silence," she suddenly found herself in the middle of a smile, "about this afternoon's little get-together is regular updates."

Rod showed his colleagues out and sank beside Kate on the sofa. "I know you'll hate me for saying it, but I think Personnel were right. Looked at from the view of cold economics, the sooner someone's fully fit the sooner they can get back to work properly. Getting a colleague to confess to you isn't the best way of building a trusting team, either."

Reluctantly she nodded. She snuggled her head on to his shoulder. She was almost asleep. "I'm not up to it, you know," she said, in a rush. "I nearly dozed off at Mr Choi's restaurant — it must have been all the exertion of having my hair cut." She sat up. "I'm scared, Rod. I wasn't all emotional like this when I had my knee operations. Not the second one, at least."

"The first was after . . .?"

"Yes, after Robin was killed. I was entitled to feel a mess, then." Anyone would, seeing her lover killed before her eyes. "But I'm happy now — never been happier. So why should I be like a damned watering-can?"

"The business with Flavia Harvey must have been . . . upsetting."

"You mean in the pub or in the car? The first, yes, I suppose it was almost funny. Why haven't the press got hold of it? It'd make a lovely story."

"Because half the lunchtime clientele are cops, maybe, with a bit of *esprit de corps*. Actually, given the average officer's propensity for gossip, it might not have been the best place for Harvey to take you, if he wanted to keep your relationship quiet."

"I don't think Graham would have had much choice in the matter, somehow. But why didn't the landlord squawk?"

"Who knows?"

"You *do* know, don't you?"

"Let's just say he owes me a favour or two. And I'd rather our personal life wasn't served up as tabloid entertainment, to be honest."

"Amen. Rod, it was very foolish of me — I'm sorry."

"If you mean lunching with Harvey, you'd warned me you might — you weren't exactly sneaking off behind my back. If you mean rescuing Mrs Harvey, I'd think you were actually rather braver than most. And more generous, considering that slitting her throat might have done the world a service. If anyone's to blame it's undoubtedly Harvey. If anyone should have undertaken the heroics, it should have been him. But after that mean-spirited little trap he set for you, I shouldn't think he's got a generous or heroic bone in his body. Did —"

"Go on."

"Did you return — his gifts to you?"

This time she was shocked to find herself laughing: when would her emotions return to normal? "Rod, Rod — I must be doomed never to have presents. None from Mr Choi, none from Graham Harvey! No. None. Ever."

"Would you like a present from me? I can't say it would make up for your previous lack but . . ." He extricated himself from her arms and got up. "It's on the bed, waiting for you. I wanted to surprise you — and not in front of my colleagues. So I let myself in and went up on tiptoe. Amazing what you hear when you come down on tiptoe. Come on, want to see?"

"Nice warm bit of stuff, that. Soft, too. Shouldn't think it weighs very much," Aunt Cassie rightly observed.

"We'll have to see if Father Christmas has any more like it for you," Rod said, treading on Kate's foot.

Kate laughed, treading back. Had the pashmina come from anyone else, she would have loved taking it off and wrapping it round Aunt Cassie's knees — but not a present from Rod.

"You won't be ruining your first Christmas, coming to see an old woman like me?" The tone was distinctly querulous.

"I can't see a visit to you ruining anything," Rod said lightly. "With Kate's hand still bad we won't be off skiing, will we?"

"Will they give you a medal or anything?"

"I hope not. I didn't deal with the situation the way they teach us. I should have talked him out of it."

Aunt Cassie cackled. "If that Flavia's anything like her mother you ought to have talked him into it."

"How did you know it was Flavia?" The blood rushed to Kate's cheeks.

"I put two and two together, didn't I? She's telling everyone a mad rapist tried to kidnap her at knifepoint and you have your fingers sliced off. Will they join up again?"

"Not nearly as bad as that," Kate assured her. What else had Flavia been saying?

"You're looking pretty peaky. Freshen her glass, will you, Rod?"

Rod and Kate winked at each other: they both knew the words that would come next. "And while you're on your feet, you might as well top mine up, too."

Rod obliged. Unusually, he topped up his own. He sat down looking the old woman full in the face.

"Cassie, I think Kate needs a bit of looking after. I'd like her to come and live with me properly for a bit."

"What?" She turned to Kate. "You'll be leaving Worksop Road empty?"

"For a while, at least," she conceded. Rod reached for her good hand and held it.

Aunt Cassie settled back in her chair. "Well, come to think of it, that might just get me out of a hole. The stock market's really let me down, and I'm going to be a bit short until it comes back up again. Which it will, you mark my words. Now, if you're not living there, Kate, my love, we could rent it out for a while. Bring us both a bit of regular cash."

"You, Aunt Cassie, not me. It's your house."

"Which I gave to you. And which you spent a lot of money on. You can't give it back to me, Kate, you should know that. We've got to think of capital gains and inheritance tax."

"But —"

"I'm tired now. We'll talk about it another day. I'll get that solicitor on to it. He might as well earn his corn instead of boring me silly. So, what are you going to do for Christmas, young Rod?"

"That's a secret I shan't even share with you, Cassie." He got up and kissed her cheek. "Now, I'm going to take this girl home and tuck her —"

"Such language in front of an old lady!" Aunt Cassie cackled.

"You know damned well I said *tuck*!"

"Ah, same as that poet did. You know," Aunt Cassie continued reflectively, "there was a time when I wished young Graham Harvey would do what any man worth his salt would have done — left that Flavia of his and run off with Kate. It would have been the making of him. And it wouldn't half have been one in the eye for Mrs Nelmes. But," she continued, pulling Rod down to her level and kissing him on both cheeks, "I'm glad he didn't. On the whole."

"So am I," agreed Kate. "On the whole."

CHAPTER
TWENTY-SEVEN

Rod's mother, Frances, and Kate, their purchases stowed temporarily in the room soon to be Kate's study, giggled their way like schoolgirls into the kitchen. It had been the easiest of days, and Kate felt almost grateful to the injury that had brought it about. They were no longer visitors in each other's lives.

The thaw had set in when Kate, gaping, pointed at a stall. "Look at all that Ruskin!"

Frances giggled. "Didn't Rod tell me you two got together when some poor old man smashed a Ruskin vase over his wife's head? He said she deserved it but the vase didn't."

"It didn't. Look at that one there — all those lovely reds and purples!"

"But that *sang de boeuf* stuff costs a week's pocket money. Maybe a fortnight's." She looked at a label. "Or in that case a month's."

Kate looked and whistled quietly. "I don't like the shape," she ventured, "as much as that one there. But even that's hardly cheap."

"Leave this to me," Frances said. She turned to the stallholder. "Tell me, what's your best on this?"

"So you *are* going to move in with him," Frances declared, raising fine eyebrows high as Kate handed over a cheque. "In that case, go for a little stroll — oh, anywhere! I have a housewarming present to buy."

"You don't mind?" Kate ventured. "He should have told you."

"Mind? My dear girl, I'm delighted! And he did tell me, to be honest, that he was going to ask you. He was just so anxious and nervous — not his usual self at all. Now, go and look at those awful vases and I'll catch you up. No turning round!"

So Kate had inspected some extremely ugly Victorian specimens, trying hard not to smile with pleasure. It would be good to have a friend, not a quasi mother-in-law.

After Stafford, they'd headed south, to find the M6 solid. The road signs announced there'd been an accident.

"Some poor bugger's Christmas ruined," Kate said.

An ambulance and fire engine followed each other up the hard shoulder.

"We could sit it out or turn off at the next exit and pick our way through Wolverhampton," Frances said.

Kate made an effort to grin sardonically. "That'll be fun, this close to Christmas."

"Quite. So what do you say to going a bit out of our way and seeing what they've got in the factory shops in Tamworth? Buy a few designer labels? Or are you too tired? You're a bit pale, you know. In fact, you're very pale."

336

"I'm fine." She refused to be exhausted by a woman in her sixties. But she couldn't shake off the feelings of unease.

"But you'd be all the finer for a glass of wine and some lunch. I know this wonderful pub. Now, you mustn't be embarrassed if they greet me like a long-lost cousin. I meet a friend here. A special friend Rod doesn't know about yet. I hope he won't mind."

"Is he nice? This friend?"

"Extremely."

"Well, tell him. Introduce them. Soon. So you can have a wonderful Christmas without worrying what he'll say. And if he says anything that isn't wonderful and supportive I'll eat that vase."

"That would be such a waste! We met through the *Guardian*, you know, and . . ."

Rod was waiting for them in the kitchen, turning serious eyes to Kate. "I'll make the tea. You two go and sit down," he said.

Kate ushered Frances out, but hung back. "You'd better tell me."

"It'll wait till Mum's gone."

"As bad as that? In that case it's Neil Drew. He's confessed."

"Worse. Or better. I don't know. Kate, he's been in a car crash. He's dead. Shit. Now you know why I meant to wait." He was almost as upset as if he'd known Neil himself. There must be more information, worse information, to come.

She nodded: she couldn't speak.

"Do you want to stay in here? I'll tell Mum you're not feeling well."

"She deserves better than that. If she asks, I'll tell her the truth. Or, at least, part of it."

Frances didn't ask. She looked from one to the other, put down her tea untouched and declared that she was tired and must head for home.

"It's not what you think, Frances," Kate said, as they stood up with her. "We haven't had a row. It's just bad news about a colleague of ours. He was in an RTA earlier."

"You police officers and your jargon. Whatever happened to car crashes?" Then the older woman's face tightened. "Not that one on the M6? While we were laughing and joking about clothes and shopping?"

"Was it?" Kate turned to Rod.

He shook his head. "I don't know. I'm sorry."

"But . . ." Kate began, trying for the right tone, not flip, not morbid, not sanctimonious. She couldn't find it.

Rod made an effort. "Did you two have a good day? You looked as if you did, when you came in. Before I blabbed that stuff out."

Frances made an equally obvious effort. "It's such good news about you two, darling." She reached up and kissed her son, gathering Kate too. "Now, which of you is going to open this? Together sounds a bit risky. Kate, darling, sit down and I'll put it on your lap and Rod can open it. There, bless you, darlings."

They unwrapped a *sang de boeuf* ginger pot: definitely one of the most expensive items. More hugs, more kisses, and a ceremonial installation on the mantelpiece. Rod poured more tea. Then, as if she valued Kate's opinion, Frances grasped her hand, asking, "Shall I tell him, Kate? Shall I? About my new man?"

Rod's pleasure, though Kate was sure it was quite genuine, was muted. He did all she'd have hoped, producing his diary and their joint calendar, and arranging dinner for them all later in the week. But it took no more than one ring of the phone to bring Frances to her feet again, and this time no one argued.

"It seems he took his kids to see their mother, who's now living near Stoke, and left them there for the weekend. He picked up the A34 —"

"Not the M6?"

DCI Smith shook his head. "Any reason why he should? There was a massive tailback after some lorry jack-knifed. No. The A34. He's tootling along and then — whoosh — he's off the southbound lane and bouncing on to a four-hundred-year-old oak. The forensic boys are going over the vehicle now."

"It could have been a genuine accident?"

"Of course. But I wouldn't bet on it. You see, he knew we wanted to talk to him. That's why he'd taken his kids away. I'd say he suddenly decided he couldn't face it and it'd be better for his kids not to have a dad who was a murderer."

"You're making a lot of assumptions," Kate said.

"You didn't see his face when I asked him to bring his uniform along, whatever he'd worn the night Bates died. Guilt written all over it. And when I said we'd got a witness, I'll swear you could see the whites of his eyes. Mind you, to do him justice, he'd packed it up ready for us: it was in a bin-liner sitting on his doormat when we broke in. It's off at Forensics now." He flicked a Polaroid print at them. "There you are. There's the rest of the house, if you're interested, Power." He handed over eight or nine more.

"Thanks." She thumbed through. Why had he taken all these? There'd be official video and 35mm photos.

"I promised you'd be kept up to speed," he muttered, as if embarrassed by his own generosity. "How's the hand?"

"Improving," she said positively. "Oh, God. Oh, my God. Look." She held out a photo of the living-room, the Christmas tree already decorated and a pile of presents beneath it.

"I know. Brings a lump, doesn't it? I'm a family man myself," he added. "When my wife lets me see them, that is."

So had a man who'd bought all his presents really meant to die before his children opened them? Or was it his way of telling his children he loved them even though he couldn't be there? For whatever reason.

"Does Mr Choi's witness know about the — accident?" Rod asked.

"Not as far as I know," Smith said.

"My feeling is that it won't do any harm to keep him in the dark about it. And I'd rather like the clothes *he* wore on the relevant evening to be subjected to inspection too. It would be nicer all round if Drew's kids thought their dad had died in a simple car crash, not a suicide bid."

"Something worries me," Kate admitted. "The bin-liner. If he looked as guilty as you say, Greg, why didn't he simply 'lose' it — why leave material evidence hanging around? I'd bet the Christmas turkey you'll find that jacket was literally spotless."

"And that the jacket in question will be . . .?"

"If he's guilty, who knows? We may never find it. If I'd been him I'd have 'lost' it days ago. Except he'd have had to explain how he came to be on patrol in a sweater when everyone else was swathed to the eyeballs."

"Machismo." Rod snorted. "Haven't you seen keenie-beanies in their beautiful white shirtsleeves when it's practically been snowing?"

"Not the macho type, Neil," she insisted. "So how come he can leave that jacket knowing it won't incriminate him? I suppose he didn't simply indent for a new one, complaining that his was torn or needed cleaning after the knife incident he's supposed to have dealt with at Digbeth. He wouldn't have needed my authority."

Smith made a note.

"I don't suppose anyone's found any documentation at Digbeth yet," Kate continued, almost wistfully.

Smith shook his head. "Has he been wearing someone else's jacket, maybe?"

"You mean, swapped the numbers and everything? Not impossible," Rod mused. He looked at Greg, and they rose as one.

"I'll get them all checked over," Greg said. "How's that Asian stabbing of yours, by the way?"

"Pretty well tied up. I rather thought I'd have the weekend off, but this is how the gods punish hubris." He bent to kiss Kate. "I'll bring something in for our supper when I come home."

"We — well, we don't really need you. This is pretty routine stuff."

Kate nearly gasped out loud. It wasn't like Smith to refuse an offer of help, was it?

Rod nodded. "I know. But the sooner we know the truth about Neil, the sooner we can work out what to tell his family."

Useless. Absolutely useless! Kate was fuming with frustration. Why was she banned from Scala House? Petty bureaucracy, that was why. She was just as capable of working with one hand as with two. She could have spoken to her team, worked with them. Now Neil was dead, they wouldn't hold her enquiries against her. She'd more than half a mind to get a cab and bugger bureaucracy!

The trouble was, as she sat down with the phone on her lap, and the directory open at the page, the numbers began to swim and she knew that all she could do was sleep. How much longer was she going to be like this? "And bugger the anaesthetic, too," she murmured.

★ ★ ★

The phone woke her, but she couldn't get to it before it took a message. It was from her next-door neighbour in Worksop Road. "How are you, Kate? Zenia here. Look, some young man turned up with a bunch of flowers for you. Royston said you'd moved, and gave them your address. Believe me, Kate, I've dinned it into him never to pass on information about you, but you know what it's like with Royston — in one ear and out the other. Anyway, catch up with you later, girl. And love to Rod!"

Kate's fingers were pressing buttons before her head knew what to do.

"Zenia: Kate. Very, very quickly. What did this young man look like?"

"Hang on — I'll put Royston on to you." Under the muffling of a hand, Kate caught the words "You got her into a mess, you get her out of it. Get real yourself."

At last Royston greeted her. "Yeah, man?"

"Royston — quick as you can. This visitor, tell me anything you can."

"Two of them, man. One stayed in the car — real smooth job. A Beamer five series."

"Wow," she said, to impress Royston. Privately she thought it too predictable for words. "Did you see them both?"

"Tinted windows, man." What a surprise.

"But the man you spoke to? How old?"

"'Bout your age. Dark hair — bit greasy, man."

"Skin. Was his face all pitted?"

"Like he'd acned for England, man. 'Cept he wasn't English."

"You've saved my life, Royston." Well, it was what he'd want to hear. She could hardly tell him he'd put her at terrible risk. "I'll tell you and your mum all about it later."

Again her fingers were in action. Rod's phone was engaged. Oxnard's? Messages only. Smith's? Jesus, if he were her last hope.

"Greg, I have reason to believe" — perhaps the old jargon would press a few buttons — "that Mihail and at least one friend are on their way round here."

"Fuck." He cut the call.

Yes, the back door was locked: she pocketed the key. All windows safety-bolted — thank goodness for Rod's paranoia. But what about fire? She could keep them outside for more minutes than a professional burglar would like to waste. But she couldn't keep out fire. And fire was as much part of their MO as the knife to the throat. She grabbed the key needed to unlock the window bolts. A window might be her only way out.

If only she could use both hands.

Front door: they could pour in petrol and . . . She must jam the letterbox closed.

But she was too late. There was someone at the door now. Bloody modern glass doors. She switched off the lights. They'd know she was at home but wouldn't know where. Dared she pull the door-chain into place? She stripped a sock and shoved it into the letterbox — but not firmly enough. A hand thrust it back. And held it open. She pushed it half closed, to be rewarded by a sharp yell and curses.

344

It became a battle. His murderous intent; her will to live. But he had two hands, she just the one. And little by little he won, wedging it open so he could thrust in the spout of a petrol can.

She pressed her hand against it, staunching the flow. Hardly more than a few drips. But alongside sneaked a long lighted taper. With her hand soaked in petrol she dared not pinch it out. Burn now or burn later? She fled. There was a whoosh as the petrol caught.

The kitchen fire-extinguisher? Or the fire-blanket? If she had to use her teeth as a substitute for the damned hand, she'd save the house. All Rod's precious things. Today's prizes. No, she couldn't bear it.

The blanket first. She'd try that. When it seemed to choke the worst of the fire, she sprinted upstairs for towels to wet. If only she'd taken more notice of fire-prevention leaflets.

Someone was on the garage roof. He was prising the double-glazing from its frame. Any moment now he and his knife would be in.

There was nowhere to run. The flames were gaining hold again, despite the blanket. And someone was banging very hard at the front door.

OK. The back. Of course Mihail's mate might be waiting for her — it wouldn't take him long to hop down — but what was worse, burning to death or a quick slit to the throat? Clutching the back-door key like a talisman, she took to the stairs again. No. Not without something wet. She wasted priceless seconds dithering — intruder or heat? Heat won. She jumped clear over the flames.

Too late.

A hooded figure was almost on her. Those *objets trouvés* of Rod's might never look the same again, but that was tough. The nearest featured a lovely spherical stone. She dived for it, holding it like a grenade to hurl at the intruder.

CHAPTER
TWENTY-EIGHT

"You hit a *fireman*! Why did you hit a fireman?" Madame Constantinou demanded, waving her fork over a cherry slice. Now that she was simply a lady lunching with other ladies she'd asked to be called Marie — not quite the French pronunciation but near enough.

"Because he was there," Meg suggested. She'd eschewed a sweet, protesting that she had to get rid of some of her Christmas avoirdupois, but had agreed that a port might go down nicely.

Kate nodded. "Exactly. I thought he was Mihail or Mihail's friend, ready to cut my throat."

"But the trusty emergency services beat him to it," Marie said happily, wiping a minuscule smear of cream from her lip.

"Like the Fifth Cavalry." But only just. Kate was still having nightmares, waking up screaming at the thought of that silhouetted figure. Rod had quietly spirited away his little heap of stones, in the hope, she guessed, that without a visible reminder of the evening's events memories would fade. The contractors had worked swiftly to erase any others: new carpets, freshly painted walls and ceilings. There was even a new front door. By some miracle both pieces of Ruskin had escaped damage. Rod had seen to everything, Kate taking refuge with Frances for a couple of days, writing joint Christmas cards and, hand swathed in a polythene bag, putting mincemeat into Frances's home-made pies. They hadn't spent Christmas with her: they were both afraid of seeming ungrateful, but Frances had assured them that having the younger generation about the place would cramp her style horribly — the man from the *Guardian* was coming to stay.

"And Mihail is safely under lock and key?"

"Absolutely. Oh, and one of your neighbours remembers *letting him* in as she left your flats, so you've him to thank for your fire, too. Are things better now?"

"All the damage has been repaired. And though I weep nightly for my little dog, Mr Bassett has given me a cat."

"What a stupid bastard Mihail was," Meg declared.

Marie winced delicately as if trying to establish herself as a verbally pure lady once more.

"If he'd had the sense to come forward and say he'd been misled by a nasty gang and could he go Queen's Evidence he'd almost certainly have got away with it, you know. Apart from sex with a minor," Meg added.

"The same goes for the whole lot, Haxhi included. It was him they found with the petrol can in our front garden." It still felt strange to say "our".

"What? Haxhi must have been in it up to here."

"We've had these long chats with the DPP — you know how it is. And apparently had Vladi simply sent

Natasha over here then joined her, he — and Haxhi — would have got away with a minimal sentence, living off immoral earnings."

"That's a mere two years on average!" Meg exploded. "But what about bringing her in illegally?"

Kate nodded. "For all that the EU wants to crack down on people-traffickers, it hasn't got round to sorting out its legislation. Of course, if he'd brought her into the country himself in the back of a van the charge would have been more serious, and the penalty — but it's not so much a loophole as a great gaping gap."

"So the lorry firm wasn't involved?"

"You sound almost disappointed. The Met got them for all sorts of violations of maintenance and driver hours. But that's all. There was quite a sizeable group of under-age prostitutes in Manchester, but they went up by coach and train. All quite legitimate."

Marie Constantinou asked, "And will poor Natasha have to stand up in court and face these terrible men who have brought so many poor girls over here?"

Kate shook her head. "She'll be allowed to sit behind a screen — possibly even give video evidence. A little irony you'll all enjoy," she added, "is that poor Vladi is so disturbed by events at home — we suspect he's annoyed a rival gang — that he's asking for asylum here."

"I hope he'll find it. For about twenty years. And then gets bunged back for the jackals to fight over him."

"A nice liberal approach, Meg! One thing, the girls are finding comfort in numbers. Manchester and Birmingham Social Services are having a professional little bicker over them, but it makes sense for those who've applied to stay over here to live together. Poor Natasha, there's no home for her to go to, not where she'll be safe, anyway." Kate stirred her coffee.

At least Meg waited till they'd withdrawn to the ladies', leaving Maria Constantinou to enjoy an unexpected cigarette, before she asked the question Kate was dreading.

"And how are things back at Scala House?"

She doubted if she'd get away with a shrug. Nor did she. "Not easy," she admitted. "We're terribly short-staffed, for a start. Jill Todd put in for an urgent transfer, on personal grounds."

"Which saved you having to do it for her, at least. Was she having an attack of conscience over all that dirt she was dishing about you and Graham Harvey? Oh, yes, all over the place."

"Not least to Graham's wife. I think even Jill was embarrassed by the consequences of phoning her to tell her about me. She sent a little note — no, I didn't quite get round to opening it, and it happened to be a casualty of the fire."

"Just happened? Well, I don't blame you for holding a bit of a grudge."

"Quite a lot of a grudge, actually." Kate raised her left hand, the scars livid. "Pain in some places, loss of feeling in others — and nowhere like full mobility, not for a few months yet, they say. It's quite hard to forgive Graham Harvey, too — his silly bravado driving his car to a place where it could be seen."

350

"But he couldn't have known it was going to be on TV."

"Couldn't he just! His wife did the PR for the event: it was her doing that the TV people were there in the first place. They've spirited him off on some training course."

"So he'll be transferred out of your hair?"

"Promoted out of my hair, probably — but into some very out-of-the-way area, I hope." It was time to turn the subject. "I'm going to be a godmother, by the way. One of my team's going to have a baby — a bab, she calls it — and wants my benign influence on the poor little thing." If it was a girl, the other godmother would be Kathleen Speed. Helen had talked about having Neil as a posthumous godfather, but knowing rather more about his end than the rest of the team Kate had suggested a living one like Dave Bush might be preferable. Zayn had even been floated as an ecumenical possibility.

However much they'd wanted Neil to be innocent, they couldn't prove him anything but guilty. The jacket in the bin-liner had been entirely unstained, but the accident investigation team had found another bloodstained one in a ditch near the scene. The theory was that Neil had been trying to sling it out of the car while it was still moving and lost control. It was all a matter of skidmarks and angles, and Kate could make very little of the reasoning, although she could no longer blame the anaesthetic for her befuddlement. Only a very few people had been told the truth: the consensus was that Neil had been a good enough

351

officer to have the edges blurred a little. Ronnie Hale had been confirmed in post as a full sergeant. She'd agonised with Kate over whether to hold a traditional celebratory booze-up. Ronnie thought it inappropriate, but didn't want to appear mean, so she'd put into the collection for Neil's family the money she reckoned she'd have spent, and everyone seemed content.

As yet, no one had managed to pin anything on Mr Choi. Kate didn't know whether to be frustrated or secretly pleased. She and Dave had persuaded him that paying for flower-bed maintenance would be the best way of thanking her and commemorating indiscriminately the dead officers — anything to stop the memorial he'd immediately wanted to erect at his expense.

It was time to return to Marie Constantinou.

As they walked across the thick carpet between the well-spaced tables — Kate had decided that it should be a memorable treat to acknowledge at least some of the effort they'd put in — Meg turned to Kate and lifted her left wrist. "And do we have to wait for this to heal properly before we see a ring?"

But Kate only laughed, pointing. Madame Constantinou, tireless and resilient Madame Constantinou, had fallen asleep and was snoring gently.